The trick or treaters' mission usually wound down at seven-thirty. When the bell rang, I expected to see the last passel of pint-sized witches and skeletons. The devil showed up instead.

"Trick or treat," Dennis said. "I need to talk to you." He wrapped his oil-stained fingers around the edge of the door. This wasn't the Dennis I was used to seeing. Dirty fingers didn't match his slick persona. Something was up.

I tried to push the door closed. "No! You cannot come into my home. You are no longer welcome here."

"Stop the dramatics, please. I'm coming in and we will talk about this. If my calculations are right, you need to hurry up and do what you need to do."

"No!" I pushed the door, but he pushed back like wind at hurricane force. I landed flat on my butt on the bottom stair, a few feet opposite the door, my bowl of baby Snickers flying everywhere. He closed the door and turned off the porch light.

"I hope my neighbors saw you. I hope they heard you. I hope they call the police!"

Indigo

An imprint of Genesis Press, Inc.
Publishing Company

Genesis Press, Inc.
P.O. Box 101
Columbus, MS 39703

All rights reserved. Except for use in any review, the reproduction or utilization of this work in whole or in part in any form by any electronic, mechanical, or other means, not known or hereafter invented, including xerography, photocopying, and recording, or in any information storage or retrieval system, is forbidden without written permission of the publisher, Genesis Press, Inc. For information write Genesis Press, Inc., P.O. Box 101, Columbus, MS 39703.

All characters in this book have no existence outside the imagination of the author and have no relation whatsoever to anyone bearing the same name or names. They are not even distantly inspired by any individual known or unknown to the author and all incidents are pure invention.

Copyright © 2007 by Pamela Ridley

ISBN-13: 978-1-58571-246-5
ISBN-10: 1-58571-246-9
Manufactured in the United States of America

First Edition

Visit us at www.genesis-press.com
or call at 1-888-Indigo-1

LIES TOO LONG

PAMELA RIDLEY

Genesis Press, Inc.

DEDICATION

For Pat:

We share the gift of being sisters
And in every season of our lives
We'll be blessed with the strongest friendship
And bound by the deepest love.

Marin McKay

ACKNOWLEDGMENTS

Lies Too Long was inspired by an article in the *Washington Post* that said, "Pregnant women and new mothers are more likely to be victims of homicide than to die of any single natural cause . . ." That is a very scary statistic. With the help of many kind people, I wrote a story with that statement as the premise. I want to thank the following people for their feedback and encouragement as well as their personal brand of expertise: Mickey Aldana, Sharon Connors, Karen Ellis, Cheryl Jones, Turgenia Knight, Lisa Lansky, William Lee, Winton Moore, Judy Quaempts, Mitchell Thomas, Patricia Ward and Sharon Wildwind. I am also indebted to Wally Lind and the Crimescenewriter group for never failing to answer my police-related questions.

CHAPTER 1

I opened the double doors of the hotel ballroom and let my aunt waddle in ahead of me. The murmur of the catering staff, who were decked out in black and white, and the clacking of silverware and china meant party time was only minutes away. Giddily nervous, I grabbed my stomach at the thought of seeing Dennis again.

"The peony centerpieces on each table are a nice touch, Aunt Olivia," I said. "The lavender, white and yellow combination is beautiful, and your decision to use tablecloths of the same colors was inspired. Reminds me there are only a few days left of spring."

"It might as well be the middle of summer. Is the air-conditioning even working?" Aunt Olivia dabbed her damp forehead and then fluffed her clipped blonde bangs. Her plump brown hand simulated a fan as she set up a staging area to oversee this fundraising soiree.

"It's cool enough," I said. "I hate it when they have it up too high." I crossed my bare arms, rubbing them to deflect future goose bumps.

"But we're expecting three hundred people. The church sold every last ticket and the mayor will be here. Everything has to be perfect." She fanned, this time with a program. "I don't know why you didn't accept an offer of the escort. You're an attractive woman, no reason you should have to come to this event with your matronly though still striking aunt."

"Yes." I smiled. "You're always striking, but I'm hoping I'll see someone I know here tonight. Don't worry."

"I do worry. You're not still thinking about that basketball player, are you?"

I never could hide anything from Aunt Olivia and I was sure the expression on my face said as much.

"Laurel, you see him at these kinds of functions now and again and yes, he's good-looking, but why waste your time waiting for someone like that to pay attention to you?"

Smarting at that remark, I squared my shoulders. "Someone like that? What does that mean? You mean he's out of my league, don't you?"

Aunt Olivia softened her voice and her frown. "Honey, no, just the opposite. You're out of his."

"He's not a bad person. He made some bad financial investments and lost a fortune, got drunk, and totaled his car in an accident that resulted in a career-ending injury, but he's not a bad person."

"I didn't say he was a bad person, he's just not good enough for you. You have to watch who you let into your life, sweetheart."

"I like him. What's wrong with me liking him?"

"Girl, you know his reputation with women and all those suspensions from other teams he played on before the Wizards. You're old enough to know that kind of man is trouble. Use your head, Laurel."

With that, Aunt Olivia took off down the hall, her white chiffon gown with the puffed sleeves I kidded her about swishing with every step. She happens to be the mayor's chief of staff. So what if she's only five feet tall and dressed like Dorothy in *The Wizard of Oz*. Power brokers can wear whatever they want. I, on the other hand, had spent hours shopping for my black dress that was long in the back, but cascaded into soft, ruffled layers in the front, stopping below my knees. I looked good, but I needed every advantage. No matter what anybody said, it was hard to find a single, straight man who could express himself intelligently and who was gainfully employed in a job that didn't place him in direct conflict with the legal system. He would also have to have the physical and emotional wherewithal to give me what I needed, but still grant me enough freedom to grow. A tall order? Yes, but one I might be able to fill if the evening went as planned.

As the catering staff set up a cheese display and a separate fresh fruit table, I walked to one of the many windows in this large room and attempted to admire the view. There wasn't much to see in Rockville,

Maryland, except brick buildings and evening traffic, so I made my way over to the piano player, a bearded white guy who looked to be in his late thirties. He looked up at me with bloodshot green eyes and lit a cigarette. "Got any favorites, young lady?"

I smiled at his generous description and wondered about the smoking regulations. "I'm open to anything."

He let some ragtime rip. "Good way to warm up," he said. His lips worked the cigarette and one eye squinted from the smoky assault while his hands tickled the keys. A couple of minutes later he stopped playing and dropped the butt into a Styrofoam cup. "Pretty dress. Where's your date?"

As I fingered the rhinestone brooch centered at the dip in my plunging neckline, I could tell by his caressing gaze he wouldn't mind doing the same thing. "Thank you. If I'm lucky, he just came in the door." I excused myself and eased into the fray of people arriving. At six-foot-four, Dennis Butler towered over most and I had him in my sights with the soft strands of a Count Basie tune as backdrop. I grabbed a glass of merlot from a passing tray to build my courage.

His neatly cut hair was trimmed into a fade. His straight nose and goatee created a well-put-together look. His black tux fitting just so transported us, hand-in-hand in my daydream, to a minister who pronounced us husband and wife.

My two favorite sports are baseball and basketball and I'd taken notice of Dennis's career the moment he joined the Wizards basketball team six years earlier. Having to declare bankruptcy before he was let go from the team last year meant he'd come through some hard times, but he was still standing. His perseverance only added to my fascination with him.

Feeling confident and feminine in my spaghetti-strap dress, I tapped Dennis on his shoulder. He turned around.

"Hel—" I began, smiling.

A woman whizzed in front of me as if I were invisible and bade Dennis to lower his face to receive her peck on the lips. "Why haven't you called me, Dennis?" she whined. "We have a lot to catch up on."

I wasn't sure which was louder, her red hair or her voice.

"You're right. And I think I can remember where we left off." He grinned lasciviously, revealing flawless white teeth. "I'll definitely call you."

"Be sure you do." The invader left us in the belch of her Jessica McClintock perfume.

"Sorry, what were you saying?" Dennis asked.

"I, uh, just wanted to say hi. You probably don't remember me."

A white-gloved server interrupted next with an offer of poached jumbo shrimp. Dennis accepted, but I didn't. This wasn't going well, but I was committed. I took a deep breath. "I'm Laurel Novak."

"I'm Dennis Butler. We've met before?"

"Yes, a few months ago at the mayor's inauguration party. Well, at one of them."

"Really? Sorry, I don't remember. Good shrimp," he said as he munched.

"Yes, I'm sure it is."

The piano player did a rendition of "Feel Like Making Love to You," matching my heart's fervent desire, or at least I thought it was my heart. Could be the overpowering physical attraction I felt for this man. More guests arrived. Old and new friends happily greeted each other.

"So, are you related to the mayor?" Dennis asked.

"No, I'm not."

He took a swallow of his wine and studied me, his bedroom eyes dark and seductive, while he waited for me to explain myself. In the interim, he snared a grilled vegetable turnover from a passing tray.

"I don't do the party scene often," I said, "but this is such a worthy cause."

"Because what?" he asked, clearly distracted.

"Because? No, I meant supporting research to cure sickle cell anemia is a wonderful cause."

"Oh yeah. Sure is. I believe in supporting what our people need. That's why I was eager to be part of the tutoring project with D.C. public schools. Will you excuse me? I think I see one of my old teammates. It was nice meeting you."

"Sure. You too—again." I wasn't memorable. I wasn't his type. Dark-skinned, flat nose, easily filling out size 12s when size 6s were the norm he probably preferred. I sighed deeply. His loss. It wasn't as if I didn't have my own prepackaged list of characteristics I wanted in a man. I couldn't reciprocate the piano player's interest, for example, just as Dennis couldn't return mine. I finished my drink and slunk away to the ladies' room.

Garbo-esque. That was the only way to describe the gown I saw when I came out of the stall. It was gold, strapless and the silk fabric gathered in creative folds over, in this case, an ironing board stomach. The woman wearing it had the quintessential Creole look: skin the color of banana pulp and wavy hair that draped around her shoulders and never needed a chemical or a hot comb.

"Neiman Marcus?" she asked in a soft, somehow round voice. Maybe she was a kindergarten teacher.

"Yes," I said.

"Pretty."

"Thank you, your dress is lovely as well. Where'd you get it?"

"Well, I go to so many of these events, being the chapter president of my sorority and all, and I have found using a seamstress gives me the options I want."

"Oh, I see." I retrieved my compact and patted on a tad of loose powder to keep the shine at bay. She sidled up next to me, opened her purse and took out lipstick.

"Of course," she said, "I just happened to have this Stuart Weitzman bag and shoes in this color. Actually, I have a few. Gold is my favorite color."

I took a moment to examine her shoes and purse as expected and to smile appreciatively.

I stuck my compact back in the bag I'd picked up at Burlington Coat Factory on sale. If you ask me, it was equally as cute as hers. I pushed my mid-length hair up from the sides, hoping gravity would stop sucking the body out of it. Darn blow-drying. I should have had it wet set so at least some curls would be left. She leaned into the mirror and straightened out an errant strand of her bang.

"I saw you talking to Dennis Butler," she said.

The warmth of embarrassment spread across my cheeks. "Yeah. I'll see you."

"Oh, wait. I'm coming. By the way, I'm Emma Yates."

"Laurel Novak," I answered automatically. What did she want? Why was she being so friendly? People who looked like her didn't hang out with people who looked like me.

"What do you do, Laurel?"

"I'm a financial advisor. What about you?" As we walked along, she said hello to everyone we passed. She seemed to know them while I merely smiled at acquaintances. I tend to be a loner and it is easy to be one living in this area. With the abundance of government employees, military personnel and people who work in the tech industry, creating lasting friendships is a challenge. Just as I get to know someone, they or their spouse get transferred. Many people simply move to where property costs less and they can get more bang for their buck when buying a home.

"We're both in sales then, sort of. I sell cars," she said.

"What kind?"

"Cadillacs."

Of course. It would have to be Cadillacs, Mercedeses or BMWs.

"I think Dennis is cute too," she said. "Too bad he didn't know you when he still had money." She laughed at her own joke. "Do you think he got caught up in drugs or something? It's a shame he lost all his money and then his career on top of that."

"I heard the rumors too, but I think the media would have harped on it if drugs had been involved. He owns a repair place and it's doing fine." I knew this because you hear things, and I had planned to take my car to him.

"Well, he's definitely fine. He's got that bad boy charm thing going on big time."

I nodded, thinking about Dennis's killer smile, his huge hands that effortlessly palmed a basketball, the way he'd looked at me even for the briefest of seconds, as if he thought the sun rose and set in my eyes.

"Speaking of media," Emma said, "here come my date and his friend." As they approached Emma whispered, "Richard's nice. A little old for my taste, but he's got great connections. He knows everybody."

A terrifically tanned former newscaster for Channel Seven approached us. Next to him was Nathan Stroud. I knew Nathan well. He'd helped get me my job at American Financial Services ten years ago. We'd even dated for a few months before deciding we were better off friends. He'd retired a couple of years ago. Nathan was the same age as Richard, mid-fifties, I'd guess.

I glanced at Emma, perplexed. Women who looked like her had no trouble attracting men, unless men were intimidated by her, which was a possibility.

"Richard," Emma said, "there you are. This is Laurel Novak. Laurel, meet Richard Wagner."

"Hello Laurel," Richard said. "I understand you know my friend Nathan."

Nathan kissed my cheek. "You look good, Laurel. It's been too long. How have you been?"

"Thank you, Nathan. I've been well. And you?"

"No complaints."

"Yes, Nathan and I go back a few years," I said answering Richard. "I hate to rush off, but I'm here with my aunt and I should check in. Please excuse me."

"I'm looking forward to meeting your aunt," Emma said. "Do you happen to have one of your cards? Here's mine." Emma removed one from her purse.

I always carried my business cards as well. My plan was to fatten my bank account and not worry about my lack of a social life. Relationships had never come easily for me, for whatever reason.

LIES TOO LONG

As I strode toward my aunt, out of the corner of my eye I saw Dennis preparing to leave with a woman. My heart clutched. I grabbed an asparagus stalk wrapped in bacon and maneuvered to stare discreetly. The woman wore a purple gown so tight it had to be painted on and heels so high I decided she must be a circus trainee learning how to walk on stilts. Where could I sign up?

CHAPTER 2

When the phone rang the next morning, I knew it was Aunt Olivia calling to make sure I was ready for church.

"You go on, Aunt Olivia. I'm not going to the nine o'clock. I might make the eleven o'clock service."

"You might make it? What do you have better to do?"

"I'll see," I said, ignoring the question. It's not that I had anything better to do, but church was full of social cliques and political hobnobbing. The idea of worshipping got lost a long time ago. It was more about what you wore, who was rich enough to buy a house in Potomac, and which ones among us belonged to Jack and Jill, a social organization where membership was by invitation only. Some Sundays I had the fortitude to keep searching for the real meaning. Today, the thought of it turned my stomach.

I thought Aunt Olivia was being dogged when the phone rang an hour and a half later, but it was Emma Yates from the party the night before.

"Hey," she said, "I know this little Latino place in Wheaton that serves the best coffee. I usually sit through half a pot and read the *Post*. Why don't you come with me? I promise to share my paper."

"I—uh." I couldn't think of a reason not to go, but if I stalled for a moment, something would come to me.

"You like coffee, don't you?" she asked.

I love coffee. "I own stock in Starbucks."

"This coffee is so good, you're going to want to talk these people into going public. So, I'll pick you up this time. You can pick me up next Sunday."

"Next Sunday?"

"I go every Sunday. You'll like it, you'll see. What's your address?"

LIES TOO LONG

Wow. I should be taking notes. Emma was a salesperson used to closing the deal. In my work, I always gave the customer plenty of space to make their own decision. I did very well, but maybe Emma was an example of why others in my office did better. Her chutzpa was impressive and hard to resist.

"5044 Quail Drive," I said.

"Quail Drive in Takoma Park?"

"Yes, you need directions?"

"No, neighbor. I live about three blocks from you on Ridge. That's too funny."

I got ready, putting on blue jeans and a shirt. I looked at my style-free hair and decided bobby pins were the answer. I liked my hair off my face because I could show off the three diamond studs I wore in each ear.

Emma pulled up in a champagne Cadillac SUV with a vanity plate that read 1GRL2NV; somehow, that didn't surprise me. Inside, it smelled like a peach orchard and she looked like a ray of sunshine in her orange shirt and pants. She wore her long hair in a single French braid today.

"You're going to like this restaurant, Laurel."

"Cute Latino waiters?" I asked.

"Uh-huh. So sexy. I love those 'please let me ravish you' honey-brown eyes."

We laughed. Good, I didn't think Emma was gay, but I really didn't know her.

"I'm glad I got to meet your aunt last night. How did she ever land that job with the mayor?"

So, it was really my aunt's connections that interested her. Was Emma a user? "Oh, she knew him when he was a child. His mother grew up in the projects and my aunt collected rent money before things became automated. The mayor would come in with his mom and Aunt Olivia used to coach him about saving his money. They kept in touch and years later when he needed someone to manage his campaign funds, he called her."

"So your aunt is an accountant?"

"Not officially because she doesn't have her degree, but she can pinch a penny with the best of them. It wasn't about credentials, but rather being around someone he could trust."

"Is her background in finance what led you to your field?"

"Maybe." Emma was good at getting people to talk, good at digging for information, but so was I. "What got you interested in selling cars?"

"I look good, I like money and I like to win. I wanted a job where I could capitalize on those characteristics and be challenged intellectually. I majored in business but, after I got my B.A., I was done. No more school and I discovered I didn't want to manage a drug store or work in a bank."

We were traveling on Georgia Avenue approaching Viers Mill.

"I just have to make one quick detour," Emma said. "Thought we'd drive by Dennis Butler's apartment."

"Why?" A reasonable question for someone on the verge of hysteria. My heart pounded a mile a minute. Did she expect me to be happy about this little side trip? To me it represented being pushed into deep water when you didn't know how to swim.

"Why not?" she countered.

"How'd you find—"

"Sorors. Sorority sisters are an invaluable source of information. You have to know it's about networking."

"Oh." So much more than "oh" was running through my head.

"I got his phone number too."

"Why?"

"So you can use this invention called the telephone. I saw you watching him leave last night. Thought you might want to try one more time. My motto is, Go for what you want and expect to get it. Isn't that yours, too?"

"Some days it is," I said.

She dug into her Coach purse and offered me a slip of paper with a number on it.

LIES TOO LONG

I shook my head. "No, that's okay." I wanted it, but not this way. This way made me feel too desperate. Dennis had never asked for my number or even volunteered his.

"You sure?"

"I'm sure." I wasn't sure.

We turned into an apartment complex. Emma pointed at the modern gray stone building, about five stories high. "That's where he lives, on the fourth floor. I'll bet that's his Monte Carlo. Cool color."

The only thing that looked vaguely like a Monte Carlo was a gold car a couple of decades old. "How do you know that's his car?" I asked.

"Sorors. Apparently he's into the restoration thing as well as repair. I understand he's good at it."

"Yeah, I remember reading about that."

"Guess what?" she said.

"You're going to tell me if he wears boxers or briefs?"

She laughed. "Give me to the end of the day. In the meantime, I've got some spray insulation in the back. We could plug up his exhaust pipe if you want."

"What?" Had I heard her right? "Why would we do a thing like that!"

She shrugged. "Maybe I need coffee worse than I thought. Let's go get some."

I stared at Emma for several, seconds thinking the exhaust pipe remark was a little strange, but since thoughts of Dennis discombobulated me anyway, I wasn't sure what to make of it. I just hoped I wasn't on a coffee date with Ted Bundy's long-lost cousin.

Emma was right about the coffee, it was wonderful. A pot later, I was bouncing off the ceiling, ready to do a mambo with our waiter.

When Emma dropped me off, she offered me Dennis's phone number again. "Take it, Laurel."

12

"Nah, that's all right."

"Do you mind if I call him then?"

"You want to call him?" I'd heard her, but needed time to think of a way to ask her not to do that, to tell her I would eventually find my way to him or him to me, but I couldn't think of how to say it. "You want to call him?" I repeated.

"Sure. Hang out. Meet his former teammates. I know some of them, but I'm in my thirties, they're in their twenties and there's a bit of a social gap there. I need all the help I can get separating them from that disposable income so they can buy a car or two. You know?"

"Yeah, I know. Sure, call him." I certainly understood the value of business contacts. "Not a problem."

"Okay. Tell you what. I'll have a party at my place and you two can bump shoulders or some other more interesting body part? How's that?" Emma winked.

"Can't wait."

CHAPTER 3

The party happened a month later, in the heat of July. By then Emma and I were practically inseparable. We had shared coffee, movies and weekend trips to the beach. She had nudged me to get Aunt Olivia to give us invitations to events the mayor's office sponsored or got tickets for. "It's a sin to have an aunt in a position like that and not take advantage of it," Emma said.

I would have been worried that Emma was only using my connection to the mayor's office to enhance her social contacts, except I really enjoyed her company.

Aunt Olivia liked Emma too. She'd be happy with anyone who, as she put it, could get me out of myself and enjoying life more. She'd said, "I've been alone thirty-one years, not something I'd recommend. I know all about hiding behind work. It's an easy escape and I want more than that for you, Laurel."

So Emma and I went to a few of these political gatherings, which necessitated hours of shopping, and they gave us more political issues and juicy gossip to debate over coffee. We also came away with several new work and social contacts. Unfortunately, Emma had begun to narrow her social focus to Dennis.

All the while she kept telling me Dennis was just a guy pal and business asset. I believed her until I saw them together at her party. Saw how she touched him. Saw how he moved closer to her when she entered the room. Their constant proximity made a statement about who each belonged to. I couldn't breathe for a minute, taking this fact in. Emma had what I wanted. I was mad enough to throw something, so I accidentally knocked a bottle of wine to the floor. It wasn't fair.

I wanted to accuse her of stealing him from me, but that was pretty hard to do when I had turned down his number twice and had to reintroduce myself to him a third time when I arrived at the party. He still didn't know my name. I left abruptly, refusing to cry. I had to get over it. Over him.

But how? I felt filleted, everything hanging out exposed, trampled on. I hated Emma. To make matters worse, Aunt Olivia decided to move back to California to take care of her brother, who was fighting prostate cancer. She was my only family in the area, the only family I was close to anywhere, so I could really start to feel sorry for myself if I worked at it.

I tried, but I couldn't hate Emma for long. I missed her. If she were gone, I'd go back to my friendless existence with my job being the only interesting thing in my life. Eventually, I understood her feelings for Dennis were genuine. I couldn't begrudge her happiness. Everyone wanted someone special. I'd just have to suck it up.

Besides, Emma wasn't the kind of woman who let a man dictate her life. She didn't disappear for weeks at a time only to explain Dennis had wanted this and such. I had gained a friend and lost an unlikely love interest. Worse things had happened. I adjusted.

From July until December, Dennis and I only nodded hello, but at Emma's annual Christmas shindig, his benign interest in me shifted in a slow, steady wave. He smiled more than necessary and gave that certain look, imperceptible to everyone except me. Wishful thinking on my part? Was he using me to annoy Emma in some petty spat? Was he bored with Emma and ready to move on to the next morsel in the candy box? He looked so good in his black turtleneck and black suit, did I care what motivated him? No, I did not.

Emma had two Christmas trees that looked professionally decorated; one in the living room and the other in the family room in the basement. The one upstairs had the magic number of shiny ornaments, white lights and gold ribbon woven to perfection through the branches. Johnny Mathis crooned about the most wonderful time of the year from downstairs, where most of the party was happening now.

"You look good tonight," Dennis said.

LIES TOO LONG

I had wandered upstairs to the dining room and reached around black snowmen and black angels festively displayed to take a chicken wing from the buffet and nibble on it.

"I make it my business to look good every night." I'd found a fabulous 1920s silk chiffon dress at a vintage resale shop in Bethesda that I was especially proud of. "But I'm glad you finally noticed."

"Oh, I noticed. I'm just finally commenting."

"Mmm hmm. Must be the brandy in the eggnog," I suggested, turning to find him nearly on top of me.

"That could be it. Or maybe it's the mistletoe I'm holding over your head right now."

My glance drifted down from the waxy leaves and red berries to his eyes, then to his lips. In an instant, his tongue enticed mine to tango. The kiss was hot enough, but when he ground his slim hips against me, I thought I'd walked into a sauna. My eyes fluttered open and I quickly left the room, thankful we were the only two there.

Two days later, my garage door wouldn't open and I couldn't find anyone to help me. I didn't need to miss any of my appointments. My work centered on retirement funds, and people liked to get things straight before the end of a tax year.

Dennis rescued me. He wouldn't accept payment and merely kissed me good-bye on the cheek. I stood in the doorway watching him leave, consigning our mistletoe encounter to too much holiday merriment, that's all. I wasn't sure if my sigh was one of relief or longing.

Months passed and before I knew it, I celebrated my fortieth birthday in April. I sat for over an hour in The Little Fountain Café, waiting for someone I'd met at a political affair to show up. I put up a good front, casually sipping my wine. When I finished my second glass, I left a ten on the table and headed for Emma's house in despair. A reasonably attractive woman with as much on the ball as I've got going deserved better, for goodness sakes.

"Where is she?" I asked when Dennis opened Emma's door. I wasn't surprised to see him. He was always at her place these days, and looked as scrumptious as ever in one of his old jerseys and blue jeans.

"She won't be home until after ten. What's the matter?"

I told him what had happened. He poured three fingers of Courvoisier from the built-in wet bar between the living room and kitchen. I accepted mine and watched him sip his. Taking off my pink suit jacket, I sat on Emma's gold leather couch, hugging one of her brocade pillows to my chest.

"You shouldn't feel bad, Laurel. He just forgot. People's schedules these days are out of control."

"Yeah, sure." We drank in silence. I used my glass to gesture toward a calculator, some catalogs and other papers on Emma's antique white dining table. "What's all that?"

"Emma's going to go over some shop stuff with me when she gets home. It needs some renovations."

Minutes later, I set my empty drink on the glass coffee table. "Well, I better go."

"Don't rush off. You have time for a birthday dance, I know." He walked over to the entertainment center and turned up the volume to a smooth jazz station. The tune, heavy on piano and sax, made me visualize a candlelit supper on a deck with a view of the ocean. Dennis took my hand and pulled me into his arms, completing my fantasy. He smelled like Dial soap. I matched my breathing to his. He kissed my ears, my neck, my eyelids and lips while we swayed with the music. My pulse raced.

"I've got to go."

"Don't." His hands trailed down my neck, settling on my breasts.

"It's your birthday. You deserve to feel good." He began unbuttoning my blouse. When it was off, he held me close to him while I quivered in his arms. He unclasped my bra. We shed our clothes and lowered ourselves to the couch. I needed him. Emma coming home early didn't enter my mind; nothing mattered except him entering me. He varied the rhythm and angle, then stopped moving altogether, our bodies and eyes locked. I came so hard, I thought I'd broken something.

The following Sunday, Emma showed me an earring over coffee at our favorite spot in Wheaton. "This is yours, isn't it?"

I looked into her eyes to see if there was anything beneath her casual tone and found nothing. I took the diamond stud earring. "Yes, where'd you find it?"

"Under a couch cushion. You didn't miss it?"

"Thanks. Yeah, I wondered what had happened to it."

From that night on, I made sure I didn't see Dennis without Emma present. But even with Emma in the room, Dennis would manage to give me an insolent smile that said we both knew what was up.

He had been nice to me, but of course, he could only be nice on the down low. Emma had that social currency with all her sorority activities he obviously valued, not to mention the look he wanted in a girlfriend. What did Chris Rock say? Men are as faithful as opportunity allows. Dennis was just being a man. I knew all of this, and still couldn't stop the train wreck from happening.

By September, enough time had passed to tell myself nothing of significance had happened. As long as it was a passing incident, I could justify never telling Emma. Why mention a minor hormonal episode that would only hurt her? That was my plan, until he rang my doorbell one night.

"Hey, Laurel," Dennis said.

"Hey." My heart did a jig. I viewed him from behind a door opened only wide enough to have a conversation.

"Just wanted to check your garage door."

"My door is fine, thank you. It's not even winter yet."

"True, but it's the coldest Labor Day on record since 1922. Nothing like a little preventive maintenance. You gonna let me in or what?"

I stepped back, knowing that letting him in was a mistake as I caught scent of his leather jacket when he brushed past me. He wiped his feet on my mat, not wanting to track dirt on my red oak floors.

To my surprise, he pulled WD 40 out of the paper bag he carried. I must admit I'd thought something alcoholic was in there, or at least whipped cream.

In the garage, he maneuvered around my lawn mower, ladder, torn screens and all manner of junk to spray in various places along the door track. He tested the door a few times before he said, "That should take care of it."

"Thank you, Dennis."

Back inside my kitchen, we looked at each other, me keeping my distance, arms crossed, waiting for him to say goodnight.

"It's a little chilly." He blew on his hands to accentuate his point. "Maybe I should check your furnace?"

"I'll remember to put gloves next to your name on my Christmas list," I said, moving toward the front door. "And, as far as I know, my furnace is fine."

"I got gloves already. This is what I want."

Four feet of space between us disintegrated; his lips fastened to mine, then to the curve of my neck. He slipped his hands under my sweater, exposing my breasts, gently squishing them together in two hands while his thumbs and tongue worked their magic.

This was the time, of course, he picked to say, "If you don't want this to happen, tell me to go."

What he was doing to me felt so good. The promise of how much better it could feel threatened to keep me from remembering my name, much less articulating a protest, but somehow I got my palm on his chest and pushed. "What about Emma?"

The tip of his tongue caressed my ear, making me moan. "Emma's got control issues. She thinks she's stringing me along until she decides to let it be known it didn't work out between us."

I ducked my head away and searched his eyes. "Seriously?" Emma's penchant for control wasn't news, but her breaking up with Dennis was. Emma, however, met a lot of men and could date at whim. That she could want to move on didn't totally surprise me. In fact, I felt relieved of a sizable amount of guilt, but still cautious. "Emma hasn't mentioned this to me."

His lips trailed up one side of my neck and down the other. "You probably think you know Emma better than you do. What she says and does is calculated. She'll tell you when it serves her interests to tell you."

Dennis kissed me and I couldn't think anymore. I had picked a red-trimmed farm table for my kitchen although I rarely cook. On it, I became a late night snack: sampled and stuffed, like the best damn turkey ever served.

He showed up for seconds and thirds in the same week. Starved for his attention for so long, I couldn't get enough of him. We were amazing together. Some people think there is only one true love of a lifetime. Could there be only one great sexual union?

My body willingly explored that question as I endured three days of solid bliss before I refused to see him again until things were officially settled with Emma. But it was too late.

When I told Dennis the pill wasn't infallible and that I was pregnant, he said it was my fault because a forty-year-old woman should have had her tubes tied years ago.

Without taking a breath he'd continued, "If I want kids, Emma and I will have them."

It took a second for that to sink in, but then I was all over him. "What! What did you say? Liar! You told me it was over between you and Emma." He caught my hand, but not before I'd slapped him hard enough to leave a red imprint.

His cold eyes barely concealed his rage. "Okay, I'll let you have that one, but don't ever do that again."

Tears of anger and frustration saturated everything they touched. "But you told me—"

"I told you what you wanted to hear. You know what you have to do, Laurel. Call me after it's over."

CHAPTER 4

Even when I had thought Emma and Dennis were through, I'd never deluded myself into thinking Dennis wanted something more than a warm place to put it. Well, yeah, part of me had held on to that slim possibility that he cared about me, but what he said and the way he said it made the truth impossible to deny.

Looking back, I couldn't even be sure I hadn't broken the garage door just to get Dennis to come over that first time; that's how demented and desperate I'd been.

My doctor said he was pretty sure I was having twins. Dennis could argue I was still in la-la land for wanting the babies, but I didn't care what he thought. He might have been my fantasy, but these babies were real.

Dennis had his own separate reality. He counted on Emma meaning more to me than the twins. What a ghastly dilemma. Emma and I had been friends for more than a year now. We talked almost every day. She would have to know what Dennis and I had done.

On Wednesday nights, Emma and I took a Chinese cooking class. After class, I started my car and backed out of the high-school parking lot space, shivering in the cold; or maybe I was nervous about what I needed to tell her.

I listened to Emma explain how she'd replaced a classmate's cream of tartar with cornstarch. Her breath blew puffs of white vapor inside the car. "Did you see her face? Serves her right. Attention hog. If she knows everything, why is she taking the class? When she eased her spring rolls into the trash, I thought I would die, girl."

LIES TOO LONG

We chuckled. Jill, our classmate, was a know-it-all, and this wasn't the first time Emma had come up with "sweet revenge" when her sense of justice demanded it. The spray insulation in her car she'd offered to use on Dennis's Monte Carlo had been left over from some other guy's blocked tailpipe after Emma had caught him with another woman. My stomach tightened. What would Emma's revenge be when I told her about the babies? It wouldn't be pretty. She'd probably come up with something special for me. Maybe she'd plaster the parking lot on my job with unflattering flyers or she'd pay someone to send me computer viruses. That I could tolerate, but it was our friendship I hated to sacrifice.

"Is something going on?" Emma suddenly asked. "You don't seem like yourself."

"There is something I need to talk about." I looked over at her in the passenger seat.

"Talk away. Is it work-, family-, or man-related? I'm telling you right now, Laurel Novak, it better not be man-related, because that would mean you have met somebody and you've been holding out on me."

I laughed, or tried to. "It's man-related, but I don't think I can talk and drive at the same time."

"Uh-oh. This sounds serious. Pull the car over and let's talk."

I almost did, but I lost my nerve. "We better not, it's starting to snow again. Can you come over tomorrow?"

"Why wait until tomorrow? We can talk at my house."

"No, tomorrow is soon enough."

A week after I told Dennis I was pregnant, he had moved in with Emma, so there was no way we could talk at her house.

"You're sure?" she asked.

"Yep. Dessert at my house. Say seven-thirty?"

"I'll be there."

A few hours later, I sat on the side of my bed with a cup of cocoa in one hand and the latest Walter Mosley book in the other, preparing to relax my way into a restful sleep, something that had been eluding me recently. Emma called.

"Laurel, are you sitting down?"

"Yeeesss," I said, drawing out the word, expecting something zany and fun. Maybe she'd dressed a snowman in one of her old cheerleading outfits again, like last year.

"Well, Miss Novak, what's small, mostly round and comes in a velvet box?"

"A clitoris?" I asked.

She howled, and then I heard her laughingly repeat what I had said to Dennis. I couldn't hear his reply, thank goodness.

"Certain extremities are involved, but that's not quite it," she said.

My heart dropped. "I see. Then it can only be that two-carat marquis diamond you picked out."

"Yes! It looks so much better at home than it did in the jewelry store, Laurel!"

"Congratulations. Emma," I said. Dennis, you conniving bastard, I thought.

"Thanks! Just had to tell you first. Got some more people to call. See you tomorrow."

I looked down at my lap. A brown stain spread over my flannel nightgown. Yelping, I leapt to my feet. Dennis's ruthlessness shocked me so much I hadn't noticed my cup of chocolate spilling. He didn't love Emma. Dennis probably didn't love anyone. I could hear him saying, "Check and checkmate," reducing our lives to a chess game.

CHAPTER 5

The good thing about being pregnant with twins by my best friend's fiancé was that a four-hundred-calorie slice of carrot cake was the least of my worries. So, I had two slices while I made decaffeinated coffee and waited for Emma's arrival.

The phone rang with her number showing on caller ID. I hoped it was Emma saying she was on her way, but it was Dennis.

"What's up?" he asked.

"Can't talk now," I said, willing a civil response. Screaming at him would only upset me all over again.

"Tell me this, Laurel. What does screwing each other's brains out have to do with bringing children into this world? You know good and damn well that was not what we were about. Why you tripping? What do you expect me to do?"

"I didn't expect you to propose to Emma just to get back at me. I didn't think you were capable of something that low."

"You have no idea what I'm capable of doing. That's why you need to come to your senses and do the right thing. I don't want you messing things up for me. Tell you what, I'll go with you, then after it's over, I'll arrange to postpone the wedding for a while, maybe forever. You think about that." He hung up the phone.

I couldn't block the number without blocking Emma's access. Shaking, I couldn't hold the coffee carafe for fear of dropping it.

I sat down at my infamous farm table and tried to regain my composure. Before long, Emma's tires crunched up my snow-covered driveway. I met her at the door and tried to act cheerful, but she saw right through me.

"I'm here," she said hugging me. "Start at the beginning."

I hung up her blue parka in the closet. "Let me see that rock first, and then I'll tell you my woes."

Emma's ring looked as if it were made just for her, not something selected from a tray of others. It would garner the right amount of attention at her next sorority meeting.

"He's the one?"

"Yeah. I mean, I didn't plan to fall in love with Dennis, but I have."

I sat down and busied my hands with a napkin before I asked this next question. "Do you worry about him seeing other women?"

"No. All that's behind him now. He's matured an incredible amount in the past year, and he understands I demand total loyalty. He's agreed there will be no more panty-throwing hoochie mamas in his life. What we have between us is real."

I cleared my throat. "Something beyond the bedroom?"

"Yes, of course beyond that." She put her hands to her cheeks. "Am I blushing? Because he definitely knows what he's doing in that department, but when I look at Dennis, I see a successful entrepreneur making it despite setbacks. I find his drive attractive. You used to too."

No comment. "But Emma, how much of his current success is due to the financial cushion you provide him?" I'd watched him worm his way into her checkbook. Dennis was a centimeter away from crossing the line between being an effective user of resources and being a con artist—if indeed such a line for him existed.

She continued as if she hadn't heard me, but her blush of embarrassment crept higher. "I think he's found his niche. He's definitely the man I want to marry. Don't make me quote Billie Holiday." She moved to the counter. "Okay, so you talk about what's been bothering you while I finish the coffee."

I could hear Holiday's lilting voice reminding people that how she handled financial issues with her man was her business and nobody else's. Sighing, I redirected the conversation. "What do you think about having two babies?"

"Girl, I know. That would be perfect, but Dennis wants to—" She looked at me. "You're not talking about me and Dennis, are you?"

I shook my head and blinked out two fat tears.

"Are you pregnant?"

I nodded, still unable to speak.

"With twins?" She came closer to me with each question. "Laurel?"

I nodded, wiping away my tears. "I think so."

"Oh my God." She pulled me into her arms and hugged me. When I looked into her eyes, I could see she was prepared to follow my lead. Were we happy, distraught or somewhere in the middle?

"The father doesn't want them," I said.

"Who is this guy? How long have you been seeing him? Why didn't you tell me about this?"

"I'm sorry. I can't tell you his name. He made me promise I wouldn't tell anybody."

She pruned up her mouth and flatly stated, "He's married."

"Yeah, sort of. But, you know, it wasn't supposed to be serious, just spending time together."

"Well, it's serious as a heart attack now." Her hand rested on my stomach. "You want to have the babies, right?"

"I do. I know it may not be fair to him, but they are babies to me, not anonymous embryos I can pretend aren't human. Besides, Emma, I'm forty. If I don't keep them, I may not have another chance."

"You never know."

"I know."

She sat down in her chair. "Laurel, I have to say this."

"Go ahead," I said, sitting again and bracing myself for the truth only best friends are brave enough to share. Well, the ones who aren't cowards, anyway.

"We've been close over a year now and never once have you talked about having kids."

"But that doesn't mean I don't want kids, Emma. I was adjusting to the idea of being unmarried and childless. You've got time. You won't be thirty-six until next year. I didn't want to whine all the time about my biological clock. How boring is that?"

"So now what? This guy is insisting you abort, but he can't make you do anything you don't want."

"That's true. He thinks that I'll do things the way he wants because, if I don't, people will be badly hurt."

She nodded.

I watched her closely for a deeper reaction and when I didn't get one, I pushed further. "Not to be overly dramatic," I added, "but lives would be demolished."

"Adultery and children born out of wedlock are not exactly a new phenomenon, Laurel. Life goes on. You plan to pursue child support?"

Her response reminded me of what I had come to know to be true about Emma. She had strong opinions about everything. This time she was on my side. But despite her seeming acceptance of babies born out of wedlock as a fact of life, what had happened between Dennis and me would hurt her deeply.

"I don't know. Either that or plan on raising them alone," I said.

"You're not alone as long as I'm here."

"Thank you." I squeezed Emma's hand, sinking farther into the abyss of deceit.

"How far along?"

"I missed my period six weeks ago."

"You saw the sonogram? Two babies?"

"Not yet. My doctor told me I had a lot of a certain hormone in my urine that is indicative of twins. I feel their presence, though, if you can believe that."

Emma's face broke into a radiant smile. "Well, of course I can. I'm gonna be a godmother."

Interpreting my weak smile as fatigue, Emma said, "Why don't we call it a day. You get some rest."

"Okay," I said, truly exhausted. With overwhelming guilt, I headed toward the stairs.

"I'll clean up and let myself out. It'll work out for the best."

"You promise?" I asked.

"Sure it will. I've got some ideas for the nursery already."

LIES TOO LONG

As I climbed the stairs, I leaned over the rail and looked back into the kitchen. "Thanks, Emma." She picked up something near the table leg and set it on the counter. A screw maybe? Stuff had a way of coming undone around here and I never knew it.

CHAPTER 6

I examined my naked stomach and growing breasts at home after my doctor's visit. The sonogram showed, to the extent it could, that I'd conceived perfect, whole, healthy babies. I was thrilled, but already nervous at the amount of work ahead of me.

Caring for twins overwhelmed parents in the best of circumstances, but I faced a truly impossible situation. How could I keep this secret and live with this guilt? How could Emma's unfaithful friend allow her to marry an unfaithful man who only wanted a meal ticket?

Actually, Emma wasn't a meal ticket; she was more of a solid business arrangement to him. If I read Dennis and his ego right, he thought Emma got the privilege of him in her life in exchange for a little moola and entrenchment into elite black society. Tall, dark and handsome, he looked good, and was well-spoken and charming when he wanted to be; he'd fit right in.

Normally, I couldn't fault Dennis for wanting to stay the course he'd picked for himself, but these babies were precious and I loved the idea of being a mother. On one level, I understood Dennis's opposition to change, but he wasn't running the show. Maybe if I offered him money he'd go away.

The trick or treaters' mission usually wound down at seven-thirty. When the bell rang, I expected to see the last passel of pint-sized witches and skeletons. The devil showed up instead.

"Trick or treat," Dennis said. "I need to talk to you." He wrapped his oil-stained fingers around the edge of the door. This wasn't the

LIES TOO LONG

Dennis I was used to seeing. Dirty fingers didn't match his slick persona. Something was up.

I tried to push the door closed. "No! You cannot come into my home. You are no longer welcome here."

"Stop the dramatics, please. I'm coming in and we will talk about this. If my calculations are right, you need to hurry up and do what you need to do."

"No!" I pushed the door, but he pushed back like wind at hurricane force. I landed flat on my butt on the bottom stair, a few feet opposite the door, my bowl of baby Snickers flying everywhere. He closed the door and turned off the porch light.

"I hope my neighbors saw you. I hope they heard me. I hope they call the police!"

"Oh yeah? Is that what you really want? No groveling for forgiveness from your dear friend before this shit blows up in your face?"

With the grip of an athlete, Dennis pulled me close to him, placing his palm against my stomach. "Let me see how they're doing. Emma mentioned something about twins."

I tensed at his touch.

"Oh, come on now, Laurel. All the things we've done and I can't see how my seed is doing? Relax."

I looked at Dennis as if I were seeing him for the first time. Why on earth would I want to be linked to this asshole for the rest of my life?

"Why are you looking at me like that? Are you afraid I'll let my hand travel south?" He ripped my pants open, and then his hand found its target.

"What is this? Something round that comes in a black velvet box?"

"Stop it, Dennis!" But he didn't.

Locking me next to him with an arm around my waist, he delivered a trail of kisses up the side of my neck. Meanwhile, his fingers were rough and hurtful.

I shook my head. "Please go. I don't want this!"

"What about what I want? It doesn't matter to you that I can't afford child support for one kid, let alone two." His shifting fingers made me groan. "Don't close the barnyard door now, baby. The damage is done."

Breathing deeply, I tried to rein in my panic. "It's not about you. It's about the babies. They deserve a chance. I'll pay you and I'll sign whatever you want me to sign. Just leave me, the babies and Emma alone."

"Depends on how well you negotiate. Maybe you can convince me." His lips chased mine until I couldn't turn away any more. "How about we sleep on it, Laurel?"

The next morning I stepped over the towel he'd left on the bathroom floor. I got under the hottest water I could stand and wept. It's not easy protecting unborn life, maintaining a savagely betrayed friendship, and being available, however reluctantly, for booty calls.

I went to work, present in body only. I managed to look busy, sifting through folders, making notes, accomplishing nothing. At the end of the day, I got on the elevator to go home, barely acknowledging a co-worker riding down with me.

"I've got to take this thing to the dumpster downstairs," Ed said. I'll need another one though." He was talking about a space heater. Our office needed work in the temperature department. Ed pushed his glasses up. "It's freezing in there. How do they expect us to work?"

"The heater just stopped?" I asked.

"No, I had to disconnect it. It works too well."

"What do you mean?"

"Something's wrong with the thermostat. It overheats."

"That's not good."

"No, it's dangerous. A fire hazard. I'm throwing it out."

The word "fire" piqued my interest. I watched Ed put the heater in the dumpster while my car warmed up. I hated myself for last night. I

LIES TOO LONG

hated that I had been so weak. I knew the chances of Dennis agreeing to go away if I slept with him again were slim to none. I should have fought harder. Never again.

I had recognized the brand name of that space heater. It was a common one. Dennis had one in his office like it. As painful as it had been, I'd gone to Dennis's shop a couple of times with Emma. A thought niggled around in my brain, but I couldn't pin it down until suddenly, it was as plain as day. I could replace Dennis's space heater with the one in the trash!

I'd have to arrange for him to sleep in the back room of his shop which had to be heated, then show up just before closing, let him think he was seducing me, put sleeping pills in his drink. Voila. Murder, she committed.

I made sure the parking lot was quiet before I looked in the dumpster. It was a deep one, but luckily more than half full. I stopped thinking and collected the space heater.

CHAPTER 7

The next morning my supervisor told me to report to Madison Research, Inc., in Delaney, Pennsylvania. Delaney is about a half hour north of Harrisburg and I didn't have to be there until the next day.

My firm, American Financial Services, specializes in tax annuities, but we handle retirement portfolios for a few corporate clients. Madison Research had over 200,000 employees nationwide. If I landed this account, I couldn't move next door to Donald Trump on the commission, but I could eat at one of his preferred restaurants.

In a county where the median family income is eighty thousand, my one hundred thousand plus was nothing to brag about, but I didn't complain much, either. Still, forward momentum in my career was a priority.

Later, while I cleaned my house, I let Emma know my travel plans and inquired how her weekend was shaping up. She told me she and Dennis had to decide today on whether to have the wedding at Shiloh Baptist Church with a reception at Christina's Kitchen, a well-known soul food restaurant in D.C., or to use the Rockville Mansion for the wedding and reception. They had lucked up on a cancellation at the mansion in Maryland, but if they wanted to reserve it, the plantation-style house required a two-thousand-dollar deposit today.

Talk about forward momentum. I wasn't surprised because I knew they had already completed the blood test required for a marriage license in D.C. Dennis wasn't wasting any time. I didn't want to know how he'd talked Emma out of the dream wedding she'd been planning since she was twelve, but I asked.

"I know, she said, "but why spend twenty-five thousand on a wedding? I mean, that's what it costs nowadays to do it right. It's just not practical. Besides, Dennis thinks we should channel every extra cent into the business and practice a little delayed gratification."

LIES TOO LONG

Mentioning that she was the only one with an extra cent seemed pointless.

Spraying Formula 409 on Dennis's fingerprints on my door and wishing I could erase him just as easily, I paused while deciding the best approach to use. Her next comment preempted any potential comeback.

"Being married and having a family with the dog and cat and picket fence has been my ultimate dream, Laurel. The dream beneath the alpha wedding dream. I'm ready. I might have to make a few sacrifices to get there, but so what? You and I both have so many exciting changes to get ready for! I have a surprise for you. I've been smiling all day."

"What?"

"You'll see soon enough. Call me when you're on your way back."

The minute I put the phone down, Aunt Olivia called.

"How've you been, girl? What's going on?"

"Hi, Aunt Olivia. Not much," I lied. I wasn't ready to tell her about Dennis or the babies. I needed someone to talk to, that was for sure, but I didn't want to add another burden to her plate. I also realized I wanted to escape her wrath. I was sure Aunt Olivia would have a word or two of admonition for me, and I wasn't in the mood to hear it. "How's Uncle Pete?"

"You know Pete—he's holding on, but the cancer is eating at him."

On the contrary, I didn't know Uncle Pete at all. I had met him once when I was seven and my grandfather had taken me to California for the summer. All I remember about San Jose was that it was windy and Uncle Pete liked waffles for breakfast. Okay, the boardwalk and water park were nice too, but that had been one summer thirty-three years ago and I hadn't seen or heard from Uncle Pete since then.

"Give him my best. How're you holding up, Aunt Olivia?"

"I'm doing okay. I spend a lot of time cleaning. Uncle Pete's got an attic full of things that need to be sorted through. What are you up to?"

We talked about my trip to Delaney and about Dennis and Emma's engagement for a while, until the subject made me ill.

"So, I'll admit it," Aunt Olivia said. "Maybe I was wrong about Dennis. From what you're telling me, Emma seems happy."

I got off the phone so I could go throw up.

At nine the next morning, I removed the space heater from the trunk of my car to make space for my suitcase. The little white knobs on the heater seemed to be staring at me as I got into my car. Had I actually thought I was going to barbecue Dennis? What was wrong with me? Hormones. Those things could be marketed as weapons of mass destruction.

I got into my black Lexus and drove. The harder I tried not to think of my situation, the more Dennis came to mind. Telling Emma the truth, sad to say, was no guarantee she'd call the wedding off. Maybe she would, based on our friendship, but Dennis was charm personified and she obviously wanted him. Out of all the men available to her, she had picked him. He'd have Emma believing he'd succumbed one time in a weak moment and she'd probably kick my butt to the curb and support her man emotionally just as she supported him financially. She'd probably assume I had seduced him rather than the other way around. God, I hoped not. What could I do to counteract his charisma? Probably nothing at this point. I had let the lies go on too long.

On Georgia Avenue, a car like Dennis's pulled behind me. A gold 1980 Monte Carlo was easy to spot. What was he up to? I went through a light and he didn't make it. I checked for him again after I pulled onto I-495. He wasn't there.

Light snow began to fall, adding to the mountainous snowplow piles already beside the road. This winter was going to break all records. I didn't mind. Winter was my favorite time of the year; something about the way the light falls tinges even the bleakest days with hope.

LIES TOO LONG

Three hours later, the busy hotel staff juggled customers reluctant to check out, and other travelers who had pulled off the highway seeking shelter for the night.

In my room by one o'clock, I kicked off my shoes, turned on the TV and dialed Bob Randall, the Madison Research accountant I dealt with. While on hold, I heard the weather guy say five to eight inches more of the white stuff was expected tonight and five more tomorrow. An extra day away from the stress of home on the company tab was fine with me. Just what the doctor ordered.

"Hi Laurel, you made it." Bob's voice always had a smile in it.

"Hi Bob. Yep, just in time. Are you going to head on home because of the snow, or can we still meet?"

"Dinner with you is the highlight of my day, sugar."

"Oh Bob, you sweet talker." I visualized Bob's chin dimple and his mischievous green eyes.

"I've got us a table at the steak house you like. I'll pick you up at six?"

The thought of a juicy rare steak made my mouth water. "Okay, if you're sure we shouldn't eat here."

"At the Ramada Inn? You got a hankering for shrimp pasta, or do you want a succulent slab of meat? One smothered in mushroom and onions, that is."

"Hmm, let me think a minute." Always the subtle sexual innuendo with the meat reference. When other guys tried that with me, I wasn't having it, but I let Bob get away with it. I'm not sure why, except there was a harmlessness about him beneath that macho crap.

I pulled back the pink, red, aqua and white spread, no doubt selected because it matched the three aqua chairs in the room. Two surrounded the round maple writing table. The third was situated for TV viewing.

The next thing I knew, ringing railed at me in my dreams. Finally, I squinted at the phone, and then at my watch.

"Bob?"

"I'm in the lobby, Laurel. You okay?"

"Yeah, just fell asleep. Give me ten minutes."

I peed for half my allotted time, then washed my face. The nap had done me good. I looked like a serious businesswoman, not a harried pregnant one. As I brushed my teeth and hair, I debated changing into my red suit, but my coat would hide most of the wrinkles of this black one. Besides, the steak house was low lit for easier adultery. Not that Bob and I were about that, but every town needed such a place. I added a red sheen to my lips and closed my door behind me.

"There she is," Bob announced, grinning. I emerged from the elevator straight into his arms and inhaled Old Spice. It occurred to me that Dennis didn't wear cologne. Womanizers couldn't leave tell-tale evidence.

Bob whispered, "Hello, my chocolate buttercup. Good to see you again." Bob and I had been wheeling and dealing for several months now. Madison Research was set to embark on a new investment strategy for their pension plan. Previously, I'd made my proposal and their board of directors had approved it, pending Bob's endorsement. He and I needed to finalize the details.

I smiled and patted his back. He was close to sixty, and had a few white strands intermingled with his black hair that he combed straight back. His face, etched with laugh lines, comforted me.

"I'm parked right out front. Shall we?" He offered me his arm.

"Let's," I agreed, threading my arm through his.

He escorted me to his white Explorer and waited until I was seated. On his way around to the driver's side, he patted his breast pocket. "Oh, wait. I made an appointment and left my pen. I wouldn't bother, but my daughter gave it to me for my birthday last month."

I tried to roll down the window, but couldn't. I pushed the door ajar. "I remember. Your initials are on it." Bob had divorced last year after fifteen years of marriage. Sarah, his ten-year-old daughter, would not be happy if he lost that pen. Little presents like that are part of the glue holding relationships together when a kid lives apart from a parent. I knew that firsthand; I had lived with my grandfather and used to see my mother only intermittently.

LIES TOO LONG

The snow angled in under the canopy as I sat in the car. I was watching it fall when someone snatched opened my door and pointed a gun at me.

"You know what this is about."

The gun prevented me from thinking clearly enough to answer, but some part of my brain assumed a mugging. I lifted my purse toward a face covered by a dark ski mask.

"Hey!" I heard Bob say.

The mugger turned. Pop. The sound was crisp, like a firecracker going off. Someone screamed. Then I heard another firecracker pop, and something whizzed right past me, shattering the driver-side window. I screamed and waited for the warmth of my own blood.

CHAPTER 8

So many questions. They kept asking me so many questions. I tried to relegate them to the "do without thinking" part of my brain while I figured out what had just happened. Every few minutes from the secluded corner of the lobby, I verified that I hadn't imagined the whole thing. "He's dead?"

Blue Suit—I didn't remember his name—exchanged looks with Brown Suit, whose name I did remember—Detective Spoon. Maybe Blue Suit's name was Dish and they would run away together. I needed a fairy tale to come true about now.

Detective Spoon answered. "He's gone, Ms. Novak. The paramedics did what they could." Then back to the questions. "Now the ski mask, describe it again."

"It was black with holes for the eyes, nose and mouth," I said, biting the nail from an index finger.

"So, from seeing this guy's nose, you know he was African American?"

"I don't remember seeing his nose. I said his voice sounded black, maybe. I think."

"And what did he say to you?"

"He said, 'You know what this is.' How many times do I have to answer the same questions?"

Spoon edged forward on the pink-and-brown-striped love seat and said, "A man is dead, Ms. Novak. We owe it to him and his family to do the job right and find the killer. When we're satisfied, we stop asking. You heard another shot and then what?"

"The window shattered. Glass was everywhere." I reached into my hair and pulled out a shard, eerily proving my point. Blue Suit allowed me to drop it into his hand. "I thought I was cut, but I wasn't."

"You were lucky," Blue Suit said. "You say his hands were gloved?"

"Black knit gloves, yes."

"And you're sure he used his right hand?" Blue Suit again. Detective Spoon looked over his notes.

"Yes, yes. When I close my eyes, that's what I see. That's all I see." But then, I saw Sarah in my mind's eye and my tears fell. "One shot killed him? He's dead?" I sniffed. Blue Suit handed me a tissue.

"Thank you. What's your name again?"

"Detective McKnight. Just call me Mac."

"Okay, thanks." Mac's left jaw was dented, like a piece of bone was missing. I fleetingly wondered why he hadn't had reconstructive surgery. His eyes were honey-brown, like the Latino waiters in the coffee place in Wheaton.

"It was a stomach wound, close range," Mac explained.

"Still, the ambulance came so quickly. Was it a large caliber weapon?"

"You know guns?" Spoon asked.

"No, I watch the Discovery Health Channel. With medical interventions being what they are today—I can't believe he's dead."

My weapon of choice was a space heater. I covered my face and bit my lower lip so the inappropriate insane laughter that threatened to gurgle up would stay submerged. I shifted focus. "Were you able to locate his wife? His ex-wife? She lives somewhere in the area. She moved recently . . ."

"Were you and Mr. Randall having an affair?" Spoon asked.

Had they been looking at me funny just now? I blinked a few times, gathering composure. "Why? What makes you ask something like that?"

"We have to look at all possible angles. Were you?"

"Of course not. Ours was strictly a work relationship. Did you find his ex-wife? Because he has a daughter . . ."

"Yes, his family has been notified," Mac said.

"It was probably just a robbery, don't you think?" I searched Spoon's white face, and then Mac's black one. "You think it was personal?"

"We have to look at every possibility," Spoon repeated.

"My head is pounding and I have to use the bathroom, and I don't think I have anything else to tell you that you can use. I'm sorry." I was numb, they had to see it. I was virtually brain—no, I didn't want to use the word dead. My brain was numb, except it wouldn't turn off, not the thinking part. If it was personal and Bob had merely interrupted something meant for me, then the nightmare was nowhere near over. Who would want me dead besides Dennis?

No, too much. Too much to think about now. I needed to use the bathroom, find something to take for my headache and rest, maybe sleep, and afterwards I'd regroup. I get a handle on everything eventually. When I was sixteen, a tornado roared over us in church. Other people panicked while I calmly ordered folks under tables. Now, at forty, I was pregnant with the twins of my best friend's fiancé—just a momentary social glitch. I would figure it out and keep my babies and my friend. My business associate murdered while I waited in his car? Not a problem. Just give me a minute, I'll absorb this and be back in the game tomorrow.

I stood up. Feeling shaky, I quickly sat back down, pointing to the trashcan. Mac knew instantly what I meant, but Spoon wasn't as quick. Consequently, I drenched Spoon's nice brown penny loafers in vomit.

People react to stressful situations by throwing up all the time, pregnant or not. Mac escorted me to the ladies' room, telling me to take it easy. I detected a slight Jamaican accent for the first time.

Alone inside the bathroom, I gripped the edges of the cold marble sink. That sharp businesswoman I had seen two hours earlier in the mirror had been transformed into a wild-haired mahogany victim of violence. When I emerged, Mac handed me a can of 7-Up and I sipped gratefully.

"You want Advil?" He held up a bottle of it. "Not sure how wise that is on an upset stomach."

"Yes, no, wait. Tylenol." I thought pregnant women could take Tylenol for sure. Why didn't I know these things? I had bought a book about pregnancy, but hadn't started reading yet. "I hate to ask, but do you think you can get me some Tylenol?"

Spoon walked toward us in response to Mac's gesture.

He handed me off to Spoon, who walked me toward the elevators. "I'll see you to your room. One of the patrolmen will stay outside your door tonight."

My mouth went completely dry in my nervousness. "It really looks like it might have been personal? Not just a random robbery?"

"Ma'am, there were two ATM's in a three-block radius, both fairly isolated. There was a near-empty strip mall a few feet from the on-ramp. Lots of opportunities for quick cash. So this guy waited outside a very busy hotel to rob someone at gunpoint? We can't rule anything out yet."

If I weren't nauseous, I would be impressed or scared out of my mind. At least this small town took what little crime they had seriously. "You need to catch him, Detective."

"That's the plan."

By the time Mac brought the Tylenol up to my room, I was almost in tears, my head throbbing like a strobe light on coke. I fell into bed groaning.

In my dream, the small, YMCA-like bedroom depressed me. Maybe it had something to do with the metal bar attached along one wall in the tiny bathroom. Something to hold onto if I needed help. In this case, something to grip if the pain became unbearable.

I settled under a thin cover in my dream. A nurse who looked like Emma carried two clear beakers, each half-filled with a reddish liquid. A mass of tissue floated near the bottom of both. She set them on a ledge. "The doctor will be here soon."

My babies. My babies were in those tubes.

I woke, my face wet and my body stiff. I gingerly straightened out as I remembered where I was, rubbing my stomach to make sure things were as they should be. The dream reflected Dennis's objective, not mine—never mine. Shuddering, I struggled to an upright position on my elbows. But, something was still wrong. Then, the horror washed over me like pus from a wound. Bob. Oh God. I collapsed on the pillows again.

I lay in bed, drowning in it, reviewing yesterday's events. Should I call his ex-wife or his mother? Would either appreciate hearing about his last minutes, or would they somehow blame me?

I hadn't eaten since lunch yesterday. I needed food to fuel my brain so I could figure out my next step. After showering, I put on my red suit and applied makeup. No one would know the turmoil raging inside from looking at me.

The patrol officer stood and nodded good morning as I left the room. "Detective McKnight would like you to meet him in the restaurant downstairs, ma'am."

I thanked him for looking out for me all night, then asked, "Any breaking news?"

"No. No news."

In the restaurant, I saw plenty of business types sitting at round brown tables with spindle-back chairs, but no Detective McKnight. When the patrolman's radio crackled behind me, customers looked at me as if I had toilet paper on my shoe. They whispered, "She's the woman . . ."

I declined a table in the middle of the room and opted for a booth near a window. I could see the canopy I'd sat under in Bob's car yesterday. Maybe this wasn't the table I wanted after all. Thank God, the angle didn't let me see where his body had fallen. Through the window, I saw Mac put out a cigarette, turn his coat collar up and put his hands in his pockets. He had on the same blue suit. He adjusted his earpiece and headed inside.

A minute later he sat across from me, earpiece gone, looking haggard.

"Have you been up all night interviewing people?" I asked.

"Me, Spoon and a patrolman. Sixty-three rooms, forty-seven of them occupied, seventy-six people to talk to."

"Where's Spoon now?"

"At home with his wife, I would imagine."

"And is your wife home in Jamaica?"

His eyebrows shot up at my question. "My ex-wives are here. Have you ordered yet?"

"No, the waitress is coming now. Here, as in Delaney?"

He turned to the waitress. "We changed our minds." Mac stretched his hand across the table for mine. I was tempted to whine about how hungry I was when he said, "I know a place with a much better view."

I hesitated. The coffee smelled so good, but I let him lead me to the lobby. Next to him, I felt protected. His presence warded off stares, contrary to what I might have expected. He pushed the elevator button.

"I'll get my coat and meet you outside," I said.

"I'm coming up with you." On the elevator he looked steadily at me and said, "I meant my ex-wives are here in this country. Since we're being personal, why aren't you married?"

"Good question. I always wanted to be."

"What? And give up your business career? I don't see you at home chasing little ones."

Hmm. Was he baiting me? Did he know I was pregnant? Either his almond-colored eyes didn't miss much or he merely equated having a man with having a family. Was Mac a throwback to another generation where women were more domestic? Well, there were trade-offs, no matter which lifestyle was chosen.

Opening the door to my room I asked, "You have children?"

"Four boys."

I watched him scan the unmade bed, the dresser, the bathroom. He opened the closet door and took my tan wool coat off the hanger, holding it up for me to slip my arms into the sleeves. I checked the mirror to see how the dark fox fur collar settled around my neck. I looked good under the circumstances. His expression of appreciation told me he thought I did too.

On the way back to the lobby I asked, "I'm not a suspect, am I?"

"Everyone is a suspect. Now that some of the shock has worn off, is there anything else you can tell me?"

"No, but I do want to pay my respects to his family today. Where are we going?"

"Mom-and-pop café a few blocks over."

Although there was no conversation on the way to his car, my thoughts clanged like cymbals in my head. If I told Mac about Dennis, he could determine if he was involved. But then Emma would have to know; or would Mac agree to keep her out of it if I asked him? If Dennis really had tried to kill me, didn't that mean all bets were off? Surely it must. Any second now I'd be on the phone spilling my guts to Emma, telling her of her fiancé's murderous intent and asking her not to hate me. Unless, of course, Dennis wasn't behind this after all.

"Mac, was there physical evidence? Anything to work with in finding this guy? Anybody get a description of his car?" Tell me it wasn't Dennis, please.

We settled into a Crown Victoria and drove away from the hotel, onto streets quiet except for the distant roar of a snow blower.

"We have multiple car descriptions, actually. We're checking every lead. We have an approximate height based on the angle of the shot into the Explorer, and we know he used a 9 mm gun."

"That's good information." They had leads. Whoever had done this wouldn't get away with it. I'd know soon enough if Dennis was behind it. "Everyone's a suspect, but I'm free to go anytime, right?"

"You wouldn't want to leave in this weather, would you?"

"The highway will be clear. I plan to leave tomorrow."

"Sure, you can leave, unless we have a reason to detain you before then. Right now, we're looking into Randall's personal life and his business dealings."

"And when you finish with his business dealings and personal life and you find nothing, where will you look?"

"We'll look at your life, Ms. Novak, to see what, if anything, shakes lose."

I swallowed hard. I should tell him now about Dennis and me. Instead I said, "Delaney seems to have a lot of resources for such a small town."

"Small town, huge tax base. Rich folks leaving the big cities in droves need a place to call home. This is it."

"How did you end up here?"

"The job. From Jamaica to Florida to New York to here. I like to think there's a master plan, don't you?"

"It would be great if there were some final explanation for what we seem to put ourselves through. Where do your sons live?"

"My twins go to the state college ninety minutes down the road."

"Twins," I restated, and smiled.

"Yes. Some of my finest work, I must admit, but I didn't stop there. I have a son in the army and my youngest lives with my parents in Jamaica, but he'll be here at Christmas."

"That's funny. He gets to have a snowy vacation while everyone else is seeking warmth."

He smiled. "Twenty, eighteen and seven, in case you're wondering."

"So you've been married three times?"

He looked at me for a long minute, as if trying to understand why I seemed so interested in his personal life. I knew why. I needed a knight in shining armor about now, and McKnight had appeared. Perhaps it was kismet, but more realistically, it was a desperate woman's longing for safety, a woman not as tough as she liked to pretend.

His ragged jaw line gave his face character and he seemed like a decent man. He'd probably be good for me, but in another time and place. Another life.

"Twice. This last time I couldn't make it happen. I'd have to pray long and hard about marrying a third time."

He hadn't married the mother of his child still in Jamaica. The good detective was fallible. Even better. Maybe he would understand how I'd gotten myself into this pickle. My stomach growled.

"You're probably starving, Ms. Novak. We'll have good, filling food where we're going."

46

"After we eat, then what?"

"I'll take you back to the hotel. Your lawyer will want to see you, I would imagine."

"I didn't call a lawyer."

"Your company probably did."

"Oh." I wondered what the home office reaction would be.

In the second restaurant, people still looked at me, or it felt as if they did, but the atmosphere was friendlier. The blonde waitress said she was sorry for my trouble. The thought of grits, ham and eggs sunny-side-up had my fork in my hand before the waitress set my plate before me.

I sopped up the egg yolk with toast. Taking a break from my half-eaten meal, I glanced around. I expected Ward and June Cleaver to walk in any minute—the place had that ultra-white, small-town kind of feel. If I lived in a town like this, I'd have to drive an hour to find somebody to do my hair. Maybe I could tell Mac my woes and he'd leave this Norman Rockwell town and come be my bodyguard in the big city. We'd rescue each other.

I took a deep breath, leaned forward and began to speak. "Mac . . ." His eyes drifted toward the window. I followed his gaze. Blue and red flashing lights whizzed by.

"We better go," Mac said.

In his car I learned that the flashing lights had been cars responding to a call reporting a 9 mm gun found under a boxwood bush.

CHAPTER 9

Just after seven A.M., Mac dropped me off at the hotel on his way home to rest. Paula Mayfield, the company attorney, crossed the lobby to meet me, delaying my plan to crawl back into bed on a full stomach.

"Oh my gosh, Laurel. I was hoping I'd catch you. You've been through an awful ordeal. How are you holding up?" she asked in her Arkansas accent.

"I'm okay, Paula, all things considered." I looked at Paula's smile, which looked surgically implanted. I expected to see worry lines on her forehead, but Botox had probably erased them.

"I'm glad to hear it." She laced her elbow around mine, her voice low and close. "I understand major work went into earning this company account so I'm here to see what patching up we need to do—damage control. I'm on my way to a breakfast meeting at Madison's."

"Oh, I'll come. I don't have any idea where Madison stands on hiring us. The investment plan I put together is certainly viable, but it's their call."

"If Madison Research makes the move to us, I'm sure you wouldn't want to be reminded of what happened each time you came to this town. You understand, I'm sure. The company has replaced you on this account."

"Oh." And me not being around as a reminder of Bob might make them feel better about going with our company. I hadn't thought about that. All my time and effort would be minimally recognized, if at all. My vertical move up in the company had come to a screeching halt. My shoulders drooped while I pondered this double whammy: Bob, and now my job derailment. By this time next week I'd be back to holding donut meetings to persuade teachers to invest for retirement through our firm. That was one more truth I needed to deal with, but compared to what Bob's family was going through, I was ashamed for even having thought of it. "I'll see you later, Paula. Thanks." I pushed the button for the elevator.

"Oh. Okay." She seemed nonplussed that I didn't want to chat more. "There's no need for you to speak with the police again. Refer them to me from now on."

"Sure," I said, waiting for the people on the elevator to exit so I could get on.

"And don't worry about sending flowers, Laurel. The company took care of that."

I nodded, then the elevator doors closed behind me and I pushed four.

The hallway was empty. No police officer standing guard must mean the threat level had lessened. I hesitated a moment before opening my door, and then told myself even if Dennis was behind this, he probably wouldn't strike twice in the same location.

In my room, I sagged onto the bed and began removing my coat. What was the answer? It would be nice if I could just run away and start my life over somewhere else. That was it. I located the hotel stationery and sat at the table. I'd write a letter to Emma telling her everything, contact someone to sell my house and its contents and move to Seattle or Maui or somewhere. Things had gotten out of hand. I'd leave with my babies and Dennis would be happy I had gone. Or would he? Would that be enough to satisfy him?

Maybe I could leave without a trace and not tell Emma anything at all. No, I couldn't afford to simply drop off the planet, not with two babies to take care of. I was a good money manager, but not that good. I threw down my pen in frustration. Running away wasn't the answer.

I could ask Mac for help or I could handle Dennis before he or one of his hired henchmen had another chance to turn the business end of a gun on me, assuming, of course, that Dennis was behind the shooting.

I'd wait until ten this morning, visit with Bob's family and then go home today. Emma wasn't expecting me until tomorrow, so that meant neither was Dennis. It was my turn to deliver a surprise, and the truth was the most powerful weapon I had.

I checked out of the hotel and drove to Bob's mother's home. She was the grandmother on every commercial on American TV, white-haired, wrinkled complexion, and spry. I told her how Bob had returned to the lobby to get his pen Sarah had given him. She responded with a teary smile and said her son was an incredibly thoughtful man and she couldn't believe God had taken him.

God doesn't wear a ski mask, I thought. Mrs. Randall spoke quietly with others who had come to share their condolences while I looked through a series of photo albums that chronicled Bob's birth, continued into his kindergarten years and on to him standing proudly with car keys in his hand. His wedding album was among the collection. And in still another album, I saw him holding a five-minute old Sarah.

I wiped my tears and made my departure by noon. To my dismay, the snow was falling again. It was a full steady snow—the kind that made highway driving less than wise, but I'd leave regardless. I started my car, and then got out to scrape off the snow.

"Can I help?" Mac took the scraper from me while I frowned, surprised to see him again. "Get back in your car, stay warm, Ms. Novak."

"Why are you here?" I asked. A brown Jeep had replaced his Crown Victoria from earlier.

"You checked out. The desk clerk made a call to the station when you did, per my request. Your timing isn't the best." He referred to the snow.

"I heard the forecast yesterday, but I thought I'd take my chances."

"Why? What's so urgent?"

I pulled my collar tighter. "I got this closed-in feeling and needed to go." That was better than explaining this cascading uneasiness in my gut telling me it was time for me to deal with Dennis. "Thanks for everything, Mac. I'm outta here."

He nodded, handed me the scraper and backed away from my car. I got in and headed for the highway. My heart rate returned to normal as the miles passed. It felt good to be moving, although I wasn't sure how I would feel when I got home. Mac was right behind me. Did he intend to follow me all the way to Takoma Park?

Mac was a nice man, too nice for a three-hour drive in a snowstorm. Part of me hoped he'd come to his senses, change his mind and turn around. Part of me enjoyed the attention and feeling safe again, as I had in the hotel restaurant.

Thirty minutes into the drive, when I had relaxed enough to put in a Norah Jones CD, the road surface started to become icy. I gripped the wheel and slowed to forty miles an hour, then gradually dropped to twenty-five. There was no way I could make it home. When Mac flashed his high beams and pulled in front of me, indicating I should follow him, I was relieved. I turned Norah off to concentrate and exited behind Mac, trailing him for two long, excruciating miles down the road. We passed one motel, and then a second one in quick succession as the streets rapidly became one sheet of ice. Maybe he had called ahead and knew they were full. My stomach was in knots. Where were we going?

CHAPTER 10

We finally stopped in front of a bed and breakfast inn with a small welcome sign on the porch overhang. Mac cautiously made his way to my door to help me out, and even with him holding my hand I still almost fell.

"This is treacherous weather," I said, trying to find safe footing.

Slowly we made our way up the salt-strewn porch. The welcome plaque above us read The Dahlia Rosa Inn.

"This is a favorite place of mine," Mac said. "I know the owner."

Inside the foyer, we wiped our feet on a mat before walking toward gleaming oak floors protected by a blue and ivory oriental rug. It was a warm and comforting space, or maybe it was the fact that I could walk without thinking 'ice rink' that appealed to me.

A fifty-ish black man with an inch of crinkly hair all around walked around a maple desk and shook Mac's hand. "Is that Wendell McKnight?"

"It's me, Gary." Mac smiled and they hugged.

Gary gave me the once-over while he pumped Mac's hand. "And who is this vision of loveliness?"

"Gary Thaxton, meet Laurel Novak."

I pulled off my right glove to take his outstretched hand.

"Laurel Novak. A beautiful name for a beautiful woman." He smiled warmly, then turned his attention back to Mac. "Man, you picked a night to visit. I'm going to have to put you two in the honeymoon suite."

"But—" I protested.

"It's the only room I have left."

"You're kidding, right?" I said. "I remember reading this plot in a Harlequin paperback when I was twelve." Both men chuckled.

Mac's eyes sought mine. "Do you really think you won't be safe with me?"

"Oh wait, I was worried about your virtue, Mac."

Mac laughed again. "Ms. Novak, I'm sure, will be comfortable in your honeymoon suite, Gary. I'm going to need somewhere else. A cot in the kitchen, maybe?"

"Oh, I see," Mr. Thaxton said. "Don't worry. We'll come up with something."

Mac went to retrieve my bag. He was such a gentleman. I looked around, smiling at a young couple with a baby and an older female couple—sisters, lovers or just friends. I couldn't tell, but they sat side by side on the sofa in front of a raging fire, drinking wine and talking about the cost of prescription drugs in Canada.

"How many guests can you accommodate, Mr. Thaxton?"

"Call me Gary. We have two regular rooms and two suites."

"Been in business long?" I asked.

"About five years now. That's when I remarried and made the move."

He took my bag from Mac. "This way, folks."

We walked up a flight of stairs and turned right onto a long hall. Gary unlocked the second door and flicked on the light, then placed the key on a small coffee table that sat between a quilted four-poster bed and a cream-colored love seat. The huge room had green wainscoting and white walls.

Gary set my bag on the bed. "You have your own bath through here. Just had the whirlpool tub installed this summer."

Mac made an approving comment.

"Dinner's at six. We encourage you to join us in the dining room, but meals can be sent to your room if requested before five. Your complimentary fruit, nut and cheese tray will be here in a moment."

"Thank you, Gary," I said, clicking on the remote for the gas flame in the fireplace.

Mac handed Gary a credit card.

"The room is on the house. Call it an early Christmas gift, Mac. I owe you one anyway, remember?"

LIES TOO LONG

"Thanks, man."

"Enjoy your stay, and Mac, this is a nonsmoking establishment now. Sorry."

"No problem. I've been meaning to quit."

"Where have I heard that before?" Gary said with a wry smile before softly closing the door.

"That was pretty hairy out there for awhile. Want me to take your coat?" Mac asked.

"Thank you, Mac. You're my hero."

That made him grin before turning toward the window. "I love the view here."

I moved next to him. Woodland lay at the back of the inn. The snow-laden trees bent under the weight. It was like being inside a snow globe.

"Lake Marion is just beyond these woods. It's a great fishing and boating attraction."

I turned to him and again our gazes held. "You should call me Laurel. Which do you do, fish or boat?"

With a surprising casualness, he put his hands on my neck, massaging away the tension from the drive. "I do both, come by them naturally. I'm from Jamaica, you know. What about you?"

I breathed in the sensations, unsure what I should do or say. "Neither." I watched his lips move toward mine in slow motion.

I moaned. I think he thought it was a moan of anticipation. It was angst. I moaned again after our tongues had taken to each other like icing to cake. Abruptly, he broke away.

"Laurel. I'm sorry. I couldn't resist. Look at where we are, the honeymoon suite, but my intentions are honorable, I promise you."

I was speechless. Mac was a phenomenal kisser, or was this my year to unleash pent-up sensuality? Maybe I could blame pregnancy hormones again.

He asked, "Are you all right? I might be wrong, but I thought you wanted me to kiss you."

"I'm not sure what I want." That wasn't completely true. I wanted him, but my motives sucked and I couldn't keep on making bad choices.

"Then, let me help you decide." He kissed me again, his arms pulling me hard into him. Again he tasted like cigarettes and chocolate and I wanted more, but I gently pushed him back. "I have to tell you something, Mac." I visualized a sword in my hand, slicing through the evil vortex that held me trapped in lies. I had to leave the dark side sometime.

"I need to sit down for this, I just know it." He settled on the love seat.

"In about seven months I'll give birth to twins."

For a moment I thought he hadn't heard me and then he said, "Twins?"

"The father isn't interested, our relationship is a mess, and I don't think it's fair to bring you into the middle of our imbroglio."

"I see. Ah, man." This time he rubbed the tension from his own neck. "That's a lot to think about." He looked at my stomach as if it had more details to reveal.

"Of course. And I'm sorry. I've been giving mixed signals. With Bob's murder and you being so nice to me—well, I needed some kindness in my life. You offered me that and I took advantage of it."

He nodded. "Any port in the storm, so to speak. I've been there a time or two myself. No harm—no foul." After thirty seconds of awkward silence he pointed at the door. "Say, I'm going to go check on that cheese and fruit tray."

"You do that." My watch said two. I didn't expect Mac to come back for a long time, if at all.

I was wired after that drive and our conversation, but I wasn't in a chatting mood. A nice walk in normal weather conditions would have done the trick, but that was out. I took my book, *Having Twins*, from my bag and read. Before I dozed off I'd learned that yes, pregnant women could take Tylenol. Thank God. I woke up at four, changed into my pair of "just in case" jeans I always traveled with and made my way to the dining room finally ready to mingle.

LIES TOO LONG

An attractive woman sporting cropped hair and large hips semi-camouflaged in a Indian-style skirt set the table. She looked up at me with a cordial smile when I entered. "Hi there, you must be Laurel. I'm Gary's wife, Melina. Gary and Mac are playing pool in the game room with Danny and Britney."

"Okay. Can I help you, Melina?"

"Sure. It's meatloaf and mashed potato night. You can help bring out the food for the buffet there." She gestured toward the massive maple buffet against one wall. "Jenny and Charlie are in the kitchen, they'll get you started."

Through an arched doorway I found a couple who looked to be in their well-preserved seventies. "Hi Jenny, hi Charlie. Melina sent me to bring out the meatloaf."

"Reinforcements have arrived, Charlie."

If Charlie owned a dog that looked like him, it would be a buff bulldog to match his hanging jowls. Jenny reminded me of a high-strung cinnamon poodle, full of energy, prancing around the room.

"She's cute too, Jenny. Quick, get the chain. We don't want to lose her like we lost the last one."

As I stood watching them a minute, I could tell they were a stitch to be around. Charlie's and Jenny's movements looked choreographed. That's what happens after years of being with someone. Would I ever experience anything close to that in my lifetime?

Charlie said, "Oven mitts to your right, meatloaf in the oven, put it in the first serving pan on your left on the buffet."

I took the mitts and got started. "This place must be serious work to run," I commented.

"We only serve breakfast and dinner, so most days things run smoothly," Jenny said. "Charlie, better get the coffee going and I'll go out to the freezer for the sorbet. Do we need anything else while I'm there?"

They seemed like a happy pair, and I envied the normalcy of their lives. "People," I felt like shouting, "my life is in shambles. A little sympathy here, please!"

I brought out the meatloaf and, on my second trip out with the potatoes, Mac took the bowl from me. "Let me help you, Laurel." I couldn't tell anything from his eyes, except they were as calming and as beautiful as ever. He assisted with the string beans, rutabaga, and cornbread.

Jenny and Charlie had a place at the table too. Gary offered grace before we made a line to serve ourselves.

The female couple, Beatrice and Agatha, turned out to be sisters, retirees from South Dakota. They each had their own room which, they said, was the secret of happy traveling. The young couple and the baby, Danny, Britney and Ian, were traveling home to New York from Oregon at their own pace. I sat next to Ian in his high chair. So beautiful. What would it be like when I had two high chairs around a table? Two high chairs, two of everything else. Ian's presence renewed my energy. I hadn't been this at peace in weeks.

"Gary, how did you and Mac meet?" I asked.

"We go way back, but we haven't seen each other for what? A year now?"

Melina nodded, sitting down, the last to be served.

"A year ago my teenage daughter, Dahlia, needed help extracting herself from a little problem," Gary explained. He moved food off his front teeth with a sweep of his tongue. "Mac made it as painless as it could have been."

"Raising teenagers is like trying to nail Jell-O to a tree," Melina said.

Everyone laughed.

"I'm glad it worked out. So, you two met because of your daughter?" I asked, still nosy.

"Actually we got acquainted during Desert Storm."

"God Bless America," Beatrice said.

Agatha said, "Dahlia is your daughter. And who is Rosa?" She no doubt had the name of the bed and breakfast in mind.

"She's my granddaughter." Gary reached in his wallet and sent around two pictures of a gorgeous, would-be baby model.

LIES TOO LONG

I ate my fill, enjoying Jenny and Charlie's down home cooking, laughing at Melina's wit and the sisters' jokes. Britney and Danny were quiet, but glancing underneath the table, I caught them playing footsie. It was encouraging to know babies were not automatic romance squelchers. I looked at Mac and smiled.

Sorbet covered with fruit-flavored liqueurs was a nice surprise for dessert but, of course, I had mine plain.

CHAPTER 11

"How much love do you have for this guy?"

I sat on the quilt in the suite, formulating my answer to Mac's question. "I have zero love for him. I let a physical attraction get way, way, way out of hand, but there's life growing inside me now. Life that I already love and that I will nurture, despite what he says."

"Okay then. My turn for confession."

"Go ahead."

"Five years ago I found a sleepy little town so I could reinvent myself. Or it was sleepy until yesterday. When you said I didn't need to be in the middle of your drama, you were right."

I felt my head bobbing up and down in agreement. That's what I had expected him to say, but it still hurt to hear it. I took a breath to fortify me and walked slowly toward the door. "You're a smart man, Mac. Thanks again for all you've done for me. Maybe one day we'll get to know each other when the circumstances aren't so crazy."

He looked at me, nodding somberly, almost smiling. "I probably made walking away from you sound easier than it is. It's been a lonely five years and I was looking forward to something new, to getting to know someone like you.

"Okay, Laurel Novak, have a safe journey, tomorrow and always. I have your address and number. One day I might call or drop by just to see how you and the twins are doing."

I shook his hand and kissed his cheek. "Please do."

I closed the door and chastised myself. "There now. You see how mature adults deal with each other, with honesty and mutual respect. That's how you treat people you care about. You care about Emma. What on earth have you been thinking?"

LIES TOO LONG

I dug out my phone, surprised by the tears on my cheeks. Must be hormones and a need for a drowning woman—me—to have someone like Mac to cling to. Even so, it was time to grow up and accept the consequences of my actions. The lies had gone on long enough. Being around Mac, Gary and the others had reminded me how far outside the realm of normal human behavior I had slipped.

My phone began singing, telling me I had messages waiting. It had been turned off since I'd been in Delaney. I would deal with the waiting messages in a minute after I talked to Emma.

"Hello, Laurel."

Dennis answered Emma's cell phone, and the wonders of caller ID had apparently told him it was me.

I couldn't speak for a few seconds. A lava-like rage came over me. "Let me talk to Emma."

"That's impossible."

I made a sound of disgust, furious he would not let me speak with my friend, but helpless to make him. "No, getting away with being an accessory to murder is what's impossible. They're going to find out what you did, Dennis. Put Emma on the phone."

"Huh? We must have a bad connection."

I hung up on him. That's fine. Tomorrow I'd be home. No, I wouldn't even go home. I'd find Emma, tell her everything, then go straight to the police and tell them Dennis Butler had killed Bob in an attempt to murder me and his unborn children.

My cell phone rang immediately; Dennis again or Emma returning my call? I had to answer to be sure.

"Laurel, don't hang up on me again. Are you on your way home? I called your office this afternoon and got your hotel number, but was told you had checked out."

"Why do you have Emma's phone? Where is she?"

"You need to get here as soon as possible."

Something in his tone made dread swirl around me like a dust cloud. "Why?"

"Emma was at your place yesterday, measuring stuff for your new nursery. The fire marshal said a faulty heater caused the fire."

"What!" I grabbed a bedpost to keep me upright. I was shaking, afraid to ask for more details, but knowing I had to. "Emma . . .?"

"Seems her clothes ignited and she jumped out the upstairs window. She's in a coma now."

I lowered myself onto the bed in slow motion. "What? Dennis, stop lying!" This could not be happening. "What? What heater?" Then I remembered I had put the broken space heater from work in my garage. Emma must have assumed it usable.

"When did you get a space heater, Laurel?"

I didn't answer him. "A coma? My God. How badly was she burned?"

"Mostly second degree burns, they say."

"Mostly? I'll be there as soon as I can. Tell her I'm coming." If I left now, driving at a snail's pace, I could be home around midnight.

I packed in record time, only pausing when I got to the front porch and viewed the menacing points on the hanging icicles. I was chopping ice off my car when Mac interrupted me again.

"We've got to stop meeting like this," he joked.

"Mac, my best friend got hurt in a fire! I have to get home!"

His expression and tone changed instantly. "A fire? I'm so sorry, but the highway isn't passable, Laurel. I've been listening to the radio. They've closed the roads."

"Well, what about the train? I've got to get to Baltimore! This is an emergency! Your Jeep has four-wheel drive. Can we get through with your police credentials?"

"No, I'm afraid not, not tonight. We'll leave first thing in the morning. I'll drive you."

"Can't we go west then cut back over? All the roads can't be closed."

He shook his head. "We could risk getting through taking an alternate route, but it would be extremely unsafe and take twice as long."

I crumpled in his arms. "Oh Mac. It's all my fault."

"What do you mean?"

"She was at my house doing something nice for me and I had this space heater and . . ."

Mac's forehead creased. "Come on. We'll find out as much as we can from this end. Has anyone suggested foul play?"

"Foul play? No, Dennis said the firefighters attributed it to a space heater." I stared at him, trying to make sense of what he'd just asked. "Oh. You're thinking because of the shooting and now the fire at my house . . . oh God." No, that couldn't be right. No one knew about the space heater except me.

"Let's see what we can find out."

We passed a congregation of anxious faces on the way to the room. I guess we'd made more noise than I thought.

"Is there anything I can do?" Melina asked.

"It's all right," Mac told her. "We'll be okay."

Back in the room, the tension was getting to me. I gripped my stomach and breathed deeply, trying to stave off the bile rising in my throat. Mac stood near the bed, using the phone. I paced.

"This is utter madness," I muttered. Just then I lost the battle with the bile, but I made it to the bathroom in time. Five heaves later, Mac helped me to my feet and offered me a damp facecloth.

"Thank you. Did you get through to anyone?"

Green-faced, Mac looked as if I'd ordered him a tasty dish of toasted water bugs as he used a second facecloth to wipe vomit from my fox fur. "I was on hold. I'll try again now."

I nodded, took off my coat, and sat on the side of the tub to make sure this episode of nausea was over. When I came out, Mac said my house was secure. Damage was significant. Preliminary reports pointed to the heater being the cause, as Dennis had said. Emma was in stable condition at Bayview, Johns Hopkins's burn unit.

"Thank you. How early can we leave?"

"Daybreak."

I rubbed my left temple, then both of them.

Mac said, "You need Tylenol, right?"

"I still have the bottle from yesterday, but a 7-Up would be nice. Thank you. You are too good to me."

"Gotcha. I'm going to start the tub for you. A warm bath will help, don't you think?"

"A bath?" I couldn't think any more. My mind felt thick yet fragile, like a mound of cotton candy.

"Yeah, in the whirlpool tub."

"Okay."

Mac came back with the soda, but I hadn't moved from my spot in the middle of the floor. With a concerned look, he walked me over to the bed and waited for me to sit. He got the Tylenol from my purse. I took it while he turned off the water.

He sat next to me on the bed and said, "Tell me about her."

"Emma? She's my best friend, Mac. She talks in this soft, kindergarten teacher voice with such expression, but she never raises her voice. She's what people would call self-directed. She's thoughtful, and funny. I don't—I don't want to lose her."

Mac squeezed my hand. "Sounds like a good friend to have. You won't lose her. Where does she work?"

"She's a car salesperson."

"Married?"

"Recently engaged."

"Nice guy?"

Here was my chance handed to me on a platter. I shook my head to the question and to the opportunity to bare my soul. "It's not a good match. If I had my way, they would never marry."

"Does Emma know how you feel?"

"Not yet, but she will." There was a moment of silence.

"Your water's getting cold. Will you be all right?"

"I think so. Do you have a decent place to sleep, Mac?"

He smiled at my implied invitation. "I'll be all right."

Resting my head on his chest a minute, I wrapped him in a loose embrace. "I can't thank you enough."

LIES TOO LONG

When Mac left, I eased myself into tepid water, turning on the tap to reheat it. Seconds later, bubbles burbled while I covered my face and cried for Bob, Emma and me.

Dressed and packed by five in the morning, I berated myself for not knowing how to reach Mac. I set my bag near the door and checked for a newspaper. I would read it until he came. He called instead.

"Mac?"

"Good, you sound like you're already up. A surprise is coming your way."

"I'm up. Surprise?"

"You hear it?" he asked.

"Hear it?"

"Listen."

The distant whirl of helicopter blades came closer and closer.

"A helicopter?"

"I've got a friend who uses a chopper at her ski resort. She'll take you to Baltimore. There's a clearing near the lake."

"The lake? But, Mac—"

"Hurry."

"Thank you, Mac. I appreciate this so much."

The pilot appeared to be stern, not the friendly outdoors type I had expected. The instrument panel intimidated me. "Pretty expensive piece of equipment," I offered.

She grunted. "Bayview?"

"Yes. Known Mac long?"

"Long enough."

I knew she wouldn't brook me throwing up on her horizon detector thingie, so I took some deep breaths and willed myself not to be sick. I concentrated on Mac and his kindness and vaguely wondered how I was going to get my car, but the bulk of my thoughts were with Emma. She had to be all right. She just had to be.

CHAPTER 12

The Johns Hopkins staff let me in to see Emma because I told them I was her sister and I'd just flown in and probably because I had the look of someone for whom visiting hours held absolutely no meaning.

She was attached to some kind of heart monitor. Her right arm and her legs up to her thighs were wrapped lightly in gauze. A cream that looked like Noxzema but was minus the smell oozed around the dressings. A clear liquid dripped intravenously.

"Oh Emma." I wanted to lean over the bedrail and stroke her face. "This didn't have to happen. I'm so sorry. Please forgive me."

Without warning, Dennis stood behind me, snug against my butt. Who else had the audacity?

I whirled, fully intending to knock him into the next decade. He caught my wrist and laughed eerily from behind his own paper mask.

A blue clad nurse walked in, her arched eyebrows giving us the I-know-y'all-ain't-up-here-clowning look.

Dennis backed away and spoke up. "How's Emma doing today, Tereka? It's Tereka, right?"

"Yeah, it's Tereka. Emma had a calm night," she said, taking vitals. "I'm Tereka Moore," she introduced herself to me.

"Hi, I'm Laurel Novak. When can I speak to her doctor?"

"She's got a couple of them and you never know exactly when they will come through, but Doctor Lewis generally does morning rounds before I get off."

"Thanks." I had a few hours to kill, but nowhere else I wanted to be. Dennis watched me from one chair; I found a second one, pulled it to the opposite side of the bed and fished for my paperback book. My nerves were shot. And what was the proper protocol for sitting in a hospital room with someone who had tried to kill you?

"Emma, I just started this one. I'll read it to you. It's called *Dangling Hearts*."

"Aw, hell no. I'm outta here. Emma, I'll see you tonight, baby." He winked at me.

Bastard. Bastard. Bastard.

"Here. You want to take care of these?" he asked.

"What?" I accepted the clear plastic bag he handed me.

"Emma's jewelry, her earrings and a necklace."

I looked at Emma's ring finger. Her engagement ring was gone.

He read my mind. "Oh, I got that." He winked again and left.

Had he paid to have me killed? I couldn't detect anything different in his demeanor toward me other than him taking advantage of Emma's eyes being closed. If he had tried to kill me, wouldn't his behavior show it? How could I be sure?

I got no further than the prologue before I decided I needed food. "I'll be right back. I'm going to the cafeteria to get something to eat," I told Emma.

Dennis slid in the elevator from nowhere, blocking the floor panel, licking his lips like a hungry wolf. I backed away. All he needed was a gun, a knife or even a hypodermic needle and it was over.

"They'll catch you. Stay away from me!"

"What? Who is they?" He looked baffled.

"What's the problem, Dennis? Can't you find thugs who know their craft? Bob is dead!"

"Oh, so I hired someone to take you out?" He shook his head, laughing as if I had told him Santa Claus was real. "That's pretty good, but wrong, Laurel. Too bad about this Bob, whoever the hell Bob is, but it wasn't me."

"I saw your car, Dennis. You followed me, then probably sent word where I'd be to your pathetic guns for hire, or whatever you call that criminal element you hang with."

"I see your car all the time too. Maybe that's because we both live in Takoma Park."

"Let me out of this elevator before I start screaming."

"Hold on. I can prove it. I picked up an antennae motor from Tolliver's Auto Supply on New Hampshire around eleven. How would I follow you to Pennsylvania and be back in Takoma Park at eleven?"

"You didn't have to follow me. Emma knew I'd be at the Ramada."

"Oh yeah. Like I'm going to ask Emma about your hotel accommodations. I had to call your office to find out where you were staying."

"Tolliver's Auto Supply. I'll check it out, or rather, I'll have the Delaney Police check it out. Now, get out of my way."

The doors opened. Dennis said, "I called around. Got this doctor's name. He's good." He handed me a slip of paper. I balled it up and threw it in his face.

I ate a perfunctory breakfast and came back in time to catch Dr. Lewis. The green shirt under his lab coat needed pressing, his orange and yellow tie was knotted off-center and several strands of sandy hair defied gravity. A man more devoted to his job, I hoped, than to his appearance. That would work for me.

"How is she doing, Doctor?"

The rumpled Dr. Lewis had skipped 'the translate to laymen's terms' class. I understood nothing except thirty-eight percent second-degree burns, and brain and spinal swelling.

"So when the brain swelling subsides, she'll wake up?" I asked.

"That's the scenario we expect, but we can't say for certain. We have some concerns about her head injury and there's a very slight chance of paralysis."

"I don't understand." I didn't want to understand anything associated with that word.

"The angle of her fall seems to have jarred the vertebrae and perhaps sprained her back. It's certainly bruised."

"But she had to fall on snow."

"That may explain why there are no broken bones, but we have to wait and see what unfolds in the next few days."

A sob burst through my covered mouth. I shook my head, wanting to stay in denial. "Dennis didn't tell me . . ."

"As I indicated, because of the coma, it's hard to be sure, but I would be negligent if I failed to mention . . ."

I couldn't hear the rest over my gagging. I ran to the bathroom and subsequently flushed away my biscuit and sausage breakfast.

"Is there something I can do for you?" Dr. Lewis asked, peeking around the open door of the bathroom.

I splashed water on my face, shook my head, but accepted his help to the chair.

This was a nightmare, I told myself. I had some mad cow beef at dinner with Bob, and this is the resulting three-day nightmare. I must be ill, thrashing to and fro in a bed somewhere, feverish and not knowing it. I'm going to wake up any minute.

CHAPTER 13

I kept vigil all morning and most of the afternoon until dozing off.

Rousing myself, I wiped sleep from my eyes and looked out the window. Seeing it was dark, I checked my watch. Five-fifteen.

Nathan Stroud, my former boyfriend, lived in Baltimore. It would save an hour's commute time if I could hang out at his place instead of going back and forth to Takoma Park. I dialed his number on the room phone, since cell phones were not allowed.

"Nathan, it's Laurel. Can you put me up for a few nights?"

"What's the matter?"

Because I started crying again, I moved as far away from Emma as I could get and whispered what had happened.

"Well, listen. You know I'd love nothing more than to have you, but I sorta have a semi-permanent houseguest. A lady friend."

"Oh, okay. I understand." He had a two-bedroom condo. Not much space.

"You're having a rough time. I heard about Randall."

"How'd you hear?"

"I stay in touch. In fact, Paula is my current lady friend."

"Paula Mayfield?"

"Yep."

"How long has this been going on?"

"Long enough."

"Oh, okay." How'd I miss that in the rumor mill, I wondered. "I'll see you another time then. I've got to call a cab."

"Where's your car?"

When I explained what happened, he said, "The least I can do is give you a ride home. I'm on my way."

When he got there, Nathan eyed me as if I were a baglady he would have preferred avoiding. "You look like hell, Laurel. Emma's going to come out of this just fine. They're doing miraculous things with burns these days, and being unconscious is just the body's way to focus on healing."

"You're right, and I'm going to stay positive. But you'd look like hell too if you'd been me the last couple of days. I get points for being vertical and somewhat in my right mind."

"When she wakes up, they'll get that physical therapy going like gangbusters if she should need it. I don't know Emma all that well, but from what I've seen, she's a tough cookie. Emma is going to get through this. I'm worried about you now."

We walked through quiet hospital corridors toward the parking lot.

"I hope you're braced," he said.

I looked at him as he held open the passenger door of his ice-green Infinity. What had he heard? "What do you mean?"

"Things happen in threes, don't they? You're already reeling. What's going to happen when the third shoe drops?"

I didn't tell him, but if I counted the pregnancy, Emma was the third shoe.

We drove south on I-95 without saying much. Thirty minutes later Nathan suggested we stop to eat. "Outback all right?"

"No thanks. I'm beat, and I have to see what kind of shape the house is in." I'd loved my colonial-style house when I bought it four years ago. But with what had transpired between Dennis and me, and now with Emma being hurt in the fire, to say its appeal had soured was putting it mildly.

When I opened my front door, the smoke smell was faint, but there. That meant I'd need new carpet, new drapes and maybe a whole new wardrobe. I looked up at the ceiling, brown with water stains in one area. Everything had to be painted.

Upstairs in my bedroom, Nathan and I stared at the black space where a wall used to be and the boarded-up windows on the other wall.

LIES TOO LONG

My bedroom connected to another small room. I had wanted to make it my office, but it was over the garage and always ten degrees cooler than the rest of the house in winter. The fire had apparently started there, since this was where the damage was most prevalent. The remains of a melted ladder formed a grotesque sculpture.

Emma had always said it was a shame to waste this room; she thought baseboard heating would make it nice and cozy. I hadn't got around to that, either. I had used the room as storage for art I'd grown tired of but couldn't part with, an odd chair, and a closet for off-season clothes. Picking up a sodden, partially unfurled roll of pink and blue bunny border, I reasoned this was where Emma thought the nursery should go. I dropped the border and went back to my bedroom, frowning at the devastation everywhere. I walked to my overturned bookcase.

"Oh no," I whispered.

Nathan began picking up my eclectic book collection.

I stooped to my photo albums, which had also been on the bookcase. They were waterlogged, but perhaps some pictures could be professionally restored. I'd meant to scan them all, but had never gotten around to it.

Nathan continued to try to salvage books, but I couldn't. I didn't want to be here. "Nathan, I'm going to take a leave of absence from work and home. I'm moving to Baltimore to be close to Emma."

"It shouldn't take more than a couple of weeks," Nathan said. "Most clean-up companies are pretty efficient about getting people back in their homes in a timely manner. Anything you want to take with you?"

I shook my head. I couldn't think what I needed or wanted. "Like what?"

"Insurance info, for starters."

"I've got my records in a safety deposit box. We financial types at least know to do that much, right?"

"Right. What about your computer?" he asked.

I showed him file storage on my keychain. "I got it covered, and I've got my laptop, but I will take my two Jacob Lawrence prints from the living room." I had one print called *Brownstone* that depicted urban street activity. Its vibrant colors would cheer me wherever I ended up. The other one was called *Tombstone*. Again, Lawrence's use of primary colors leapt off the canvas. I liked how it captured the cycle of life with the birth and death symbols it contained, but Emma had always thought that one was rather morbid.

Nathan removed them from the wall. "Okay, I'll hold onto these for you until you find a place. Where next?"

"The Holiday Inn, I guess." I'd wash out my underwear and go shopping for new clothes tomorrow.

"What about a car?"

"I'll rent one through the hotel."

Back in the car Nathan said, "Call me if you need help finding a place to stay in Baltimore."

"Thanks."

By ten the next day, I'd dealt with my leave of absence, contacted the insurance company and rented a car.

Charlie from the B&B called and told me to meet him at ESPN Sports Center in Baltimore to pick up my car. Perfect. The hospital was only fifteen minutes from there, max. I'd buy Charlie lunch and then spend the afternoon with Emma.

While I picked up a week's worth of outfits at City Mall, I kept thinking that at least Emma's face wouldn't be scarred. But, oh my God, to have to tell her about Dennis and me and that I had intentionally brought a defective heater home. She'd never, ever forgive me. Not in a million years, and I couldn't blame her.

The drive back to Baltimore would take an hour. En route, I called Tolliver's Auto Supply to do some research. I pretended to be in charge of Mr. Butler's accounts payable.

"Sir, we have an illegible receipt." I gave him the date in question. "Please tell me the items purchased, amount, and time of purchase."

"Time of purchase. That's a new one. Let me check."

He verified what Dennis had told me.

"Thank you," I said, "he's a funny guy, isn't he? Likes those overalls and plaid shirts, wears them everyday."

"Who?"

"The guy who bought the motor," I explained. "What's the name on the receipt?"

"Dennis Butler. I didn't see him though. Wasn't here that day. Sounds like quite a character."

"He is. Thank you for your help."

Dennis could have sent somebody to get that motor. Or maybe Emma had the Ramada Inn address written down some place. To know for sure if he had been at Tolliver's, I'd have to go there, find who was working then and show Dennis's picture. Police work was tougher than it looked, but I was used to hustling.

I'd had plenty of pictures of him and Emma, but they had been on a bookcase in my bedroom. I'd have to find another source.

CHAPTER 14

As I looked at Emma's empty hospital room, a fear seized my gut as if I had been entrusted with something extremely valuable and I had no idea where I'd put it.

My puzzled expression asked the question for me after I'd fumbled my way to the nurses' station.

A nurse answered, "Emma Yates is on the other wing now."

"The other wing?"

"Yeah, follow the blue line on the floor straight ahead to room 22-B."

"Why?" My mouth suddenly dry, I stuttered, "Did-did something happen?"

"Her condition stabilized. Patients in this wing need more care than she does at the moment."

I reveled in this good news for the length of the hall, but when I pushed open 22-B, another surprise awaited.

Vivian Reece's face was a mask of frozen horror under a remarkable feathered and bejeweled black hat. "Isn't this just too tragic for words? Dennis said she was doing something at your place when a space heater caught fire. That's how it happens, you know. Somebody leaves something cooking or candles burning or it's one of those dang space heaters."

She was a short, stout woman dressed in a navy blue designer suit. It was good to know they made them in that size because by the end of my pregnancy my waist girth would match hers.

Emma had beaten Vivian twice in the run for president of their sorority chapter. Not a lot of love lost there, so her worry was probably feigned.

"Hi, Vivian. Yeah, well . . ." I walked over to Emma. She looked like something the cat had dragged in. Hair in disarray, her legs and right arm secured so she wouldn't hurt herself more if she flailed about unconsciously. Beeping machines were attached to her with tubes and wires.

I smoothed back her hair the best I could. I'd buy her a comb and brush as soon as I got the chance. "Emma's on the road to recovery. When the paramedics first saw her they thought her burns were more severe than they turned out to be, and that's why they brought her here instead of to another hospital. That's the good news. The bad news is that she hit her head in the fall."

"My Lord. That's a crying shame. Jumped out a window. Burned and in a coma. Umph, I will certainly keep her in my prayers."

"Thank you."

"I—I mean we, our chapter members, are going to hold a special meeting later this week and I'm going to shoulder the responsibility of the chapter presidency. We've got the scholarship ball before Christmas and the winter retreat after it. The voter registration rally at Temple Hill Baptist Church is on Doctor King's birthday. Somebody needs to be at the helm to make sure everything goes as planned. I'm willing to make the personal sacrifice and do what has to be done, even though my daughter is visiting from Italy."

Emma had told me Vivian's daughter had received a dishonorable discharge from the army for leaving her post while on duty in Italy, but I wasn't supposed to know that. "I'm sure Emma appreciates you stepping in." Yeah, like Al Gore appreciated George W. Bush.

"No problem. Emma's going to need some time to recuperate and adjust to the changes." Vivian settled in a chair near the window.

"There shouldn't be any lasting changes, Vivian. Second degree burns heal completely. All her injuries are temporary." I spoke with confidence based on faith and being up most of the night doing research on the Internet.

Her expression indicated she thought me delusional, but she'd go along with it for my sake. "If you say so, you poor thing. You must be just riddled with guilt. And your poor house! What a shame."

I nodded and gave up on the idea that I didn't need to sit and chat for a few more minutes. I sat across from her, thinking how kind she was to state the obvious.

"Well," Vivian said, "I'll be coming regularly and I expect this place will be jam packed with visitors."

"I'm sure she knows everyone is rooting for her. There's a two visitor at a time limit." I made up that second part. I knew Emma wouldn't want to be on display, and a two-person limit sounded reasonable. But that wasn't the only reason I'd said that. Emma's sorority friends tended to see themselves as uniquely special and a tad better than the average Jane or Shiniqua. Having identified myself as average all my life, being around a group of them made me uncomfortable. Sure, their sorority causes were community-oriented and noteworthy, but could they get over themselves already?

Of course, Emma didn't seem to mind; in fact, she fit right in. Hearing their chatter might help bring her out of her coma faster, but I'd made a selfish decision, something I seemed to be doing with greater frequency when it came to Emma these days. I refused to be knee-deep in sorority sisters for the duration of Emma's recovery. I already had Dennis to contend with, and endless versions of Vivian were more than I could handle at the moment.

"Okay. I'll spread the word."

"Will you? I'd appreciate it."

We sat smiling stiffly at each other. I glanced at my watch.

Vivian shrugged. "With her being up here in Baltimore, many sorors might wait and see her when she gets home."

"That might be best."

"When do you think that will be? When will she be home?"

"Predictions are hard to make, but you know Emma. Once she sets her mind to something, she can't be stopped."

"Now that's true. She does have a certain pit bull quality about her. I hope it serves her well. So you're here all the time, huh?"

"Yes, I plan to be."

LIES TOO LONG

"Where's that handsome fiancé of hers? I see her ring is off for safe keeping."

She meant why wasn't Dennis keeping a twenty-four-hour vigil, and could she please have something else to gossip about?

"He's around, you know. Keeping his shop going." Plotting my murder.

"I sure hate I missed seeing him. That is one fine man."

I smiled again and stood. Thankfully, she followed suit.

"Call me if there's something I can do."

"Yes, I will. Thanks for stopping by, Vivian."

"You have my number?"

I gave her yesterday's newspaper. "Write it on here." The paper and her number shared equal value in my book.

At the hospital the next day, Emma looked tousled because they'd just changed her dressings. The coma was good for something, otherwise the pain would be excruciating.

"I'm here, Emma." I braved a kiss hello. "I've got the rest of *Dangling Hearts*, I've got Patti LaBelle, Bony James and Norah Jones." Fortunately, my car was well-stocked musically. "So what do you want to hear first? Who? Bony James. Okay, we'll listen and I'll check the newspaper for a place to live close by."

I must have been exhausted because when I woke, it was after eleven. The crick in my neck clicked louder than the soda can I crushed and threw in the trash.

I massaged my neck and gazed at the Baltimore skyline. The moon hung low and orange in a dark blue sky. Mac had been good at rubbing my neck two days ago. Was that just two days ago? I wondered what he was doing right now. Despite the corniness I hummed, "Somewhere Out There" from that animated Spielberg movie.

"Hi, I can rustle you up a cot if you're gonna be here all night."

I turned to Tereka's voice. "Hi. Oh, thanks, that would be great. Did Dennis come by tonight?"

"I come on at seven. I haven't seen him."

"Okay." I wondered how long he'd keep up the façade. Emma wasn't in a position to write checks, so Dennis was effectively cut off. Maybe he would shrivel up and blow away.

Tereka rolled my cot in and helped me open it.

"Thanks." I accepted the fresh bedding.

Tereka glanced at the food tray I'd converted into a desk. I'd been looking through rental ads in the *Baltimore Sun*.

"You looking for a place near here?"

"Yeah, you got any suggestions? It would just be until Emma is better."

"Yeah, I do. I can hook you up. It's nothing fancy, but they finally got the roaches in check."

"The ro—"

"Girl, I'm just messing with you. You should see your face. It's a two-family flat and my cousin was gonna rent out the bottom floor to this man last month, but he changed his mind. She's hurting for rent money 'bout now. There's some basic stuff there, but I'd get a new mattress if I were you."

"You bet. And the neighborhood is pretty safe?"

"Pretty safe. Where you from?

"I grew up in D.C."

"So you know what to expect and how to be careful. It's a mostly white, working class, poor neighborhood. Blacks have been moving in for the past ten or fifteen years."

"Oh, okay, sure." I knew how to live in an urban environment, not taking unnecessary risks, but not being afraid either. "Do you live near here too, Tereka?"

"No, I live in northeast Baltimore for now. I plan to move to Columbia as soon as my money gets right. Better schools for my daughters."

Columbia, Maryland, was a planned community midway between Baltimore and Washington, D.C. "Oh, how old are they?"

"Four and five. Anyway," she took out a pad from her purple top pocket, "it sounds perfect for you for a couple of months. Here's my cousin's name and number."

Tereka's cousin Rachel pushed open the door to her lower flat. Her smooth sepia skin complemented her coarse gray hair, which was pulled back and piled high, librarian-style. Her black, rectangular glasses added to an air of seriousness.

The door thudded and bounced against the doorstop. A medley of smells greeted me—Lysol on top of new paint on top of a pervasive fried food smell. The dirty, pale orange carpet was probably culpable for the last one.

"Here's the coat closet." Rachel pulled the door ajar.

"Okay," I said. I pulled on the light chain, peeked into the stuffy darkness a second, then closed the door. Rachel opened it and pulled the chain once again.

The living room was a good size and a large picture window let in a lot of light. Light and city noise. This house sat ten feet from the curb on a semi-busy street named Addison Court. The kitchen was on the right and beyond that were three doors. The walls were stark white.

Seeking something positive to say, which meant overlooking the furniture, I came up with, "Nice window, and the paint job is nice too."

The kitchen, big enough for a small table and two chairs, had the typical, nondescript appliances. I checked the counter for mouse droppings and the cabinets for scurrying roaches. I didn't see either. The hot and cold water worked.

I considered the living room again. Rachel must be the master salvager of post-eviction furniture as witnessed by the black vinyl couch, mismatched end tables, the gray plastic rectangular coffee table reminiscent of the '70s, and one mauve lamp with no shade.

The black lacquered dresser in the bedroom confirmed it. It was huge, leaving just enough space for the fake brass bed and a floor lamp. Where was the decorating team from *Trading Places* when you needed them?

I contemplated the black-and-white-tiled bathroom that could be accessed from the bedroom and the living room. Let's just say I would be investing in new flip-flops and taking only showers for the duration. At least it had a linen closet.

The sun porch was a bright spot. The French door that led to it added a whisper of charm. Someone had left a wind chime, which tinkled gently.

Rachel stepped out beside me and together we looked through the bank of screened windows. "It's not heated, but it gets the morning sun," she said.

The neighborhood had seen better days, but that was true in any big city in America. In the waning evening light I saw overturned trashcans and a fence that looked as if people walked over it rather than around it. The proximity to Bayview and downtown Baltimore couldn't be beat. The property itself was gold. It was only a matter of time before somebody bought up the whole block and made a fortune.

Turning to Rachel I said, "Instead of paying you six hundred a month, I'll spend two thousand on furniture and other improvements, and you can keep everything when I leave."

"No," she shook her head and folded her arms across her chest, "that won't work. I need the cash. What? You got your own furniture?"

"I will have it, yes."

"All right, I can get somebody to take what's in here out, but that's gonna cost you a hundred. And when you move your stuff in, be careful with my walls."

"The tub and sinks need to be caulked." I was not about to pay six hundred dollars a month to watch fungus grow inside cracks. "A burglar alarm has to be installed."

"I'll have the caulking done, but you're on your own with the burglar alarm. Tell them to put the control box inside the coat closet. I don't want them messing up my new walls. I just had drywall replaced."

LIES TOO LONG

"What about the carpet?" I asked.

Her eyebrows bunched and she looked at me over her glasses. "I just had it cleaned."

You win some, you lose some.

CHAPTER 15

I spent time with Emma, needing to be there for her while trying to stay upbeat and stifle my growing depression. Too much uncertainty to cope with.

During trips to the hospital cafeteria, where I had unrestricted use of my cell phone, I arranged for repairs on Addison Court. The burglar alarm company couldn't come until the end of the week. I gave my new address to Nathan and asked him for help finding someone to do the floors. The fifteen-year-old icky carpet had to go, and restoring the wood floors would actually be cheaper than getting new carpet installed.

After discovering that computer jacks were available in the cafeteria, I shopped online for my new furniture. Luckily, Rachel was usually home so I didn't have to be there in person when someone showed up to do or deliver something.

Five days after Bob's murder, I drove back to Emma's house to get a picture of Dennis to show the clerk at Tolliver's Auto Supply. Dennis usually worked at his shop all day Saturday, but still, I stopped every five seconds and listened for signs of life other than my own rapidly beating pulse.

Emma's photo albums were in the den, but once I was inside, curiosity got the better of me. I headed upstairs to their bedroom.

Vestiges of Emma's French Country décor were buried under Dennis's clothes, which were scattered everywhere. I smelled his Dial soap and Emma's peach-scented bath products. I'd buy some for her. Having the smells she loved around her was good therapy, according to information I had been reading on the Internet about coma patients.

This snooping wasn't so bad. I considered taking Emma a couple of her gowns, but I couldn't for the same reason I didn't take her bath gel; I didn't want Dennis to know I'd been here. If he didn't know I had a key, I didn't want to tell him.

I opened a brown wooden box on top of a chest of drawers. A receipt from Johnny's Pawn Shop for a diamond ring rested on Dennis's cuff links. It was dated yesterday! My God. Had he no sense of propriety? But then I remembered, propriety wasn't exactly my strong suit either.

When the shock lessened, $50 jumped off the receipt at me. What? Oh my God, her diamond must have been a cubic zirconia! I was surprised Emma hadn't taken it to a jeweler to have it appraised for insurance purposes, if for no other reason. Dennis, Dennis, Dennis. What a slime ball. He needed to be dealt with.

Downstairs again, I found the photo album and sat at Emma's desk while I paged through it. I took a picture of Dennis posed on a basketball court and put the album back where I'd found it.

I drove to Tolliver's Auto Supply, parked and got out only to discover it closed at four on Saturdays. Drat. But it was only four-fifteen. I tried knocking. Didn't they have to take care of the day's receipts and clean up?

A man, black, around my age, yelled, "Come back Monday, we're closed."

"I just have a question. It will take ten seconds. Please?"

"What is it?" he asked, coming closer to the door.

When he wouldn't open the door for me, I held up Dennis's picture to the glass door. "Did this man buy an antennae motor from you five days ago?"

"What?"

"I know it's a strange question, but it's really important."

He pursed his lips. "Hold on."

I could see him explain what I wanted to a younger white guy who came over to me.

He looked at the picture and smiled. "Yeah, that's Dennis Butler. He's a former Wizards player. I know him. He comes here a lot."

"Do you remember if he was here last Friday?"

"Friday? Yeah, I'm pretty sure it was Friday. Bought an antennae motor for a '96 Camry."

"Okay, thank you."

"Why'd you need to know?" he asked.

"Oh, just running down some details. Thanks for your help." Now what?

On Sunday Nathan brought me a spider plant for my sun porch because he kept statistics on how long it took me to kill anything green. "The place looks damn good, Laurel. Red couches, huh?"

I shrugged. "Why not? And only one is a couch; the other one is a chaise."

"It works. *Metropolitan Homes Magazine* needs to take some pics." He held up an adhesive guaranteed to attach the prints to Rachel's walls without putting holes in them. "With these prints on the wall, you'll have it laid out."

When we were done, we stood back, shoulder to shoulder, admiring the paintings. They did a lot to jazz up the place.

"Have you had lunch, Nathan?"

"I could eat," he said.

We ordered Chinese. While we waited, I mentioned the neighborhood being a golden investment opportunity.

"You're absolutely right," Nathan said. "As a matter of fact, I've been working 'round the clock putting a deal together to make a move in that direction."

"Get out! You're in a position to put that much capital together?"

"Me and a few partners."

"Who?"

"Mostly contacts I've made doing consulting work since I retired."

I stared at him with awe, then toasted him with my Diet Coke. "I had no idea you were wheeling and dealing with the big boys, Nathan."

LIES TOO LONG

"Well, never hurts to dream as long as you are able to execute. If the chips fall like I planned, we'll wrap this deal up soon."

When the food arrived, we sat down to eat and, between bites of orange chicken, I said, "I hear Madison Research decided to stay with their original investment portfolio."

Nathan helped himself to his egg fu young patties. "Where'd you hear that?"

"I stopped by the office one day last week. Some paperwork snafu with my leave I couldn't get straightened out over the phone. Saw Ray."

"How is old Ray?"

Old Ray or Raymond De Leon was my supervisor and Nathan's former one.

"He's good. I thanked him for sending flowers to Bob's funeral. But I don't think he knew what I was talking about."

"Probably didn't. His secretary or Paula probably handled it."

"Yeah. How's Paula?"

"She's good. How about you? You seeing anybody now?" Nathan asked.

"No time for that, really." This meant, present craziness aside, I couldn't find anybody to love who wanted to love me. Talking to Nathan reminded me that I missed having someone to confide in. I almost told him about the babies, but he'd notice soon enough. I figured I'd be in elastic-waist pants and big sweaters before much longer. "I'm worried about Emma, Nathan. It's been a week and she's still in the coma."

"Guess she's not in any hurry to wake up, but I bet her burns are healing nicely and the spinal and brain swelling are decreasing every day."

"Stupid, stupid, space heater. I can't believe how stupid I was." Every time I thought about it, my head shook with mortifying regret.

"Oh, come on now." He pulled me into his embrace. "I make it a policy to never date stupid women. And I know Emma knows you are there for her every day. That will make a difference. She'll pull out of it."

CHAPTER 16

The next day, *Parenthood*, one of my favorite movies, was on a cable channel. I could definitely relate to the grandmother's theory that a roller coaster was a metaphor for life. About the fifth time Keanu Reeves said *Dude*, Emma groaned. At first I thought I had imagined it. I pushed mute and held my breath. She did it again, softer than the first time.

"Emma," I called gently. "Emma." I said louder. Shaking her good arm, I pushed the call button and shouted, "Send somebody! She's waking up!"

Seconds later, Dr. Lewis and one of Emma's day nurses, Cheryl, jogged into the room.

"She groaned twice!"

Dr. Lewis forced me aside. "Emma, I'm Doctor Lewis. You're in the hospital and you're going to be fine. Can you open your eyes? Open your eyes, Emma."

She groaned again. I looked at them to make sure they had heard her. They had.

"Oh, Emma! Open your eyes," I pleaded, wringing my hands.

"Mmmm," she moaned, her brow scrunched.

"Is she going to wake up, Doctor? Why won't she open her eyes? Is she moaning because she's in pain?"

They ignored me, focusing on Emma.

Cheryl took her pulse, Dr. Lewis checked her pupils.

Suddenly, Emma yawned a wide, tongue-fluttering yawn. Then Cheryl rubbed a chip of ice on Emma's chapped lips and Emma licked the wetness! She was so close. Could she come all the way back?

When Emma's eyes flew open, the emptiness in them made me step back, but the way her vacant eyes darted to every corner of the

LIES TOO LONG

room made me want to ask if she could see. I could handle only one answer to that, so I couldn't risk the question.

I stepped in front of Dr. Lewis and held Emma's face between my hands. "Emma, look at me. Look at me!"

Finally, her gaze found mine. "Do you know who I am?"

"Am?" she croaked, partially echoing me.

"Emma?" I turned to look behind me, more alarmed about her response than my earlier fear of her being blind. Panic threatened to overtake me. "Doctor?"

Cheryl put her arm over my shoulder and walked me to the hall. "It can take days before a coma patient is completely lucid."

I wiped tears away. "She's going to be all right, isn't she?" I felt weak. I needed to sit down or fall down.

Cheryl led me to a waiting room with yellow plastic chairs.

I hugged myself and rocked. My emotional pain was like the worst toothache known to man. "Please." That's as far as I got in my prayer. I didn't know what else to say that God didn't already know.

Cheryl brought me some water. I didn't want it, but took it anyway. Maybe she knew I'd have to stop rocking or spill it all over me.

"Is there someone I can call?" she asked.

"Is she awake?"

Sympathetic eyes told me the answer was no.

"It takes time. Her body is fighting its way back, but it takes time. Do you want me to walk with you to the chapel perhaps?" Cheryl asked.

"Chapel? No, thanks. I—uh . . ." I sighed. Energy-depleted and speechless, I sat looking at the hard yellow chairs, the two payphones side by side and the one vending machine. I craved Mac. But no. If I called him, and if he came, I would only add misery to his life too.

Back at home, I did what I did most nights, researched everything I could about comas on the Internet. I gathered patients were rated on a point system and the fact that Emma was moving and talking, even though she was disoriented, was a good sign.

I listened to the news at eleven, the first half. When the sports came on, I took my shower. I didn't enjoy sports highlights anymore because they reminded me of Dennis. When I stepped back into the bedroom with only my towel on, I immediately felt a chill. Picking up my flannel gown from the bed, I began to put it on before I checked the thermostat.

"Don't bother."

I swung around with my head trapped inside my gown. I cried out before I fought my head through the opening and was finally able to see him.

"Shut up. It's me." Dennis pushed me on the bed and covered my mouth with his hand.

My heart was pounding as if I'd run up five flights of stairs. "Get off me!" It was muffled, but he knew exactly what I had said.

"I'm not doing anything until you get control of yourself. Don't yell and I'll let you go."

I screamed again. He straddled my chest, holding me down, keeping my mouth covered. I fought with everything I had.

He whispered close to my ear, "You'll get tired eventually, but if you want to wrestle, I'll get naked and we can have some real fun."

Tears of frustration ran down the sides of my face. After a few more futile attempts to break free, I gave up.

"Good." He scooped my breast free of my nightgown, squeezing an already pregnancy-tender nipple. I winced and attempted to squirm out from under him again.

With his hand still covering my mouth, he sucked hard on my nipple, then let it pop free, "That's got to be an inch long. Damn. If I take my hand away, are you going to scream?"

I shook my head no, agreeing to keep quiet. He removed his hand from my mouth.

"Get off me," I said.

"We need to talk, and I like having your full attention."

LIES TOO LONG

His weight pressed against my stomach.

He said, "You mentioned money before. Two hundred thousand."

"What? Plan B after killing me didn't work?"

"Can you say broken record? Get it straight, Laurel. I never tried to kill you. You give me five hundred thousand and sign what my lawyer will draw up releasing me from paternal responsibility for all time, and we have a deal. I'll be gone the next day."

"I don't have that kind of money. Are you crazy?"

"Sell your house or tap your IRA or something. You have a week."

"A week?"

"Not my problem. This is a one-time offer. I hear Emma had a good day. When she comes around, I'll say that in a weak moment I did what men do. Men don't turn this down when it's offered."

He pushed my gown up. While he talked I tried to keep my legs closed against his probing hand.

"I'll beg her for forgiveness, we'll get married and she will help me pay child support times two for the next eighteen years and she'll hate you for the rest of your life.

"I've barely touched you and you're wet. Are you sure you're not a slut, Laurel? Is there ever a time you don't want it?"

I jerked and twisted again. I had to get free, but when I moved, he held both my wrists down again. We noticed the blood on his hand at the same time. He wiped it on the front of my gown, scrambling off me like he'd seen a rattlesnake.

I sat up in shock, wondering if I needed a sanitary napkin or bath towel and if I had enough time to get dressed before I drove to the emergency room.

"Get out!" I screeched at him. "I swear to God if you ever touch me again, I will kill you!"

He laughed. "Right. Hey, I'd take you to the hospital, but this is for the best. You'll see."

I threw the closest thing I could find, the CD remote, at his head and watched it shatter against the wall.

I tested the amount of flow with my gown, and it didn't seem like a lot. I didn't think I was miscarrying, but I sobbed, scared I might be. No cramping had to be a good sign. I pulled on my panties, stuffed paper towels in them, and threw on some sweats. I wanted to call Dr. Patel, but he'd only tell me to go to the emergency room. I'd get there and let them call him.

Panic rose a notch as I drove to the hospital. I remembered once when my mother had visited with a friend of hers. Her friend had come out of the bathroom saying she'd just lost her baby. I had been about nine then and couldn't wait to check out the toilet to see where her baby went.

Tears fell like rain. I'd come this far, almost through my third month. I wanted my babies, despite who their father was. I couldn't lose them now.

"I'm still in my first trimester and I'm bleeding."

The emergency room intake person phoned for immediate help. I was on a gurney in five minutes. Fifteen minutes after that, the emergency room doctor snapped off his latex glove and depressed a foot petal on the metal can to the left of my stirrup.

He said, "The bleeding was minimal and it appears to have stopped. Any pain at all?"

"No."

"No sense of pressure? Any cramping in your belly or back?"

"No. None."

"I notice some bruising in the vaginal area and on your wrists."

I averted my eyes. "I'm okay. You saw both babies on the sonogram and they're fine?"

"Yes, they're fine. The heartbeats are strong. Ms. Novak, were you sexually assaulted?"

"No."

LIES TOO LONG

He took a few beats, maybe considering how hard to press. "Sometimes spotting is normal, but it should never be ignored, especially considering your age and the fact that you're having twins. Bed rest is recommended for the next couple of days. You can get dressed now. The nurse will come back and speak with you in a few minutes."

A few minutes turned into twenty, but my mind was incapable of holding another thought, neither Dennis's cruelty nor his offer/threat for me to buy him out. I felt nothing but grateful the babies were okay.

"Okay, Miss Novak." The nurse who had been with me during the doctor's exam was a fresh-faced, energetic young Latino woman. "The doctor wants you to check with your OB/GYN tomorrow, just to make sure everything is okay. Can I have his or her name for our records?"

"Dr. Prajeet Patel."

"You are to go straight home and get in the bed. Stay there for a couple of days if at all possible. You want the babies to have every advantage." She peered at me closely. "You have bruising around your mouth."

I tapped the tender puffiness around my lips. "Is it anything a little makeup won't hide?"

"No, probably not. And you don't wish to report any kind of assault, correct?"

"No, I wasn't assaulted." Of course I had been, but I had no desire to press charges and have to deal with the court system and Emma's recovery at the same time.

"Even if it was someone you know . . . violence is unacceptable."

She had to be all of twenty-two, lecturing me about what could be my preferred sex habits as far as she knew, but I knew better than to take my anger out on her.

"Thank you. Do I need to sign something?" I asked.

"Yes." She handed me the clipboard. While I read over my discharge notes and signed them, she tore a sheet off another pad and gave it to me.

"Here's a list of women's shelters in the area. Just in case."

I hesitated a moment, and then took it. "Just in case."

"Is there someone I can call for you?"

"What?" Déjà vu took me back to the waiting room at Bayview.

"Is there someone you want me to call?"

I scratched my head and thought a second. Mac. I needed him. "No, I'm good." I stood up and folded my list of shelters into my purse.

The security guard walked me to my car. I wanted to pay him to come with me until my burglar alarm was installed; I didn't feel safe going back there tonight. What if Dennis came back?

But where could I go at quarter to one in the morning? I thought about the shelter list in my purse, but that would be way too depressing and I was already teetering on the brink. I'd go home to Takoma Park. Most of the repairs should be complete and I had been planning to drop by anyway to check on the progress.

After I let myself in, I walked from room to room, touching things for the last time, knowing this wasn't my home anymore. My bedroom was stripped bare. I turned off the lights and went back to my car unable to force myself to spend the night. Though I'd list the house for sale tomorrow, it had nothing to do with Dennis's latest affront and his plan to blackmail me. It was just that this phase of my life was over. Tonight it was back to the Holiday Inn.

I fell into my hotel bed feeling like a homeless wanderer and part-time dishrag. I dreamed about Mac and me watching the snow fall outside our window. Two little kids were building a snowman when a man in a black ski mask began chasing them. Startled awake, I glimpsed the time. Three forty-three A.M. It occurred to me that nothing in Dennis's deal protected me from his changing his mind and coming back for more money. He could blackmail me with the threat to reveal everything to Emma from now until kingdom come.

I needed to be with Emma until the aftereffects of the fire were only a dim memory. Then I would tell her everything. But what should I do about Dennis in the meantime? Though I had repeated the same mental lap countless times, the answer still eluded me.

I fell to my knees, calling out to God. I hadn't prayed for longer than two seconds in twenty years, and not on my knees in thirty. "I didn't plan these babies, but I think You did. If You give me the chance, I will love them and teach them about Your love for them. Help me to know what I'm supposed to do, God. Help me to do it."

I didn't say anything else because God knew my heart. I listened because I wanted to know His. Maybe if I did, I'd find out how to stop making a mess of things.

I got up, stiff, not any wiser, but more at peace. I took a bath for the first time since the bed and breakfast inn. Enjoying the warm soak, I fell asleep in the water.

At seven I dialed 411 and got Mac's home number.

CHAPTER 17

"I've been calling you, Laurel." His Jamaican accent made my name sound like a running brook. I winced as I smiled, my mouth still sore.

"I haven't been at my house."

"I tried reaching you at your office, too, so I wasn't sure if you just decided not to return my calls."

"No, it wasn't that. I took some time off from work. Why didn't you try my cell phone?"

"How much phone rejection do you think one man can stand?"

We laughed.

"Did the fire do a lot of damage to your place?"

"A considerable amount, but it's been repaired. I'm not comfortable there anymore and I'm going to put my house on the market."

"You are? Then what?"

"Well, I haven't thought that far. I'm renting a place in Baltimore now so I can be close to my friend."

"How is Emma?"

"Emma is getting better slowly. I see the progress."

Silence. I stopped pacing in the dark and touched a gold lamp base. An arc of light illuminated the pale green carpet.

"I called because I miss you, Mac. I know where our boundaries are, but I've been thinking about you."

"And me you, obviously," he said.

More silence, then I heard his slow exhale.

"What's the situation with you and the father? Anything change?"

"No, it's the same. I, uh . . . I had a scare last night. Some spotting."

"But everything's all right?" The concern in his voice warmed my heart. He cared about me and my babies.

LIES TOO LONG

"Yeah, except I'm going through this alone. I mean, that's what I expected and, uh . . . but I did pray about it."

"That's good, Laurel. You won't feel so alone that way. So you are okay?"

"Yeah, mostly."

"I have to be on duty at eight. May I use this number to call you later?"

"Yes." A tiny step forward, but we were making it together. A giggle escaped.

"Write down my cell number and program it into your phone," he instructed.

"Okay." I smiled. "Take care, Mac."

The day was crisp and clear. Doctor Patel was able to see me right away. The babies were fine. It was good to have that confirmed even though he said not do to any heavy lifting and to stay off my feet as much as possible.

Going back to Baltimore, I was held up by an overturned tractor-trailer on I-95 that tied traffic up for miles. While I sat immobile, I called the alarm company and explained if they wanted my business, someone would have to install the system today and not Friday, three days from now. They agreed to add one more stop to their installer's day; they'd come between seven and eight tonight.

When I finally got to Emma's room at noon, I couldn't believe my eyes. Cheryl and another nurse had just helped Emma into a wheelchair.

"Emma!"

Cheryl gestured me out to the hall.

"Laurel, she's been awake since six this morning, but she's not one hundred percent yet. Remember what I told you yesterday. We've been gradually getting her into an upright position all morning and she's doing great."

I took a deep breath. "It's a process."

"Good girl." Cheryl patted my shoulder as we walked back inside the room.

I looked at Emma again. "Cheryl, the gauze is gone too?" Her right hand and both legs were a mass of peeling skin.

"Yes. Doctor Lewis took a look and decided today was the day. The next step is to get her standing. She's making progress."

"Yes, she is." I pulled a chair in front of her. "I'm here, Emma. Sorry to talk about you like you're not in the room. Are you feeling better? You look good."

Her gaze focused on my face, but her expression remained vapid. My hands outlined her hair and then her shoulders, hoping to confirm the real person I used to know was in there. I got the lotion that matched her peach-scented shower gel and rubbed some on her left arm.

"I'm Laurel. Do you know who I am? I'm your . . ." I was going to say "best friend" but I didn't deserve the title. "I'm Laurel."

After I figured out how to unlock her wheelchair, I rolled her to the bathroom so we could look at our reflections and practice. "Laurel." I pointed to my reflection. "Emma." I pointed to hers. "Can you tell me your name? Say Emma." No response, but she did look at the mirror.

"Hold on." I ran and got her comb and brush. I brushed Emma's long hair back, and put it into a French braid. "There," I said when I finished. "Probably feels good to have your hair off your face and neck. You look beautiful," I told her reflection. "You want your earrings." I went to get those from my purse. She always wore some version of hoop earrings.

I lifted her chin. "Gorgeous," I said. "Thanksgiving is in a couple of weeks. I'll bet if you work really hard, Emma, you could be home for Thanksgiving. Wouldn't that be great?"

"I know what," I said, backing her out of the bathroom. "You're probably bored with this room. You've been here for nine days. That's a long time. Why don't we go for a walk, maybe up and down the hall? Would that be good?"

LIES TOO LONG

"Don't leave yet, I just got here." Dennis came in carrying a dozen red roses. "Emma? How are you, baby?" He flinched when he looked at Emma's splotched arm and legs, but tried to pretend he hadn't. "These are for you." She studied the flowers stuck under her nose. He handed them to me without taking his eyes off Emma. "Put those in water, will you?" He lifted his Starbucks cup to his mouth and slurped.

Put them in water your damn self, was my first thought, but negativity in any form wouldn't do around Emma. When I didn't take them, he took a vase already in use, dumped my bouquet from yesterday and put in the new one. He added water from Emma's water pitcher.

"What's wrong with her, Laurel?"

When I didn't answer, he thrust his head outside the door.

"Nurse?" he called.

Apparently he didn't see anyone so he turned back to me. "I got a call saying she had improved. She's just staring, not saying anything. What does that mean?"

I had deemed him invisible, never worthy of seeing or speaking to again in life, so it took all I had to make eye contact with him. "You need to talk to the doctor, but as I understand it, there are different stages in coming out of a coma. This is the beginning stage."

He set his coffee down, put his hands above both his knees and bent down at her eye level. He scrutinized Emma as if she were a frog he wanted to dissect, but was afraid to touch. He straightened up. "When will she be her old self again?"

"Eventually."

He looked as if my answer inflicted pain.

That did it. "Why does it always have to be about you, Dennis?" I spat at him, thoroughly fed up. "Grow up for goodness sakes!"

He swelled like one of those puffer fish. "Let me tell you something—"

"Somebody called for a nurse?" Cheryl stood in the doorway.

Dennis rubbed his brow and ambled in her direction. "Yeah. So like every day she'll come out of it more and more?"

"We hope so. The doctors will talk to you about that." Cheryl grinned up at him like most women do.

"Yeah, sure." He looked at his watch. "I'll catch up with him tomorrow. I've got to get back to the shop."

Yes, please go back to the shop. You're useless here, I thought.

"Walk with me, Laurel." he said.

He had to be kidding.

He gestured with a flick of his head, indicating he really expected me to go with him.

I folded my arms, tilted my head, and wished vultures could peck out his eyes. "No."

He came toward me, whispering his coffee breath in my face. "You don't understand. Emma and I had a lifestyle. Certain financial obligations are going unmet. I don't mean for things to get out of hand, but I'm under the gun here."

"I know the feeling." And it was more that Emma had a checkbook rather than him having a lifestyle.

"I keep telling you I had nothing to do with that mugging." He shook his head like I was the densest creature he'd ever seen. How did he know it was a mugging? Had I told him about that?

We stood toe to toe. The way he sized me up, I knew he knew I was still pregnant. He went on, "I'm not a bad person. I mean, I'm no angel either, just a guy trying to have things go my way for a change. I've got a business that's actually making a profit. You get that? Not just breaking even—making a profit—and I own it. You want me to deal with all kinds of changes that I never agreed on from the git go."

I put my finger to my lips. "Keep it down."

He shook his head at me as if talking to me was useless because I'd never get it. He strolled out of the room with a gangsta limp, came back, got his cup of java and left with a "See you later, Emma."

LIES TOO LONG

Emma and I took our walk up and down the hall. Afterwards she rested in bed, while I read a batch of her newest get-well cards to her.

Scanning the *Washington Post* next, I skimmed pages looking for short interesting articles to share. I stopped when I came across a story in the real estate section headlined "Baltimore Tycoons in the Making." I read it aloud.

Real estate investing has historically been one of the most consistent ways to achieve great wealth. Helin-Stroud Investing, a corporation dedicated to neighborhood revitalization, purchased twenty houses along the Eastern Avenue corridor in Baltimore City. Roscoe Helin, CEO of Value Mutual, and Nathan Stroud, a financial planner, intend to return the neighborhood of dilapidated row houses to its former status times fifty. Helin stressed the company would not rely on proven strategies for buying and selling properties quickly (called "flipping"). Stroud commented, "While this method may be effective for a quick cash return, we are devoted to bringing families back to the inner city by creating a planned community called Newcom." Newcom will be a gated community, with stores, schools, recreation and homes starting at $400,000. Construction is scheduled to begin in sixty days.

"Emma! That's my Nathan!"

Emma's eyes remained closed. She'd had a full day.

I meandered over to the chair near the window, rattling my paper along the way. Not only was that my Nathan, I was familiar with Value Mutual because Bob Randall's company, Madison Research, supported them in a big way. Madison Research was one of the last major investors to stay with Value Mutual, which had a few pharmaceutical holdings, but was mostly tech-oriented. That's why I had wanted to adjust Madison's portfolio. If Madison had followed my advice, a sizable portion of their pension fund would have been reallocated to construction companies rebuilding Iraq and companies that make large-diameter and long-length pipes for oil pipelines.

Madison Research helped Value Mutual stay in the black, which, no doubt, helped Mr. Helin get his three-million-dollar bonus while other CEOs in a similar environment could only long for the gravy train days of yore.

Nathan must be having one heck of a party tonight. I checked my watch. After six. I hurried home in case the burglar alarm installer came early.

During my drive to Addison Court, I thought about Newcom. Four hundred thousand would only be enough to frustrate. Deeper pockets would be needed to pay for the attendant privileges such as a private community center, the private school, not to mention the private trash collection. And that was assuming residents didn't mind living in a fish bowl on lockdown.

On the flipside, it was a prime location. Not spending hours and hours commuting was priceless. Nathan was on his way to becoming a real estate tycoon, just as the newspaper article had stated.

Tereka came out of her cousin's flat when I opened my car door. She wore a cinched-at-the-waist puffy white jacket with a fur-lined hood. "You all right? Rachel and I were worried."

"I'm fine." She must have been referring to the incident with Dennis last night. "Emma's sitting up now." I hoped my topic change marked the end of the questions.

"Good. She was awake, well, her eyes were open this morning when I checked on her." Tereka followed me into my place, uninvited but not totally unwelcome.

"You have a nice way with decorating, Laurel. Place looks good. I'm surprised it's still intact."

"What do you mean?"

She stuffed her hands into her jacket pockets and confronted me. "Rachel said she heard yelling down here and she had to get up in the middle of the night because the sun porch door was banging in the wind. The thing of it is, Rachel doesn't want the drama.

LIES TOO LONG

"I told her you were a quiet businesswoman type. She doesn't want anybody entertaining all loud and then going off leaving the house open to the world. She wants you gone by the end of the week."

"What?"

"You heard me."

What I heard was my pulse pounding and *The Simpsons* TV show coming from upstairs.

"But . . . but . . . last night was a fluke, Tereka. There was an unfortunate incident with someone I used to know. With a burglar alarm, he wouldn't have gotten in. I'm not the irresponsible type, going off leaving my things unprotected. If I can talk to Rachel, I'll convince her to give me another chance. It won't happen again."

Tereka folded her arms. "Rachel showed me the bloody nightgown she found when she came in here. She was scared shitless she'd be tripping over your dead body next."

"It was nothing." I would be on extended leave without pay soon. That wouldn't be a problem for another two weeks, but I couldn't afford to keep moving and spending money on hotel rooms. The thought of needing to use my shelter list scared me into lying. "A bad nosebleed."

She looked at me, her gaze hard. "If it happens again, we're gonna set your crap out on the sidewalk. Believe that."

Tereka let the burglar alarm guy in on her way out. Turning back to me she said, "Rachel is going to want to know how to disable that. If something triggers that alarm by mistake, that whooping noise will drive her nuts."

Mac called me later that night. His voice helped iron out a few wrinkles from my day. I filled him in on Emma's progress, told him my burglar alarm had been installed, but left out the rest. "You sound tired, Mac."

"I am. Hungry too. I got me a nice piece of cod frying now."

That reminded me that I hadn't eaten anything but crackers from the vending machine at the hospital. To make it worse, Rachel was cooking greens and the smell was starting to make me nauseous. I fought it by pulling out a pint of Ben and Jerry's butter pecan. "Any news on the case?"

"Looks like we have the break we were looking for. We've taken the shooter into custody."

I had a spoonful of ice cream halfway to my mouth but suddenly had no appetite. "He was someone for hire, wasn't he?"

"Yes."

"Who? Who hired him?"

"The guy we caught implicated someone named Roscoe Helin."

"Roscoe Helin?" Not Dennis? "Really?"

"So you know who he is?"

"Yes, he's the CEO of Value Mutual. Bob Randall's company, Madison Research, has a sizable portion of their pension funds invested with Value Mutual. I wanted to persuade Bob to make some investment changes I thought would be profitable."

"I have to come to Baltimore to get a more complete statement from you and Mr. Helin. He's headquartered there."

"Please come. I'll do whatever I can to help get to the bottom of this."

"I'll be there Friday morning by nine. And Laurel?"

"Yes?"

"I'm looking forward to seeing you again."

I hung up thinking that seeing Mac would be great but, oh my God. Dennis really hadn't tried to kill me? I sat at the kitchen table to let that sink in, reeling from this revelation. Dennis had been telling the truth this whole time? Could it be possible?

But what did this new development mean? If Bob had agreed to restructure the Madison Research portfolio, Value Mutual would have been heavily impacted. Helin had an interest in seeing that Bob continued to do business with Value Mutual so their stock didn't fall and

LIES TOO LONG

his CEO bonus remained healthy. Greed is always a good motive for murder.

Uh-oh. Implicating Helin put Nathan's real estate investment plans in serious jeopardy. Since we had been good friends through the years, I owed it to Nathan to talk to him before his name got dragged into this. I just hoped he hadn't been in on it from the beginning.

Nathan wanted to put me off until later in the week, but when I mentioned strife between Bob Randall and the folks at Value Mutual, a space magically opened in his busy schedule the very next day.

Camden Yards, visible from Nathan's office window, awaited the Orioles opening game in spring. I had enjoyed sitting along the third base line many times. Maybe one day I could enjoy sports again. But with caring for his children, would there ever be a time I didn't think about Dennis?

Nathan's plush office, decorated in muted tones, knocked thoughts of Dennis out of my mind and made me think of hallowed ground. I spoke softly, respecting such a revered space. "You are really making it happen, Nathan. I'm proud of you, I just hope it didn't cost a man's life."

Nathan, in his gold vest and crisp navy blue suit, ushered me onto his sable leather settee.

"Laurel, what the hell are you talking about?"

I proceeded to bluff, taking an educated guess. "I'm talking about Bob being murdered because he asked for financial favors in order to veto my investment strategy."

"You know better than to go around spreading unfounded rumors. Have you lost your mind?" His expression was much like Dennis's yesterday—pained.

"As much as you love the good life, Nathan, I have to believe you would draw the line at killing someone."

Nathan sat on the edge of the settee, his torso angled to face me. "Did Bob mention something specific to you?"

I continued with my hypothesis. "With Bob out of the way, the decision to drop Value Mutual stalled and as a result profits for Value Mutual stayed strong. You can't tell me you don't know what I'm talking about. Were you in on it? Was Helin? Answer me, Nathan."

His grimace softened into his poker face.

"Is Paula involved? Is that why she barnstormed into Delaney to make sure I was reassigned?"

"If there were any substance to this, wouldn't the police be here now?" Nathan asked.

"Maybe they're coming. Maybe that's why I'm here."

"Laurel?"

"What?"

Nathan stood and flicked an imaginary piece of fluff from his blazer sleeve. "Let me show you the door."

I left not knowing what to think. Nathan appeared guilty. Dennis appeared innocent. Nothing was as it seemed any more, except that Bob was definitely dead.

CHAPTER 18

Emma listened to a CD through headphones later that morning, her upper body swaying like a metronome. She smiled, but her eyes still had an unfocused look unless I got her attention.

I tapped her arm and waited for her to pull her earphones off with her unburned left hand—something she couldn't do a couple of days ago. "Emma, I'm not going to stay long today. Mac, this police officer I met in Delaney, is coming tomorrow and I want to rest up. Being pregnant wears a person out. Well, in the beginning anyway. I understand the second trimester gets better."

"Coffee."

"Did you say coffee? Oh my gosh! Emma! You want coffee?"

"Coffee," Emma repeated.

"That's wonderful! That's fantastic!" I clapped in joy over the first word she'd spoken without prompting since the fire.

I flew to the cafeteria. Emma and I had had many important talks over a cup of java, and we would again. When I got ready to pay, I realized I had left my purse upstairs. Fortunately, since I'd spent so much time in the cafeteria, the cashier knew I was good for it.

"Here we go," I said when I returned with the coffee. I had filled her cup half-full and put lots of milk in it so she wouldn't have to worry about it being too hot. "To conversation," I said, offering a toast. Emma held her cup without drinking.

"Emma, this is so great. You're going to be home by Thanksgiving," I said. "I just know it."

"Milk," she said.

Yes! Two words, but then I worried she was only throwing out random words without meaning.

"I put milk in, Emma. You want more milk?"

"Milk," she said a second time.

I went to the nurse's station and luckily, some was available. I brought in the small carton and added more milk to Emma's coffee before sitting down for our chat.

"The physical therapist says the x-rays of your back look good. Did she tell you about getting you standing as soon as possible? She also said that within the next couple of days they would move you to a rehab facility not far from here. You're doing so well, you don't have to stay in the hospital anymore."

The thought of Emma moving to a rehab center secretly frightened me. What if it represented the beginning of her life permanently altered? What if her motor and language skills never got better? But I had trained myself to shoo thoughts like that out of my head as soon as they surfaced. I focused on the positive and stayed in the present. Right now, I yearned for more words from Emma. For several minutes, she said nothing, and she didn't drink her coffee, but finally I got my wish.

"Bathbed," she said.

As soon as I left the hospital, I checked my phone messages.

"This is Paula Mayfield. We need to talk."

Nathan had sicced her on me. He wouldn't do that unless I had hit a nerve. "Oh Nathan," I sighed.

When I called her back she said, "If you care anything at all about Nathan, you'll meet me at Fuddruckers on the Pike."

I didn't know how I could help at this point, but I did care about Nathan. What could the harm be in meeting in a public restaurant? "I'll see you at the Fuddruckers in Rockville. Give me an hour."

Rockville Pike is a main corridor in Rockville, Maryland, going all the way into D.C. to the south and up into the next Maryland county, Frederick, to the north.

LIES TOO LONG

We'd missed the lunch crowd, but the place did good business throughout the day. I only wanted tea, but Paula asked for a Swiss melt when our orders were taken at the register. She was her contemporary Southern belle self, dressed in a winter white pants suit and a fluffy periwinkle blouse. She filled me in on office gossip I had been missing, biding her time like a spider weaving a web. I excused myself to the restroom, intentionally stepping on one of her juiciest tidbits of gossip.

When I came out, her food and my tea were on our yellow and white checkered tablecloth. I had exactly two swallows before she lit into me.

"If the things you said leaked to the wrong people, you could undermine the success of Nathan and Helin's real estate venture. You want to see Nathan's dream crumble like crackers in soup? What's the matter with you? You're not allowed to go around spewing crap all over the place."

"I'm not allowed! Excuse me! A man is dead, Paula."

"Look at it this way. Even if Bob wanted to be paid to keep Value Mutual online, that's just the cost of doing business. Wouldn't it behoove Value Mutual to have someone like Bob doing their bidding? Why have him killed?"

"I don't know. Maybe he had a Swiss bank account he expected Helin to feed indefinitely. I think it's interesting that you conveniently showed up for damage control after Bob's death. You moved me out of the way and kept things running as they had been. I don't get it. Are you screwing Nathan *and* Roscoe Helin?"

Her face turned tomato red. "That's just plain ridiculous. And when who I'm screwing becomes your business, there'll be a space colony on Mars, preferably with you living on it. If the police can't find anything to charge anybody with, don't go creating needless turmoil with all this unfounded speculation. I'm warning you."

"Somebody created needless turmoil for Bob and his family and I could have died that night as well."

"You didn't, but I've got to tell you, making waves like you're doing, you're asking for trouble. So much is riding on this real estate deal for so many people. If I were you, I'd keep my mouth shut."

Back in my car, my head hurt, and with good reason. If Helin, Nathan and Paula were guilty, this fiasco could be the biggest blow-up since Enron. With police involvement, there was no way they could keep a lid on this, so Paula's personal threat to me was probably baseless. Still, it upset me. Why didn't they get that I was trying to help? I fished in my purse for the bottle of Tylenol.

I threw back two tablets and swallowed some bottled water while I waited at one of those four-minute traffic lights. Tapping impatiently on the steering wheel, I realized I probably should have eaten something because it was almost three and I'd be starving by the time I made it back to Baltimore. A McDonald's fish sandwich called my name just as a surge of nausea threatened to overcome me. When I rubbed my brow, my hand came away wet with sweat. Lowering my window to get some fresh air, I tried to talk myself out of throwing up. "Laurel," I said, you have been doing so well for the past two weeks. Deep breaths, that's it."

By the time I pulled into two parking spaces on the McDonald's lot, I had to cover my mouth to keep from throwing up in the car, but I made it to the bathroom.

Inside the stall, I stood with my hands pressed against the wall behind the toilet, panting between regurgitations. Wiping my mouth with the back of my hand, I banged my way out of the stall to the sink. A look in the mirror told me a raccoon going a couple of rounds with the heavyweight boxing champ looked better than me. I decided to throw some water on my face, sit out in the restaurant and wait for whatever this was to pass.

Suddenly, my breathing became shallow and fast. What on earth was the matter? The floor swam up to meet me and my head hit hard on the wall near the stall. I had time to register that the tile floor was cold and the grout needed a good scouring before I passed out.

LIES TOO LONG

". . . so I was like, no, this bitch didn't get in my face with some . . . oh damn!"

"Are you all right?" the voice asked.

With one arm, I pushed up to a sitting position. "Can you help me?" I said. "I think I fainted."

"You sure you don't want a doctor?"

"No, I just want to sit down a minute." Two girls helped me to my feet. I felt a plum-size knot on my scalp.

"Why'd you faint? You got the flu or something?"

"No, I don't know," I moaned.

"I'm Kimberly, this is Marcie."

"Thanks for your help. I'm Laurel." They were both sixteen going on thirty with blue jeans below the navel under expensive-looking outerwear and two hundred dollars' worth of makeup on their faces. School must be over for the day, I thought, as they helped me into a booth.

"Could be your blood pressure is up. That happened to my sister," Kimberly said. "Can I call someone for you?"

That question again. I wet my lips. "No, thanks. Maybe something to drink?"

Marcie said, "Okay, I'll get a Coke."

"Make it a Sprite, please."

"Maybe your blood sugar is low. Are you diabetic?" Kimberly continued to help me diagnose my problem.

"No, I'm not diabetic. I just felt really sick to my stomach and woozy." I thought a second and remembered experiencing those same symptoms out of nowhere when I was a kid.

"Maybe you're allergic to something or ate something that made you sick," Kimberly persisted. A medical career loomed ahead for this one.

Bingo. Codeine. That could be it. I'm allergic to codeine.

Marcie brought me a soda and she wouldn't let me pay for it.

"Thank you. You both have been very nice."

"No problem. You be careful."

I waved goodbye to my two rescuers while I sipped my Sprite and tried to figure this out. I had taken Robitussin with codeine when I was twelve. Would it still affect me the same way? Or was this nothing more than pregnancy-induced nausea compounded by not eating since six this morning?

Of course! There was such a thing as Tylenol with codeine. I didn't even look at the pills. I'd just tossed those babies back. I pulled out my Tylenol bottle and checked the contents. They all looked like the regular ones to me. I took only two, so if this was where the codeine came from, wouldn't there be more in the bottle? I was confused; who would do that to me anyway?

Who knew I was allergic? Emma knew, maybe Dennis did too. Nathan knew, so Paula might know. But when had I taken codeine? How?

Dennis had had access to my purse the night he'd broken in. I suppose it was possible to have taken the only two pills in the bottle. But that wouldn't make sense for another reason. If Dennis hadn't paid to have me killed in Delaney, he had even less motivation now, especially when he thought I could get him money. But maybe he was cleverly covering all the bases. I hadn't left my purse alone with Paula, but she could have put something into my tea.

After twenty minutes of sitting in McDonald's, I felt completely fine, still confused but physically fine. Even my headache was gone. Still, I called Dr. Patel, hoping he could see me since I was in Rockville and his office was too. He was at the hospital, so I made a semi-emergency appointment for tomorrow. Before I could replace my phone, it rang.

"Hey, I passed your place and saw the for sale sign," Dennis said. "Good girl. Someone will snap it up. You want to meet me at my attorney's office tomorrow and sign those papers?"

It was time to make a stand. Mac was coming tomorrow and he might have an idea about the best way to confront Dennis. "Sure, say around this time tomorrow afternoon?"

I hung up and got in line, having decided I needed some fries for the road.

CHAPTER 19

Overnight, the plum-sized knot on my head became a walnut-sized one. I slept in, but when I finally got up, I felt better than I had since my pre-Dennis involvement days. Maybe it had something do with being hydrated properly because I had come home and drunk a lot of water, wanting to flush my system of whatever was in it that shouldn't be.

Mac called to say he would be delayed, but that worked out perfectly for me. I had managed to get up and dressed an hour before he rang my doorbell.

"You're here," I said, easing myself into his arms.

"I'm here and bearing gifts." He gave me a gift bag with pink and blue tissue paper flowing over the top. Inside the bag were two teddy bears dressed in Christmas finery. So cute. Before I could say anything else, Rachel opened her door and said, "Good morning, Laurel."

"Oh, good morning, Rachel."

"I'm glad to see that you're all right from the other night."

"I'm fine, thank you. Sorry for the disturbance."

"All right. As long as it doesn't happen again. Have a good day."

And of course the first thing Mac said was, "What happened the other night?"

"Thank you, Mac. These I will treasure my whole life." My first baby gifts, if I didn't count Emma's attempt at the nursery. I took my teddy bears and put them on my bed.

Mac followed me. "You're welcome. What happened? What was the disturbance she mentioned?"

He wasn't going to let me avoid it. "Dennis broke in."

"Dennis? The babies' father?"

"Yep."

"He hurt you?"

"He—it could have been worse. I'm all right."

"Did you file a police report?"

"No."

"Laurel, that only encourages him. If there're no consequences, he can harass you anytime he feels like it."

"You're right, but I had my reasons."

"I'm listening."

I took in a deep breath. "There's a whole lot going on. And I can't believe how nice you are for bringing me teddy bears."

He looked at me, waiting. It was time he knew more details. "Come on, Mac, let's go for a walk. I have a lot to tell you."

The day was sunny but brisk. I pulled the hood of my leather jacket up and tied my white scarf around my neck for the trek along the narrow street. We walked quietly for several minutes, passing houses which were a variety of colors: some green, some cream, some blue. Tall trees, their roots shifting concrete walks in spots, spoke to the age of the neighborhood.

"This Dennis guy is married?" Mac asked, jumping right in with the same assumption Emma had made when I first told her about the babies.

"No, but he's Emma's fiancé."

"Whoa." He stopped walking. His expression said I probably liked being dipped in cheese and placed in rat-infested sewers too. "What happened to loyalty, Laurel?"

"When last seen, it was jetting out of here along with common sense and self-respect." I walked on and so did he.

"Emma forgave you?"

"Emma doesn't know."

For a minute, I thought he might run screaming in the opposite direction.

"And this guy is harassing you, yet you didn't report him. What's his full name?"

"Dennis Ivan Butler. He doesn't want me to rock the boat. Emma is underwriting his auto repair/restoration shop and much of his life."

"Dennis Butler? Not *the* Dennis Butler?"

I nodded.

He whistled. "And he's this broke now? After all those millions?"

"Yep. So I'm a threat to what little he has, not to mention child support payments."

"What are you going to do?"

"I want to tell her. I'm not intimidated by him anymore—especially if he's not trying to kill me."

"What? It's gotten that serious? He's threatened you?"

"Well, no. Earlier, I thought he might have been behind the incident in Delaney. Before I can tell Emma about my pregnancy, she has to recover. Initially, I wasn't strong enough to tell her, but now she really isn't strong enough to hear it."

I didn't tell Mac the second half, about the space heater. It was too much all at once. My heart threatened to spring out of my chest as it was.

"Emma doesn't have family?"

"Well," I sighed, "her parents passed on a while ago. She has a mentally ill brother in New Haven. She had an older sister who died of kidney disease a couple of years ago. I'm her family."

He whistled again. "Complicated."

"Unbelievably so."

Silence. I stared straight ahead, waiting for something like, "It's going to be all right, Laurel." Nothing came.

I took a long shaky breath and looked at him, thinking that might trigger a response when he felt my gaze. It didn't. "You're quiet, Mac."

"It's not because I'm judging you. I would never do that. I've made my share of dumb, selfish mistakes. I'll just do the police work—what I'm qualified to do—and be your friend."

He wasn't going to take me into his arms and tell me he couldn't live without me and whatever it takes, we'll get through this together?

Of course not. That's what happens when you grow up reading Cinderella stories. Unrealistic expectations abound. Someone, preferably a knight on a white horse, was supposed to swoop down and make it all better. Real life doesn't work like that. I needed to rein in my fantasies. Mac didn't really know me, and I didn't know him.

"Thanks, Mac. I need a friend. And for the record, I couldn't have asked for a better one. You've come through for me every time I've needed you."

He reached over, put his gloved hand on my hood and pulled me to him, planting a warm kiss on my lips. "You're welcome," he said.

I traced my lower lip with my finger. So we were kissing friends. Hmmm. We headed back.

I said, "Emma will be all right, my babies will be fine, and Dennis will fade into black."

"What makes you think Dennis will just go away?"

"I don't think he has the fortitude to hang around through Emma's recovery. He's asked me for five hundred thousand dollars."

Mac stopped walking. "What? Laurel?"

"If I give him five hundred thousand and agree to never acknowledge his paternity, he'll go away."

"But you're not going to give him money, right? Lying is one of the things men like Dennis do best."

"I considered it, and I came to that same conclusion. Any ideas?" We started walking again.

"All we have to do is get his complicity on tape and Dennis will be out of your hair for all time. You'll still have to tell Emma, but Dennis can't come back to haunt you."

"Why didn't I think of that! But he's not stupid. If I try and get him to tell all, it will sound stilted and he'll know I'm up to something."

"Just get him talking about what needs to happen. What he wants from you will come out. We'll go to Radio Shack and get a voice-activated tape player."

"That's perfect. I knew you would think of something. I was too close to think it through."

LIES TOO LONG

Back inside the house, Mac made himself comfortable. He took out his laptop and worked at the coffee table. "I like the artwork. Did you get to see Lawrence's exhibit when it came through at the Phillips Collection?"

"Yes, I sure did. Did you come down to D.C. for that?"

"I had planned to, but something came up. Listen, this guy, Kendrick Truman, the one we caught. He's been in and out of the legal system several times and he's only twenty. He's the one who implicated Roscoe Helin. Does his name ring a bell?"

"Kendrick Truman? No, I don't recognize the name."

"He's from Baltimore."

"I don't know him. Backtracking to find out who in Value Mutual authorized a hit will take more than a notion. I think it's a safe bet Roscoe Helin didn't speak directly with this Truman guy. Is that what he says happened?"

"Yes, that's why it's important you tell me everything you know. I mean *everything*."

I gave him the Helin-Stroud Investing newspaper article. After he'd read it, I said, "Nathan is a former boyfriend. He retired from American Financial Services two years ago. I'm not sure what he knows, if anything. His girlfriend is Paula Mayfield, the lawyer who came to town after Bob was murdered. She and I had a run-in yesterday. She's thoroughly pissed with me."

"Why?"

"I may have let her think I knew something about her or Value Mutual's involvement in Bob's death. If Value Mutual is involved, this real estate deal they're cooking will fall apart."

"But you don't know anything?"

"Nope." Matching Mac's confused look, I shook my head. "I faked it. Bob is dead. I wanted to do something to make that right, but I also wanted to give Nathan a chance to tell the truth if he was involved or prepare for the fallout if Helin is." I threw up my hands and flopped on the couch next to Mac.

"Your pregnancy, Bob's death, the fire, dealing with Butler and now worrying that Stroud is involved . . . you're a strong woman, Laurel Novak. Lesser women would be trying on a straightjacket about now."

I laughed, registering new heights on the music scale and doubling over with it before my hysteria turned to tears, and I boohooed like there was no tomorrow. I thought about telling him someone had just tried to poison me, but I didn't know that for sure. He held me and finally I exhaled deeply, pulled myself together and blew my nose. "As you can see, I'm not that strong. I can't undo Bob's death, but I want whoever killed him to pay. If it's Nathan and Paula, so be it."

Mac got on the phone to follow up on the arrangement with the Baltimore police to question Roscoe Helin. Nathan and Paula were added to the list of people he wanted to interview. I got busy preparing brunch.

Chicken soup is in my repertoire because all I have to do is add chicken to the frozen soup mix. An hour later I said, "Soup's on."

I set two steaming bowls of soup and a basket of the cornbread I like to make on the table for two in the tiny kitchen.

"Milk? Orange juice?" I asked as Mac eased into the tight kitchen space.

"Whatever you're having. This is cornbread like I like it. How'd you know?"

"I didn't. It's how I like it too."

"It's got the onion and peppers I love."

"Guess we have something in common," I said, smiling.

I poured milk for both of us. Mac lifted his glass in a toast. "Here's to friendship, the foundation of all great romances."

I almost dropped my glass. Who was sending mixed signals now?

"Tell me about your family, Laurel. Other than Emma."

"I have an aunt in California, and maybe some cousins scattered to the four winds and that's it. I knew my mom, but we were never close. My grandfather raised me from when I was a baby."

"Where were your parents?"

"Annie Mae, my mother, was around. Had a little problem with the booze on and off. She died in a car crash when I was fifteen, and then my grandfather died two years later. My dad, who I never really knew, was killed when I was ten. It sounds really bad, but I was happy growing up."

Mac broke apart his second piece of cornbread. "I know. Nikki Giovanni says black love is black wealth. My parents were coffee farmers until my mother hurt her back and we had to move to Kingston to live with her brother. Twelve people in a house meant for four sounds horrible, but most of the time, we were happy."

He asked for a second bowl of soup. While I refilled his bowl at the stove he said, "Kids are resilient, that's for sure. Doesn't take a lot to make them happy."

"So your youngest son is with your parents. You're so lucky to have them both."

"Yes, I'm blessed. Lindbergh and Madeline McKnight are doing well. And I have three sisters and one brother."

"I always wanted a large family," I said.

"Yes, Drew is with them. No longer in Kingston though. My siblings and I built a new home for them ten years ago and my dad grows coffee beans on twenty acres. He and my uncle are having the time of their lives because it's more of an avocation at this point."

"A coffee farmer? That is so cool. Emma and I are coffee aficionados. Where's Drew's mother?"

"Drew's mother does something important at the Kennedy Space Center in Florida. Her work is her passion and priority, more so than being a mother and wife, but she sees him regularly.

"I admire you, Laurel, for wanting to keep your children. Keeping Drew was not Felicia's first inclination. I had to beg her to do it. I'm going to be bringing him to live with me permanently this summer."

"That's good, Mac. When I was his age, I wondered why I didn't live with my mother and father. When you are too young to understand fully, it hurts to think you aren't wanted. In June, I'll be a full-time parent too. Something else we have in common."

"I remember when my twins came home." He shook his head, smiling and frowning at the same time. "You think your aunt will come help you? And let me beat you to it this time. Twins, we have that in common too."

"Yeah, I'm sure she'd come if I asked her. Or I might go out there to live. It depends."

"On what exactly?"

"Like I told you, I don't want my house anymore, and by the time the babies are born, Emma won't want anything to do with me because she'll be on her feet again and I will have told her the truth. If Bob's murder turns out to be connected to work . . ." I shrugged. "The only good thing left on the East Coast will be you, Mac, but you might enjoy visiting California. You and Drew, that is."

"Who knows? We might."

Mac made some more calls after lunch. I drifted off to bed for a short nap, just me and my teddy bears. One was a girl dressed in a red velvet gown trimmed in white and the other teddy bear was a boy dressed in a black velvet tux. Would I have two boys, two girls or one of each? Did I want to know or be surprised? We just need an hour of rest at the most, I told all interested parties, rubbing my stomach. Three hours later, I awoke to the smell of fish.

Mac had gone out and bought what he needed to make ackee and salt fish for dinner. "If you're Jamaican, this is what you want to eat every day," he said.

Ackee is a fruit, and salt fish is cod. It was pretty good, but I might have to work at acquiring a real taste for it. Not to mention I was becoming more sensitive to smells. But no guy had cooked for me in years, so it was delicious from that standpoint.

After dinner I said, "I'm going to see Emma, Mac. Here's the code for the burglar alarm and a key. You're still going out, right?

"Yes."

"I'll be back home by nine. Make yourself at home. You'll find what you need to be comfortable on the couch in the linen closet. There are sheets, towels and extra toiletries."

He gravitated toward me. "If you're going to be later than nine, call me," he said.

LIES TOO LONG

I swayed closer, pleased that he would worry about me and readied myself for the kiss that never came. Men are so fickle. If I live to be a hundred, I'll never figure them out. Chagrin hastened my departure.

I stopped at the gas station, filled my tank and got hot chocolate for Emma and me. In her room she sat facing the window, humming "What a Wonderful World It Would Be."

It was one of the songs we harmonized on a lot. "Emma?" After I finished gaping in shock, I picked up a line and started singing along. When we stopped I said, "Emma? You're humming! It's about time we reactivated the only world-class singing duo in the state of Maryland."

Her back was to me, and she didn't turn around, but the humming ceased.

"I brought you hot chocolate," I said, coming to stand in front of her. Her face was red. Had I snuck up on her and embarrassed her? She narrowed her eyes and swiped at the chocolate I extended to her. The hot liquid flew everywhere.

"No!" she screamed, huffing worse than a pig-seeking wolf.

"What's the matter, Emma?" I ran to the call button. When Tereka came in, I vaguely registered that she must have switched shifts with Cheryl.

She surveyed the mess. "What happened?"

"Is she all right? She's all red in the face and she knocked the drink out of my hand."

"Emma?" Tereka put her hand on Emma's shoulder, scrutinizing her.

She took Emma's blood pressure. "It's 140 over 80. She's okay, a little upset but okay." By then, Emma's face was no longer red and her breathing had returned to normal.

"This sudden agitation is part of the coma recovery process, isn't it, Tereka?"

"Yeah, we see a lot of agitation. Could be the coma or just the residual effects of her head injury. Patients become frustrated when they can't find the language or the mobility they used to have. It comes out as rage. Don't take it personally."

"Mobility. Oh shoot! I missed the physical therapy this morning. How'd she do?" I held my breath, afraid it would be bad news.

"Oh, that's right, you missed it. I heard she got tired really quickly, but in a week or two, Emma is not going to remember this wheelchair, right, Emma? It's going to be a bad dream from your past."

"That's fantastic news! Emma, you're home free!" Her burns would heal, she'd be walking. The old Emma was coming back, but it had to be a maddening experience—having a freak accident interrupt her life. "Maybe she's upset about leaving. This is her last night, isn't it? Did the doctors tell her?"

"Yeah, you know, don't you, Emma?"

Emma gave no visible response.

"They'll transfer her sometime between nine and twelve tomorrow. You or Dennis might want to get her personal belongings and take them to her after she gets to the rehab center. There's a plastic bag you can use and there are more at the nurses' station if you need them."

"At the rehab center, will she have a speech therapist?"

"They'll evaluate her and give her what she needs."

"Okay, she was humming when I came in and that's great, but her language is still limited."

"I don't want to give you false hope, Laurel, but I think Emma will be fine. Language can come back all of a sudden. She'll be talking in two word sentences, then in the next breath, she's talking like she was before the trauma. I've seen it happen."

"Thanks. That's good to hear."

When Emma and I were alone again, I pushed her chair so she could face me and the TV. I surfed to an *I Love Lucy* rerun. "I don't know if Lucy can help, Emma, but maybe. You're almost there, try not to get discouraged. I'm going to be with you every step of the way. I got really sick. That's why I wasn't here this morning. Remember I told you about the time I had bronchitis when I was twelve and almost died from the codeine in the cough medicine? Well, I didn't really almost die but I was sick as a dog yesterday. I think Nathan's girlfriend slipped me some codeine. Don't ask."

Emma looked amused, as if I were speaking pig Latin.

"I'm sorry I missed you up and out of this wheelchair, girl. Can't wait to see that."

A man from housekeeping came in to clean up the chocolate spray. When he left, I sat on her bed. "Mac's here, Emma, at my place. They found the guy who killed Bob. He was hired to do it. Only twenty years old. It looks like Value Mutual is behind it, but proving that is going to be a whole other story.

"Hurry up and get better, Emma. I need all the help I can get to figure this out."

I went to get another bag for Emma's other items I would take. When I came back, Dennis was there. If our meeting tomorrow went as he expected, I was sure he'd skip town immediately, so maybe he was here for his swan song. As I got closer, I could see the checkbook he had put in front of her.

"What are you doing?" I asked him.

"I told you. I've got obligations, we both do. I just want to see if she can sign her name to pay some bills, is all."

"Can she?"

His hand sawed back and forth across his lips and chin. "No, dammit!"

Good. He'd just have to make do.

I glanced at the check. It was made out to him, not the mortgage company or even Pepco, the electric company, and it was for five thousand dollars. I didn't want to be in the same room with him.

I busied myself collecting her clothing, cards and plants. "Emma, I will bring your things to the rehab center tomorrow morning."

On the way out I told them at the nurses' desk that Emma was ready to get back into bed. Anything I could do to keep Dennis from hounding her, I would do.

CHAPTER 20

Soft, rhythmic grunts came from somewhere in my living room. Perplexed, I called out, "Mac?"

"I'm here. You're late." Hidden by the couch, Mac was on the floor doing crunches in gray sweat pants and a red T-shirt. "Two hundred, two hundred one, two hundred two."

He counted for my benefit, I suspected. We laughed as I sat down on the couch to watch. Probably his count was closer to fifty, but he didn't have an ounce of fat on him and with his washboard stomach, two hundred was not out of the question.

"Did you have any luck?" I asked.

"Surprisingly, Helin and his three attorneys spoke to us without a fuss. Swears he knows nothing about nothing. Volunteered for a lie detector test. He'll be in Delaney on Monday."

"If he were behind Bob's murder, he wouldn't sully his hands with a phone conversation to Truman, but maybe, if he knows anything at all, it will show up. What about Nathan and Paula?"

"They are out of town this weekend."

"How convenient." I sighed, folded my arms and paced. Mac didn't even breathe hard through his sit-ups. If I had tried to join him, I'd wheeze like an asthmatic husky on the Iditarod Trail. Physical exercise beyond a nice, brisk walk or exuberant lovemaking was simply unnecessary torture in my book.

"We put it out they are wanted for questioning. It would be bad PR for Stroud to refuse to cooperate with a police investigation, but we'll see. As an attorney, Mayfield knows cooperating or not is her call. Unless there's outside pressure, I'm betting she'll decline to say anything and we don't have enough to arrest her."

LIES TOO LONG

"Yeah, maybe American Financial Services will prod her to do the right thing. Our company reputation could be on the line," I said. "If she knows anything, that is."

Rolling gracefully to his feet, Mac wrapped a towel around his neck. "I admit what we have is sketchy, but it's about getting in the game, Laurel. If we wait for something more concrete to fall into our laps, we'll be waiting indefinitely. Many times something as simple as seeing the head honcho questioned makes the peons nervous. Nervous people make mistakes."

"I understand," I said. Noticing the linen he'd harvested from the closet, I snapped loose a sheet for him to make up the couch as a bed.

Taking one end of the sheet he asked, "You usually go to bed this early? It's not even ten."

I yawned on cue. "Sorry. I sleep a lot these days." I felt bad there was no TV in the living room to entertain him, but he could hear the low murmur of Rachel's if he listened hard.

"Well, get your rest. When and where is the meeting with Butler tomorrow?"

"In Silver Spring, back down I-95, I'm afraid. It's at four."

"I thought I'd hang out. Maybe your friend Nathan and his girlfriend will come back tomorrow. I don't mind driving to Silver Spring, by the way. Did the visit with Emma go okay?"

"Yeah, sorta, not really. Nothing I'm not used to."

"Was Butler there? Did he say something to upset you?"

"Don't worry. This will be resolved soon. I don't want to talk about it now. Goodnight, Mac."

Exhausted, I leaned my head against the bedroom door as I locked it. Dennis was a leech. His type is the reason women across the world lock their bedroom doors at night.

Turning off the light, I tossed my top and bra into the hamper and shimmied out of my jeans and panties. The jeans were still clean for at least another day and I folded them neatly on the chair, thinking I'd have to do laundry soon. I pulled on a clean, oversized T-shirt.

In the bathroom, I washed off the day's dirt from my face and brushed my teeth. I considered taking a shower, but was too beat. I smiled at the thought of jockeying with Mac for first dibs at the hot water in the morning. Then I locked the bathroom door on my bedroom side.

A couple of weeks ago I had been willing to share a bedroom with Mac.

But tonight, since Dennis's home invasion, the locked doors had become my last bit of protection in case the burglar alarm system didn't do what it was supposed to do. Should I get a gun? No, no way. I didn't want one of those around, did I?

I sighed as I climbed under the covers. I would be locking doors, not to mention my heart, for the rest of my life.

I dreamed Paula and Emma had planned their weddings on the same day. Compelled to attend both with nothing to wear, I shopped at the big women's shop. It was the only store open and all they had was a black floor-length gown covered in red and purple irises. Desperate, I bought it, hoping the flowers would camouflage my protruding stomach, which, in my dream, I thought important to conceal. I got purple shoes to match.

When I got ready to put on my shoes, I discovered I had a red one and a purple one and I had exactly twenty minutes to get to the first wedding.

"Laurel?"

"What?" I shot straight up in the bed when Mac's shadowy image appeared in my doorway.

"What wrong shoe?" he asked.

"What do you mean, what's wrong with me?"

"No," he chuckled, "not with you. You said 'wrong shoe' in your sleep."

"I did?" I rubbed both arms briskly, not because the room was cold, but my dream had chilled me. I folded my arms around my bended knees. "I had a bad wedding dream."

"Let me get you another blanket." He took one from the linen closet in the bathroom and tucked the extra warmth around me.

LIES TOO LONG

"Thank you. I've been having lots of weird dreams. I don't know if it's stress or being pregnant. Of course, I haven't been able to separate the two, but the dreams do seem especially vivid. I could have sworn I locked that door."

"You did." He pulled a credit card from his sweat pants pocket, then stared at me a second. "I would like nothing more than to climb in there with you and hold you until you go back to sleep."

I flushed, but only had to think about it for three seconds. "That's a bad idea."

"Too much temptation."

"Yep," I agreed, my eyes fixed on his. Electricity zigzagged between us, but I quickly turned off the switch. "And, if you noticed, I don't do temptation well."

"Well, maybe I can sit here with you." He grabbed a teddy bear, pulled up a chair, and used my bed as an ottoman.

"At least put your feet under the covers, Mac." When his cold feet touched mine, I laughed as if he'd tickled me and moved my feet away. But at least his toenails weren't stilettos like a few other male toenails I'd encountered along the way.

"Go back to sleep now, Laurel."

I settled back on my pillows and looked at him, wondering if he was going to tell me a story with the bear as a prop. When he didn't, I elicited one. "Tell me how your jaw was injured. Did it happen in Desert Storm?"

"No, nothing that noble. I was twenty-three, took a wet curve going forty-five miles an hour on a motorcycle and shattered my jaw. My body rejected the artificial bone the doctors in Jamaica tried to repair it with. An infection set up. There were no other medical resources I had access to at the time. I decided to just live with it."

"Sorry. Was it a long recuperation?"

"Long enough for me to know I wanted to divorce my wife and marry my nurse."

"Wow. The silver lining theory at work. What happened with your first marriage?"

"Let's see. Take your pick: I didn't feel loved. All I heard was nagging. We fought all the time. And if you asked her, I'm sure she'd say the same thing."

We laughed. "Relationships are extremely tough, even when you start out in love, aren't they?" I said.

"Yes, and getting married at nineteen was ill-advised to start with."

"And what happened with the second marriage?"

"Yolanda was medicine for what ailed me while it lasted. We still talk once a week. Our son, Alexander, wants to use the army to pay his way through dental school."

"And your twins, what do they want to do?"

"Other than party hearty and drive their old man to an early grave? Adam, the older one, wants to go into sports medicine. Adrian is going into communications. Wants to own a radio station."

"Adam, Adrian, Alexander and Andrew. Say, that's pretty good, Mac. You managed to have them in alphabetical order."

"Not something amateurs should attempt."

"And Drew. I bet I know what he wants to be."

"What?"

"A police officer, like his dad."

"Beautiful and psychic."

"Oh please, I'm not beautiful, Mac. Just average with an attitude."

He laughed hard, slapping his knee. "Well," he said, "you're beautiful in my eyes."

I was? "Thank you. Would you say I was character-actress beautiful, Mac?" I teased.

He rocked his head from side to side, considering. "No, I was thinking you were more aging-newscaster beautiful."

I threw a pillow at him and readied a second one.

"Hey, careful! I'm holding a defenseless bear. In ten, no twenty years, I meant. And only in the top markets—D.C., L.A. or New York."

I threw the second pillow.

"The anchorwoman, of course. None of this roving all over the place. Staying put is best."

LIES TOO LONG

We laughed and then exchanged another electrically charged look. I didn't think we were thinking about TV reporters anymore. He brought my pillows and teddy bear back.

He kissed me on my cheek as I settled under the covers.

"Goodnight, Mac." I fell asleep happy for a change.

The next day I climbed into Mac's Jeep and queried him about Kendrick Truman's statement implicating Roscoe Helin. That bugged me. "What kind of idiot gives a name to a hit man anyway?"

He shrugged. "Truman came up with the name Helin; we can't ignore it."

"No, I guess we can't."

I gave him directions to the rehab center. "We've got a full day ahead, Mac. After we leave here, we go to Radio Shack, my doctor's appointment and then my meeting with Dennis."

"You sure know how to treat company," Mac joked.

I gave him a sugary smile. "Tours run daily."

Emma looked up from her wheelchair when we walked into her room at the rehab center. "Hi, Laurel."

"You said hello. You said my name. My God." I hugged her. "Yes! Mac, she's better already. Must be the homier atmosphere." Two adjacent windows with white mini-blinds offered a view of the melting snow on the grassy areas outside. The tan walls, blue blanket and the upholstered maroon chair blended well. Two bouquets of flowers, one yellow and one pink, added more color to the rainbow.

I introduced Mac and began putting her things away.

A birch armoire combined with shelves for displaying books or pictures sat at a right angle to the windows. I placed Emma's belongings where I thought they should go. This was home to many people for months at a time. I wondered who the last resident was, and hoped she or he had fared well. Emma would leave within a couple of weeks. I refused to believe anything different.

A nurse had given us a schedule of daily activities. Mac and I looked it over; every hour was planned. Breakfast, bathing, doctors' visits, physical therapy, occupational therapy, speech therapy and counseling were slotted.

"The program is certainly structured," Mac said. "You'll get a lot of good help here, Emma."

"You won't have to stay long. You're improving every day. You can already stand, you're more aware of your surroundings and your language is coming along. Everything is going to fall back into place soon and we can put this chapter behind us. Your skin looks great, doesn't it Mac?" It was splotched in a multitude of colors ranging from brown to fuchsia, but it got better with each passing day.

Mac nodded. "The burns are healing nicely."

"What did you have for breakfast, Emma?" I asked.

"Breakfast." She nodded and smiled at me, making solid eye contact.

"Did you have eggs?" I prompted.

"Eggs." She put on her I'm-trying-to-remember face then said, "Eggs, bacon, toast and eggs."

I grinned at Mac. "Still some trouble forming sentences and remembering, but this is undeniable progress."

Soon the three of us moved to a huge, gray-carpeted therapy room. A set of practice steps led nowhere in one corner. Stationary bikes, treadmills and waist-high parallel bars filled the other corners of the room.

Two physical therapists, sandwiching Emma, assisted her into a standing position between the parallel bars, making sure she had her balance before releasing her. Then one therapist positioned one of

Emma's hands farther along on one bar, and encouraged her to lift her 'stepping leg.'

She took one step, said, "Walking," and smiled. On her own she slid the other hand forward and repeated the process, making it halfway to the end of the bars, arms shaking with effort, before her therapists guided her wheelchair under her. "Tired. I'm tired," she said.

If I had had my pom-poms from high-school pep squad, I would have been doing a cheer.

At Radio Shack, we found a recorder as long as a pen and a tad wider. I also picked up a replacement remote control for my CD player, having destroyed the other one when I'd thrown it at Dennis's head. Mac put the batteries in the recorder and slipped it into my purse. Then it was on to the doctor.

Dr. Patel always started his visits with a mini-conference in his office. I had assumed Mac would sit tight in the waiting room, but when the receptionist called my name, he stood.

Surprised at his intention to join me, I dropped my magazine. We bent to get it at the same time, bumped heads and then laughed.

He had no trouble reading my surprise. "Is this all right?"

"Sure, I guess," I said, happy but still caught off guard.

Dr. Patel and Mac shook hands, introducing themselves.

"Oh, Ms. Novak, so nice to see you've come with the father this time."

"I'm Ms. Novak's friend, but not the father," Mac said.

"My mistake." Dr. Patel bowed slightly.

He sat down and folded his hands on his massive wooden desk. "So, Ms. Novak, the babies are almost at twelve weeks. Tell me, how have you been feeling?" His clipped English and Indian accent set the gold standard for verbal efficiency, and his brown eyes danced with secret merriment.

I told him about the fall I had taken at McDonald's.

The merriment went away. He began tsking as he made notes in my file. "Ms. Novak, you cannot be the heroine in an action movie and expect to deliver healthy babies. Shootings and trips to the emergency room and now this fall? I have to be frank. You may have noticed you are not twenty-one anymore. Babies do not fare well under stress in the best of circumstances. What is your line of work again?"

Gee, Doc, thanks for sugarcoating it, I thought. "I'm a financial advisor, which is not exactly stress-free, but I'm on leave taking care of a sick friend."

"Oh, and what's the matter with your friend?"

"She was injured in a fire in my home."

Again the tsking with an added headshake. "If I haven't been clear before, let me be clear now. At your age and carrying twins, this is an at-risk pregnancy. That bleeding, though slight, is considered a threatened abortion. You want a calm existence for the next six months, or as close as we can get to full term. All this crazy havoc must stop."

Mac gave me a series of encouraging nods. "She's going to take care of herself, Doctor."

"I'll do my best, Dr. Patel. I'd love to sit on a beach somewhere, but I don't see that happening. I'm taking my vitamins," I added weakly, hoping that would atone for a few sins. "Codeine wouldn't hurt the babies, would it?"

"Vitamins are good. Sometimes they can have the effect of added nausea, but please be consistent in taking them. And if it was codeine that made you feel faint, that one-time exposure will not harm your children. So that is good."

"Very good," I said.

"Anything else?" Doctor Patel asked.

"No, that's about it."

"Very well. My nurse will show you to the exam room."

"Should I come with you, Laurel?" Mac asked.

"Uh . . . Yes, give me a minute." I couldn't see getting undressed with him in the room, but I'd be grateful for a hand to hold, especially now that I was vying for the title of world's worst mother despite all my efforts.

A few minutes later, Dr. Patel stood at his end of the exam table next to his nurse, and Mac smiled down at me from the other end. He reached for my hand before I could reach for his. His firm yet gentle touch was something I could easily get used to.

After several long seconds Dr. Patel said, "Your babies are doing fine. Strong. Here, put on the stethoscope and listen to the heartbeats."

As relief overtook me, I brushed at the tears tickling my ears while I listened. I passed the stethoscope to Mac. His smile started in his eyes and spread all over his face.

When Mac and I were alone, I took my feet from the stirrups and sat up, holding my paper top together in front while trying to hold the drape that covered my bottom half together in back. I was torn between being embarrassed at my state of undress and being grateful for his presence.

Flustered I said, "Dr. Patel is great, don't you think?" I glanced at him shyly, my rising blush heating my cheeks.

Mac gave me a reassuring smile. "I like him. I like honesty." He lifted my chin with his hand, forcing me to look him squarely in the eyes. "You're glowing, Laurel. You really are beautiful."

"I am?" Grinning, I held my breath as his hand left my chin and moved to my stomach. The drape was no barrier to the warmth of his open palm or the tingling sensation that coursed through me when his hand made a circular motion.

"These babies are so lucky. You'll be a fantastic mom."

"I'm going to try, Mac. I want to be the best mother I know how to be." Looking down, I put my hands over his and felt like weeping. Such simple acts: his support, his belief in my ability to be a good mother, his gentleness, these were all things I desperately longed for.

My top parted when I let it go, leaving my breasts partially exposed. As Mac's gaze rested on them, feelings of passion that had absolutely nothing to do with me loving my children made me breathe faster.

Without thinking, I took his hand from my stomach and brought it to my breasts. Seconds seemed to pass with our gazes locked. His hand moved beneath the paper and his fingertips, like the softest feathers, grazed first one nipple, then the other. Inhaling sharply, I closed my eyes and threw my head back, thinking this was the sweetest prelude to lovemaking I'd ever known. Except we weren't about to make love in the doctor's office, or were we?

Abruptly, he pulled his hand away.

My eyes flew open. "Mac?"

"I'm sorry." His voice was hoarse at first and then he cleared his throat.

"No, don't be sorry," I whispered.

When he spoke again he sounded angry. "Get dressed, Laurel. I'll wait outside."

I stared at the door as it closed behind him. What had just happened? It was me, I lamented. I'd been too forward crossing lines he'd clearly said he wasn't prepared to cross.

Back in the car I jumped right into conversation, hoping to prevent any kind of barrier being erected between us. "Thanks, Mac. Have I told you lately that you are a nice man?"

His smile was like sunshine on a rainy day. He brushed my hair into place. "We have time to kill before our meeting with Butler and the lawyer. Can I see your house?"

"My house? Sure." And I supposed that intimate moment in the doctor's office was forgotten. That was probably for the best. I thought about asking why he wanted to see my house, but I knew why. He was a policeman first, and he was curious.

As the other cars and the roadside landscape rushed past my window, my uneasiness grew. I feared that within the walls of my house, I'd have to tell him how Emma came to be burned in the first place.

CHAPTER 21

I clicked on a lamp in my living room and hurried to the thermostat to turn up the heat. It wouldn't do to have a pipe burst. But I knew it wasn't just the temperature that made it cold inside my house. The ghosts of my mistakes had taken up residence.

I looked around. Everything was spotless thanks to the cleaning company I'd hired to make the house ready for potential buyers. Mac walked over to my green sofa and took his coat off.

His hand trailed across the back of my wing chair as he wandered to the kitchen, opened the garage door, observed everything with his policeman's eye. When we came down from the newly repaired upstairs, he asked me what I thought had happened.

"I didn't know Emma was coming over, but she had mentioned a surprise and decorating the nursery must have been it. Seems she wanted to take some measurements and try out a few borders. I picture her getting the ladder from the garage, seeing the space heater and taking it up with her. The room is right over the garage and a little colder than the other rooms."

He frowned. "A cold room doesn't make a good nursery."

"No, but Emma had been trying to convince me to install baseboard heating. She said it was a great room, great windows and a shame to waste the space."

"Go on."

"I can only guess. She must have plugged the heater in, too close to something, and it started a fire. When she tried to put it out, her clothes caught fire. She panicked and jumped out the window."

"Yeah, makes sense. When adrenalin kicks in, jumping out of a second-story window is nothing."

Mac seemed lost in thought a moment. Immersed in silence, my heart pounded.

"And the heater was broken?" he asked.

How did he know? "What do you mean?"

"Well, why was it in the garage?"

I sat on my couch and covered my face with my hands. Mac sat next to me, ready to take me into his arms. I momentarily considered telling him the garage was where I stored it. But he had been so sweet to me, I wanted to be honest with him.

"The heater wasn't working and instead of letting it sit in my garage I should have pitched it." I shook my head, thunderstruck all over again at my stupidity.

"Why didn't you?"

"I intended to. I didn't have the chance. And once again, my choices ended up hurting Emma."

"At least the second time it wasn't a conscious choice."

That stung.

"Not like the first time," he prodded.

A slap to the other cheek, but I met his gaze. "Yeah, you're right. I have rationalized my involvement with Dennis a few times, but there's no excuse. I feel guilty about the fire, and I should."

"Not just the fire. Your best friend's boyfriend was clearly off limits. I think when we step outside boundaries, we invite all kinds of consequences."

"That could be the understatement of the year from where I'm sitting," I said.

"But you know," Mac said, apparently trying to soften his verbal blows, "we can't necessarily see the big picture. It takes a lifetime and a God to know how it all works together for good. As long as you have learned and changed your way of thinking, however you rationalized it, it'll be okay. That's what I've done in my life. You move on."

He knew just what to say to make me confess all. "I planned to take the broken space heater to Dennis's shop and arrange for him to die in a fire. That's the real reason I kept it."

"What?" He recoiled and walked around my coffee table, looking at me as if I'd morphed into an alien species.

"It was a dumb idea. I knew I couldn't go through with it as soon as I got home. Dennis's manipulation pissed me off. I responded to it."

"Are you sure you weren't just looking for physical comfort in your relationship with Dennis? Do you do that sort of thing often?"

"What do you mean? Are you asking me if I sleep around? Is that what you think?"

Mac fiddled with his keys in his pants pocket, looking down at his shoes.

"Let me explain, Mac. Dennis was eye candy I had been looking at with my face smashed to the glass for a long time. When he finally opened the door and let me in, I wasn't strong enough to say no. When I first saw him, he was a big-time basketball star and even when his fame fizzled, his charisma still lit up every room he walked into. Look at me. I'm an average woman who puts her career before relationships because relationships never work out. When this charismatic former professional basketball player finally paid attention to me . . ." Suddenly, this whole conversation felt futile. "Mac, you know what? You should just go. I cannot bear that look on your face."

The groove in his brow deepened, then his eyes widened in surprise as if he had no idea what I was talking about.

I shook my head, got up and stood behind the couch, looking across at him. "I'm never going to be anyone other than who I am. And I can't change my past. You shouldn't be here. I can't let you make me feel worse than I already do." I pointed to my purse on the couch. "I'll call a cab, you take your Jeep and go back to Pennsylvania."

He stayed on his side of the couch and met my troubled gaze. "You want me to leave?"

"Yes."

"Are you saying you won't allow me close enough to care about you and tell you how I feel about whatever the topic is?"

"The topic? Give me a break. We're not discussing politics. You want to give me a character makeover and you know it."

"Given your situation, you don't agree there would have been a more honorable way for you to conduct yourself?"

"I-I'm not saying there wasn't. I'm saying I don't like feeling you think it's your job to correct me. To fix me."

"That's not my job, although I think it's pretty obvious something is broken somewhere and needs fixing. I can't do it, but I want to help, if you'll let me."

"Oh," I said, not trying to contain my anger. "So now I'm broken."

"Laurel, did you even hear the things you told me yesterday and today? You slept with your best friend's boyfriend and you seriously considered burning him alive. I mean, you've got to admit that's pretty heavy-duty stuff. I'm not unsympathetic, but things happen for a reason. It could have something to do with not having your mother around when you needed her."

"Oh God!" I walked away in disgust, but came right back at him. "Don't try to psychoanalyze me! How dare you take my personal details and try to turn them against me? Yeah, I know I didn't have a mother or a father, but I had a grandfather who could plait hair and iron clothes with the best of them. He could make a lemon pound cake that would curl your toes and he came to every recital and school performance I ever had!"

I got my second wind and could not have stopped my "sistergirl" neck roll if I'd wanted to. "And, I'll have you know, he was vice president of the PTA and ran the spring fair all through elementary school." By now my chastising finger was in his face. "So don't you dare go there. I thought you understood. My upbringing was better than some rich kid's who gets sent off to boarding school. I was loved. Get out of my way so I can call a cab."

"No."

"No?"

"No."

"Why not?"

"I don't want to." He put on his coat. "Let's go."

LIES TOO LONG

I glared at Mac as he backed out of my driveway. *I don't want to.* What the heck was that supposed to mean? Too angry to speak, I retreated into memories of my grandfather.

He wasn't a tall man, maybe 5'8" with his shoes on, and he had big, expressive eyes that reflected his mood more clearly than anything he said or did. Granddaddy liked the simple pleasures: sitting on the porch listening to crickets in the evening, slices of lemon pound cake right from the oven. He loved a clean house. And he loved me. Only after he'd made sure I had everything I needed did he tend to his lady friends.

He always had at least two girlfriends and, as I recalled, they rotated frequently. One was to sit with in church and to go to her house after church for a full-course Sunday meal. Then there was the other one, to take out on Friday nights and bring home for a "sleepover."

Could that be the reason I'd had an easy time crossing that boundary with Emma and Dennis? Between friendship and betrayal? I'd seen my grandfather play fast and loose with moral guidelines my whole life. That, and my mother drifting in and out of my life, had taught me emotional ties were tenuous at best. Maybe that's why part of me fought so hard to maintain my relationship with Emma. I sought that permanent connection somewhere in my life.

I looked at Mac again, my anger subsiding. I was surprised he'd stuck with me this far. Maybe his ability to handle emotional commitment was stronger than mine. That would be a good thing.

CHAPTER 22

"Hello, I'm Gayle Marklin, Mr. Butler's attorney." Gayle Marklin, two inches taller and probably thirty pounds lighter than me, had a head full of blond curls and huge gray-blue eyes. She shook our hands, smiling. Her gaze lingered on Mac before finding its way back to me.

"I'm Laurel Novak, Ms. Marklin, and this is my friend, Wendell McKnight."

"Friend?" She studied Mac further. "Will you be represented by counsel today, Ms. Novak?"

"No, I'll just have moral support. I do have something I would like to speak to Dennis about before we start." I made sure my tape player was at the ready.

"He isn't here yet. Please make yourselves at home." She gestured toward her reception area which was filled with comfortable chairs, bonsai plants and the fading afternoon sunshine.

"Coffee or tea, perhaps?" she offered while turning on matching lamps next to gurgling table fountains.

"Some tea would be nice, thank you. What about you, Mac?" I asked.

"Tea is fine," he said.

Ms. Marklin beamed. "Oh, reggae, reefer and rum."

"Excuse me?" Mac said.

"I'm sorry. I didn't mean to be politically incorrect. Your lovely accent transported me back to my last vacation in Jamaica. Which parish is yours?"

"I'm from St. Thomas Parish. You know Jamaica well?"

"Not as well as I'd like to. I loved rafting on the Rio Grande. You guys have so many mountains, rivers, caves and beaches." She turned toward me. "Have you been?"

LIES TOO LONG

I shook my head no.

"You must go. In addition to this great geography, they have fifty spas. I like the Milk River Bath in St. Elizabeth."

"One day." I smiled.

"It's such a treat. The sunset alone is worth it. Well, let me get that tea. I'll be right back."

I watched Mac study the back of her tan pants and how her red shirt tucked in at a tiny belted waistline.

Oh, great. Jealousy rearing its ugly head. I beat it down like it was a pop-up villain in an arcade game. I reminded myself that when "mines" are stepped on, they explode. Don't remember where I read that, but the point was not to get clingy. And what was there to get clingy about in the first place?

Five minutes later, Marklin came back with a wooden tray filled with orange cups of steaming tea. Green tea, she informed us. She poured milk into our cups after asking, then into hers. I sipped mine, holding my orange saucer under my cup.

"Have you known Dennis long?" I asked.

"I met him when he and my husband played basketball in college, so that's been more years than I care to remember."

"Oh," I said.

"Well, my ex-husband, that is." She set her cup down and rubbed her empty ring finger. Then she threw up her hands. "Who can you trust these days?" She glanced at her watch. "Excuse me again, I'll just call to make sure he's on his way."

Mac adjusted his jacket and sat up straighter. I pretended I didn't care about his need to look erect and dignified for the willowy Ms. Marklin while I examined my fingernails. I needed a manicure. The past couple of weeks had been hectic. I decided to make appointments for my hair and nails and see if I could get back in touch with my feminine side. Better than that, I needed a day at a spa. Perhaps Ms. Marklin had gone past small talk into throwing a hint my way.

At four-twenty, Mac got up to stretch his legs.

"I don't know what happened. He's not answering at home or his cell, and his work number is busy," Marklin said, coming back into the room.

I positioned my hands on the armrests and prepared to hoist myself from the luxury of the club chair. "I hate to have to reschedule this, Ms. Marklin, but we've waited long enough."

"Yes, certainly, but before you go, could I have a word with you alone?"

I remained seated, my gaze sliding from her face to Mac's and back again. "No, it's okay. Mac can hear whatever it is you need to tell me."

"Dennis and I played phone tag for a while, but I finally caught up with him last night to talk in detail about what he wanted to accomplish at this meeting. I had to explain to him that a parent may not sign away paternal responsibilities. The child's interest must come first. It's the court's responsibility to make sure adequate provisions are in place."

"Well," Mac said, "that explains it. When Butler heard that, he probably decided to ditch this meeting. If he can't sign away his parental responsibilities, what would be the point?"

"No, no, he said he didn't want to waste an opportunity to come to a financial agreement," Marklin said. "He mentioned how he would appeal to your fair-mindedness, Ms. Novak, seeing as how he never expected to be a father. He stated vehemently that you would agree with this assertion. He hoped the three of us could draft a preliminary agreement."

"I see. Just preliminary?" I asked.

"Until paternity has been established, to do more would be spinning our wheels. Now, I will admit the idea of declaring his paternity voluntarily gave Dennis pause, but I'm surprised he hasn't shown up. He wanted to be here."

―

Mac waited for an opening in traffic before pulling onto Colesville Road. "Is his shop far?"

"Less than ten minutes from here," I said.

LIES TOO LONG

"Okay, because Butler needs to know new ground rules have been put into play. I'm not going to let him harass you, and it doesn't matter if there's an agreement in place or not. It stops now."

As we stood in front of Butler's Automotive, the orange, red and green 7-11 convenience store logo half a block up on the other side of the street seemed especially bright. When a bird squawked behind me, I turned, but couldn't see it in the leafy camouflage of low bushes. A hint of uneasiness made my heart beat faster.

Mac tried the front door. With his hands cupped around his eyes, he peered through the door pane. "I don't think he's here. The phone must be off the hook."

"The phone sits on the counter right in front. You see it?"

"Yep."

"Is it off the hook?"

"Looks like the receiver is half on, half off."

Mac walked five feet to the left and tested both red, windowless service-bay doors. They were locked.

"Wait here. I'm going to get my flashlight and take a look around back," Mac said.

I didn't want to be left in the chill of dusk with just my creepy feeling for company. "No, I'll walk with you."

He hesitated a moment, then we fell in step, our feet crunching on white gravel. He gestured to a cluster of four cars parked in the rear, probably finished or needing repair. "Do you see his car?"

I shook my head. The Monte Carlo wasn't there. We stopped at the back door which led to the little room where I'd planned to cremate Dennis. I turned the knob, but it was locked.

"There's one more window on the side. Maybe we can see in, I don't know," I said. We walked the short distance, rounding the corner. The window shade was drawn. I stopped short.

"Might as well try the window while we're here," Mac said.

I grabbed his wrist, my anxiety refusing to be put down this time. "I've got a bad feeling, Mac. I want to go."

"Let me just check. I have to go back home tomorrow and I'd like for you not to have to worry about this joker after I'm gone. Come on."

I let him take my hand. The window wasn't locked. Mac pushed the shade aside and shone the light around a small bathroom. He climbed in, then opened the back door for me.

It smelled as if a toilet hadn't been flushed. Instinctively, my hand covered my nose and mouth to filter out the funk. Walking toward the front of the shop, we came to the first bay. Mac's flashlight beam hit on a pair of work boots attached to blue-jean–clad legs.

"Dennis?" I called out.

Dennis didn't answer. The light swept up from the jeans. We took a step closer and could see why he had remained silent. A car pinned the lower half of his body to the ground. His face was horribly swollen and dried blood caked his ears and nose. Suddenly a mouse scurried across his chest.

"Jesus!" Mac and I exclaimed in unison. I bolted to the front door, fumbled with the lock, desperate for fresh air. I stumbled to my knees and let the nausea take over.

"This is not what Doctor Patel ordered. Are you going to be all right?" Mac asked as he brought me a chair outside.

I nodded, noticing I felt more respite than sorrow. My blackmailer was dead, and the gigolo vulture nipping at Emma's checkbook was no more, yet the father of my children had died a horrible death.

Mac called 911, identified himself as a police officer and reported what we had found.

Five minutes later, three patrol cars and two unmarked police vehicles pulled up. Here we were again. Just like in Delaney. My stomach tightened.

A big man nodded tersely, showed us his ID as he walked past us to the service bay. Detective Marquis Woodson, black, appeared to be about thirty and looked as if he worked out every day and twice on

LIES TOO LONG

Sunday. His neck, the circumference of my upper thigh, was my first clue. We could hear him speaking to the medical examiner. "How long has he been dead?"

"Less than twenty hours, more than twelve, my guess."

Mac and I looked at our watches.

"Sometime last night or early this morning, someone cut the air hose that operated the jack. He was caught under the Chevy and crushed."

"What a way to go," the detective said. "Thought these things were hydraulic?"

"Most are these days, but this place hadn't been renovated in a while. Don't see a lot of air jacks anymore."

"I know why. Not too safe," Woodson said.

"Check his tools carefully," the medical examiner said. "Look for whatever cut the air hose. Looks like a razor edge. The killer knew the exact spot to cut, right underneath the turn-on valve."

"Wouldn't it have taken the car several seconds to fall? I mean, wouldn't it have been a slow descent?"

"Evidently not slow enough. Still caught him from the waist down."

Blue, red and white lights continued to flash, and we could see the media gathering, so Mac and I moved back inside. The murder rate in the county was around twelve per year, making Dennis's death big news. Wait until they found out a former Wizard had been murdered in his place of business.

"Shit," the detective mumbled coming toward us. "Is someone here to do PR? Extend the crime scene tape along the entire perimeter of the property. Get another team out here to help read the scene. Someone call DMV and get Butler's tag number so we can know which car belongs to him."

"Dennis's car isn't here, Detective. His Monte Carlo isn't here," I said, volunteering this information.

"We need to locate that car ASAP, folks. It's not here, so maybe someone took it. Let's find out." Detective Woodson didn't seem to be speaking to anyone in particular, yet uniforms scampered.

144

Woodson focused his bullshit radar on Mac for a long moment, and then on me. "You two found the body. What's the deal?"

"When Butler didn't show up for a four o'clock appointment, we came looking for him," Mac said.

"You found him," the detective stated. "Must have been a pretty important meeting."

Neither of us commented. Finally Woodson said, "We'll take your statements momentarily. You won't mind if we search your vehicle first, will you?"

Mac said, "No, come with me."

A middle-aged officer steered me away to Dennis's back room. I sat on a brown metal folding chair, staring at the gray industrial tile that was new fifty years ago. A twin bed with a green sleeping bag on it was pushed against a wall. There was a floor lamp, a full-length mirror leaning against one wall, and a space heater like the one I had taken from the dumpster. Officer Nadine Lipton stood over me, note pad in hand.

I wondered why policewomen wore ponytails. Wouldn't they be easy to grab and hang on to? After she took my basic information she said, "You knew him? He was a good ball player. Sad to see it end like this for him."

"Yes, it is."

The incredulity of two murder interviews in the same month made me want to pinch myself.

"Take me step by step through what you did after you got here."

I filled her in.

"When was the last time you were here before tonight?"

"Um, maybe four months ago."

"Who were Mr. Butler's enemies?"

I shook my head. "I'm not sure." Besides me? Did Gayle Marklin do criminal law?

"Butler owned this shop?"

"Yeah."

LIES TOO LONG

"Did anyone work for him?"

"I'm not sure now. I haven't been paying much attention lately."

"Married? Girlfriend? Family?"

I told her about Emma. "He has a brother who lives in Harper's Ferry. Um. Officer Lipton, someone should check out Emma's house if Dennis's keys are missing."

"Yeah, someone has been dispatched. We'll notify the family to get the locks changed. I heard you say you had a meeting with Butler today. What was that about?"

"Well, we had something legal to work out. I needed to sign some papers."

"Papers for what?"

I plucked at my eyebrow and then bit my thumbnail. Marklin had given me her card. Was I a suspect? "I'd rather not go into those details if I don't have to. I didn't kill him. Detective McKnight and I were together yesterday, all night and all day today. Before that, I visited Emma at the hospital and Dennis was there."

"Got somebody at the hospital who can corroborate?"

"Tereka Moore."

Detective Woodson interrupted us, summoning Officer Lipton out of hearing range. They looked over at me and down at their notes, whispering. Then the detective approached me.

"McKnight told me you're pregnant and that Dennis Butler was the father."

I opened my mouth to say something but nothing came out.

"He also says you had an unpleasant run-in with Butler a couple of days ago. Is he right on both counts?"

I sighed. Did Mac have to cooperate *that* fully? "Yes."

"So you could have a motive and you could have opportunity."

"No, I was at the hospital and then at home with Mac all night. I didn't have opportunity." Motive, that was another matter.

"McKnight admits you two didn't sleep in the same room. You could have snuck off and come back at some time during the night."

"That's ridiculous. Is that what Mac said?"

"No, that's what I say. We are going to search your place and your vehicle, getting the warrants now."

I dialed Marklin's number on my cell phone, thinking Mac was right. Dr. Patel was not going to be pleased.

CHAPTER 23

Mac took off his jacket and covered my head, keeping his own lowered as we pressed through the mob of clicking cameras to his car. Sitting at the first stoplight away from the murder scene, Mac and I looked at each other.

"I hope you understand that I had to be completely honest. I'm a cop."

"Yeah." I understood, but I was still pissed. It wasn't exactly betrayal, but close to it. On the other hand, I knew he was a principled man, so what did I expect?

"You didn't kill Butler. You don't have it in you. I know that," Mac said.

"Good." As we drove and reality slowly seeped in, I shook my head in disbelief. Two men, each with their own set of redeeming values, were dead. Of course, a person would have to search harder to find the good in Dennis, but he had some good qualities. I looked down at my stomach.

"You can tell them their father was a fine athlete and businessman who died before his time."

I glanced over at Mac, not surprised that he was in tune with my thoughts.

"Mac, I want to get Emma's locks changed. On top of everything else, she doesn't need to have her home burglarized."

"Okay."

I made the necessary calls and we sat in front of Emma's house with the car running, waiting for the locksmith.

"Was the cash register empty?" I asked

"At Butler's? I don't know."

"Dennis indicated he had money problems more than once. Last night he tried to get Emma to sign a check."

"What time was that?"

"Around eight. He could have been into drugs, or maybe he had gambling debt—something like that could have gotten him killed. Could we take a look inside? I'd feel better knowing whatever his problems were, they won't spill onto Emma. Maybe we can find something useful."

"You have a key?"

"Yes, Emma and I exchanged keys."

"But if Woodson's team finds us inside Butler's house, it won't look good, Laurel. They'll want to make a quick arrest. We shouldn't do anything to draw attention from the real killer."

"Right. If I hadn't been with you, I think he would have arrested me." After a few minutes I said, "Would I sound evil if I said a burden has been lifted? Now I don't even have to tell . . ." I realized too late who I was talking to.

"What? Not tell Emma the truth?"

"Dennis is gone. Emma cared for him, and now she needs me more than ever. Before she'd have him if she wanted him. Who does she have now besides me?"

"Lies like that bite when you least expect them, Laurel."

"Yeah, you're right. A week after she's back at work, I'll take her out to dinner, tell her the truth, and destroy her world all over again."

"Despite your sarcasm, I hope you don't really believe you have a choice. It won't be easy whenever you tell her, but sooner is better than later."

"There's always a choice. Stop trying to tell me what to do, Mac. She's my friend."

"I'm sorry," he said. "Some days I'm better at keeping my opinions to myself than others."

"I respect what you think, but hasn't she been hurt enough?"

"Do you want to go to the rehab center when we leave here?" Mac asked, obviously tired of my merry-go-round dilemma.

"I would like to be with her, yes. That's probably better than watching the police go through my things."

"As for Emma, when they find out her condition, they might wait until morning to try to question her. If I could venture an opinion again, I'd say let's call it a night after the locksmith comes. Your place will only take an hour at the longest to search once they get there and that's including your car. You don't have much stuff. You should go home and try to relax when we leave here. Doctor's orders."

Back in Baltimore, the police asked for my shoes. They were the only pair that had gravel on the soles and they wanted to check them for blood. They went through my belongings and Mac's looking for a sharp knife or a razor. They took two knives from the kitchen. They tossed my car and dug out bits of rock from my tire tread.

Later that evening, I climbed into my bed grateful for an oasis of peace in the raging storm my life had become. Cocooned beneath the warmth of the covers, my hands roamed the bulge in my belly. I needed the concreteness of the twins to affirm for me that the world wasn't spinning off its axis. Mac tapped at my bedroom door, one I hadn't wanted to lock tonight.

"Yes?" I answered, reaching for the lamp.

He came in dressed in his "visiting" pajamas—gray sweats and a yellow T-shirt. "This has been a horrible day and I want to make sure you're all right and to tuck you in."

All right? Would I ever remember what all right felt like? I rolled onto my side, stretching my hand toward his. "You're spoiling me. What am I going to do when you're not here?"

"I don't know. I don't like to think about that." His thumb raked back and forth across my knuckles, before he bent and kissed them. "So . . ." he continued to hold my hand, looking at the back of it before flipping it over, his fingertips teasing my palm. "I have something important I want to say to you, but I think maybe my timing is bad. If you're too tired . . ."

Extracting my hand slowly, I sat up, revealing my sleep shirt, a charming matronly number Aunt Olivia had given me. "Bring the chair closer." While he moved the armchair closer to the head of the bed, I tried to figure out what was on his mind. So much had happened; I mentally skirted a plethora of possible topics. His demeanor said it was something difficult to broach, and there was a melancholy in his expression—almost one of grief. My stomach clenched and I felt my breathing turn shallow. This was going to be where he told me for the second time that my life was too complicated and he couldn't hang. I'd lay money on it. "It's okay. Whatever it is, just say it. I can take it."

I crossed my arms as he lowered himself into the armchair now next to me. Suddenly riled, I couldn't bear prolonging this conversation one minute longer than necessary. If he needed to go, then that's exactly what he should do. It wouldn't have worked between us in a zillion years—him with all his do-good honesty and me with my various and assorted character flaws. Indulging in any thought of an "us" for a second was further proof of my insanity.

I could take whatever Mac had to tell me. He wouldn't be the first man to disappoint me, or the last. Disappointment and relationships went together in my world like day and night, like death and taxes, like Bobby and Whitney.

Mac settled into the chair and looked at me curiously. "Do you know that you deserve a man who loves and respects you, Laurel?"

What? Surely he was reading from the wrong script. I narrowed my eyes hoping to zero in on what he was getting at. "I know you respect me. You've shown me that from the beginning."

"I'm not like Butler. I would never take advantage of you."

Drawing in a deep breath, I tucked my hair behind an ear, unsure of his point, but willing to go along for the ride. I averted my gaze from his for a second while I shared an uncomfortable truth. "He . . . well, I got myself into that . . . this situation with Dennis, so in a sense, we took advantage of each other."

LIES TOO LONG

Mac bobbed his head slowly like a patient teacher eliciting a correct answer from a challenging student. "Why were you with him? What were you looking for?"

"Didn't I already explain that?" I asked, exasperation scraping my voice.

"I know what you said about him being eye candy, but what were you really looking for?"

Baffled, I stared into his copper-colored eyes. "What do you mean?"

"I'm just wondering if you understand that no man, even one who loves and respects you, will be able to make you love yourself—no man on earth, that is." He looked at me with brows raised and his forehead furrowed—his way of silently asking if I concurred.

I closed my eyes briefly and sighed—my heart ready to gallop out of my chest. On some level, I'd known for years that I was trying to fill an emptiness by choosing men who were inappropriate or unavailable, no matter how forced or fake the involvement proved to be. I had needed something and accepting crumbs had been better than having nothing at all. Those days were over—I would never go back to that.

I had kept the truth knotted in lies, never wanting to unravel the emotional threads all tangled up inside me, but Mac knew. Moreover, he was the first person to ever say it out loud. He saw my vulnerability. Saw who I really was, and yet he stayed. My throat ached from holding back the tears. No words would come.

"I'm falling in love with you. If I could make you see what a smart, capable, beautiful woman you are I would, but that's something you have to know for yourself."

Emotions welled, transformed into tears and then spilled, leaving wet trails down my cheeks that I didn't have the energy to wipe away. He moved closer and gently wiped them for me. Two images of Mac swirled in my blurred vision. Had he said he was falling in love with me, or was I only hearing what I wanted to hear? I didn't dare jinx the moment by asking. "I know," I said, pulling myself together. "That self-esteem thing—it's something I'm working on."

A twinkling admiration replaced the sadness in his eyes. "Laurel," he began in that lilting, trickling brook way he had.

"Mac," I said smiling, caressing his jagged jaw line. Our lips were only a breath apart, but then, cruelly, the doorbell interrupted us.

"Who could that be? It's almost ten o'clock." I tied on my robe as Mac and I hurried toward the front door.

The peephole revealed the mystery. "It's Nathan and Paula," I whispered. "Maybe I can get them to say something useful if they don't know you're here, Mac."

"Good idea. Record them and I'll be in the bedroom."

I fumbled in my purse for the tape recorder while they buzzed a second time. "I'm coming."

Nathan greeted me with blazing eyes and a raised voice. "I talked to Helin today. What the hell have you done, Laurel?"

My hands went up as a shield. "If we can discuss this civilly, that's one thing, but you're not coming in here yelling at me."

They looked at each other, him in his black pinstriped suit and Paula in her mink stole over a purple leather jacket and skirt. Nathan cleared his throat and guided Paula to the couch.

"I didn't do anything except try to warn you, Nathan. They found Bob's killer. He came up with Helin's name. You are linked because of your business connections. If you know anything, you should talk to the police."

They exchanged a look. Paula was as pasty as a flour tortilla. "The shooter is spewing this nonsense? This is not good. It doesn't take much to scare investors." With a heightened level of desperation she said, "We've got to get a spin out on this, Nathan. We have to take control of the situation."

Nathan nodded gravely, looking me up and down. "If you're so innocent, what's wrong? Are you sick?"

"What do you mean?" I asked.

"Your expression, Laurel. I know all of them. And it's only ten and you're in bed."

LIES TOO LONG

"I, uh—got some bad news, some more bad news I should say. Emma's fiancé was murdered."

"I told you things happen in threes. Bob, Emma and now this. Damn."

"Nathan," I said, "I can read your expressions too. You look scared."

"We should go, Nathan. People around Laurel have a way of meeting with harm," Paula said.

"Whatever, Paula," I said.

"It's called negative karma and you get what you give, bitch."

"Shut up! You make me sick, literally. I was miserably ill after lunch with you. Did you put something in my tea?"

"Please. Keep your negative karma and your paranoia in check, will you?" Paula stood and sauntered over to the door. "Let's go, Nathan."

Nathan shook his head with disdain. "You think Paula tried to poison you, Laurel? You're way into left field these days. It must be stress-related. When Emma gets well, you may need to take her place in that hospital bed."

Was he threatening me?

Nathan got up, hovered over me, his gaze burrowing. "You're supposed to be on my side. Happy I'm getting a chance to play in the big league. I don't feel the love, Laurel. Why didn't you just tell me what the police found out instead of jerking me around?"

I stared right back at him. "I didn't know what to believe so I went on a little fishing expedition. Don't forget, I was shot at too." I glowered at Paula. "It wouldn't be the first time greed, lust and power led a man in over his head."

I stood to open the door for them, but Paula beat me to it. "Have a good evening. The police will be in touch."

Mac and I listened to the tape. The recorder had worked well, capturing the conversation.

"What did she put in your drink?"

"I don't know for sure, that's why I didn't mention it to you. It could have just been one of those pregnancy things. Maybe I went too long without eating. I'm not worried about her. Do they sound guilty? They both looked scared, but I can't know if it's because of murder or greed. Maybe Nathan was scared at the prospect of losing all that money. What do we do with the tape, Mac?"

"We hold on to it. Consider it a piece of the puzzle that will create the final picture."

He kissed my forehead. "Rest well. I'll see you in the morning."

"Who can sleep? I'm all wound up."

"How do you normally unwind?"

"With a pint of Ben and Jerry's. How else?"

He laughed. "For me it's cigarettes, but I'm working at giving them up. Is this your first pregnancy craving? Because I'm used to them and don't mind going out for some ice cream."

"You don't have to go out. A single woman knows she must have emergency pints in reserve. You can sit beside me while I focus on being present in the moment, yet project myself into the future and dream of the day all of this is behind me."

I got the ice cream, two spoons and joined Mac on the couch. "Man oh man, what a night. So much has happened. And, on top of everything else, did you hear that face-lift poster child call me a bitch?"

I shoved my spoon in the carton and left it there.

"What's the matter?" Mac asked

"Dennis is dead." It finally hit me, but I still couldn't cry.

CHAPTER 24

I arrived at the rehab center bright and early in the morning. The sun streamed in from several skylights, creating a cheery atmosphere in the dining hall. The horror of last night seemed like some fleeting nightmare. Emma transferred an individual pat of butter into her oatmeal then said, "More butter, please."

I maneuvered around parked walkers and wheelchairs and retrieved the butter for her. She smeared her toast and I was happy to see her back doing the simplest things we take for granted. On my tray were two boiled eggs, toast and juice that sat untouched. I dreaded having to tell her about Dennis, and I didn't think I could on a stomach full of breakfast. As she spooned up the last of her oatmeal I said, "I've got some bad news."

"Dennis is dead," she said flatly, right before her last mouthful.

Guilt swatted at me for not following my first inclination and coming to be with her last night. "My God, did the police tell you?"

"I saw TV."

"You saw it on TV?"

She nodded.

"Oh." I hadn't thought of that. I held her left hand. "I'm very sorry, Emma."

"Thank you."

I studied Emma as she extracted her hand from underneath mine. Was it just the brevity of her sentences or was there a real lack of emotion?

"The police," she said.

"What about them?"

"He's here."

I looked around and sure enough, Detective Woodson was approaching our table.

I turned back to Emma. "You're right. How'd you know?"
"Saw him on TV."

Woodson made eye contact with me and I nodded to his unspoken question. Yes, Emma knew about Dennis, but could he read the panic in my eyes?

"Ms. Yates, I'm Detective Woodson. Sorry for your loss, ma'am." He showed her the badge attached to a chain around his neck. "If I could escort you to your room, I'd like a few words with you."

"Okay," Emma said and off they went, him pushing her wheelchair.

I called out to them. "Emma, do you want me to come with you?"

He swirled around so they both faced me. "I need to speak with Ms. Yates alone for a few minutes."

"Just a second please, Detective Woodson." I waved him over to an unoccupied corner of the dining hall.

I stared into the deep brown and alert eyes of a man who knew to expect the unexpected. "Emma doesn't know that Dennis is the father. Please, you don't need to mention that, do you?"

"Are you asking me to compromise the integrity of this investigation to tap dance around your personal issues?" He walked away.

Embarrassed, I glanced at the others in the cafeteria and nervously fluffed my hair, looking for something pleasant to think about just in case it was my last chance to do so before I'd have to face Emma with the truth.

I sat back down, sighing as I relived the pleasant intensity of Mac's kisses. Sensuality was good, but clear, honest communication was better. I had learned that lesson. Mac and I would have to revisit where our relationship was headed.

"Miss Novak?"

I swiveled when an aide spoke my name minutes later. "Yes?"

"Detective Woodson would like to speak to you in Lounge B." She pointed me in the right direction.

Lounge B was a tiny conference room with Renoir prints strategically placed on lemon walls.

"How's Emma? Did you have to tell her?"

"She seems fine. Frankly, I expected her to be more broken up, but people react to news like this in a multitude of ways."

"And she's still recovering."

"Yes, there's that. As it turns out, I didn't need to be explicit about you and Butler."

"You didn't? Oh, good. That's a relief." Maybe Detective Woodson had a heart after all, or maybe he was just an officer who played it by the book and didn't let the craziness of what he dealt with every day faze him one way or the other.

"I have more questions, Ms. Novak. Sit down."

His request sparked the thought of needing Gayle Marklin present, but I doused it. I didn't kill Dennis and I had an alibi, plus I knew from Bob's murder that the police ask the same questions over and over again.

"The last time you saw Mr. Butler alive was . . ."

"The day before yesterday at the hospital."

"After you left the hospital, where did you go?"

"I went to Radio Shack, thinking they closed at nine, but they close at eight. Then I went home. As you know, I had an overnight guest."

"Couple of the nurses at Bayview state you and Mr. Butler had ongoing tension between you."

"Yeah." I crossed my legs and then folded my hands on the table.

"Why was that?" he asked.

"Why?" My crossed leg swung back and forth for two beats. "We had areas of disagreement. Mostly about the pregnancy."

"And your landlady, Rachel Edwards, says you and Butler had a major row a few days ago."

Only a few days ago? Seemed like months, so much had happened since then. "Yes, we did. That's the incident Mac mentioned yesterday." How did Rachel know it had been Dennis? Maybe she'd been shown a picture of his car? Or maybe she and Tereka had figured it out.

"She mentioned a bloody nightgown."

I looked at my hands. My cuticles were really in bad shape. "Yes, there was a bloody nightgown. My blood."

"He hit you? You fell? What?"

"I told Tereka, she's Emma's nurse and Rachel's cousin, it was a nosebleed, but I actually was bleeding, spotting."

On his pad he'd written Tereka Moore and Rachel Edwards and underlined the names. "You mean from being pregnant? A spontaneous kind of thing?"

"Dennis had um . . . gotten physical and I think that caused the bleeding, but fortunately, I'm fine."

"But you just said he didn't hit you."

"He was on top of me. I tried to fight him off."

"Are you saying he raped you?"

"I think he would have, but the bleeding scared him. It was a kind of sexual assault. I'm not sure it was technically rape."

"But you elected not to report it."

"That's right."

"Who else might want Mr. Butler dead, besides you, that is?"

Rachel had apparently heard me screaming at Dennis that night, too. "I didn't kill Dennis."

"But you had a reason to want to kill him."

That comment didn't seem to require a reply.

"I understand you were a victim of an attempted mugging gone bad in Pennsylvania a few weeks ago where someone lost his life."

"Yes."

"The murder in Pennsylvania, Miss Yates's fire at your home, and Mr. Butler's air jack sabotage—all this in less than a month . . . Doesn't that strike you as odd?"

Was he questioning my karma as Paula had? "Yeah well, what? You think I'm cursed or something because I knew all three people?"

"Who needs voodoo when we can look at statistics? When too many otherwise random events congregate around one individual, it's time for that someone, or maybe the police, to pay attention."

"But it's possible they are unrelated events."

"Sure, but let's search for an underlying theme, shall we? These are all people you . . ." His hands took on a rolling motion for me to complete his sentence.

"All people with whom I had a relationship."

"You don't have a stalker, do you? Someone who wants you to himself or herself? Someone capable of systematically removing people from your life?"

"No." Roscoe Helin, Nathan Stroud, and Paula Mayfield were involved in Bob's murder. The defective space heater hurt Emma. Dennis's shady dealings got him killed.

"No secret admirer? No notes, flowers or calls?"

"No."

"Is there anyone trying to intimidate you? Manipulate you? Force you to do something you're not comfortable doing?"

I shook my head. Not any more. Dennis was dead.

"Okay, Ms. Novak. Stay close. You have my card. Call me if you think of something."

I stood to leave.

"Oh, just one more thing. I'm going to need your fingerprints and a DNA swab."

"What? Why?"

"Why, Ms. Novak? You have probable cause written all over you. It's your association with a fellow police officer that's keeping the cuffs off right now."

"But, I didn't . . ." Declaring my innocence was getting old and getting me nowhere. Maybe he'd found more evidence. "Detective, did you find what cut the air hose?"

"I don't think there will be any problem with us going to a station right here in the Central District. No need to go all the way to Silver Spring."

Ah, the good detective could not divulge information. "Now? I don't know if I should leave Emma."

"I'm afraid I'll have to insist."

"Fine." My thoughts raced. There was no way the killer had left fingerprints on the murder weapon. Only a complete idiot would do that. What other evidence could they have? "Did Dennis's car show up?"

He looked right through me, his face a milk chocolate stone.

"Let me tell Emma I'm leaving."

Detective Woodson attached himself to my side while I sorted through this in my mind and said goodbye to Emma. I didn't remember being in or even touching Dennis's car, so there would be no prints. DNA meant body fluids and hair. I should be safe there too, unless a strand of my hair had transferred to Dennis's clothing and then to his car. I could explain that. I had nothing to worry about. Did I?

CHAPTER 25

Detective Woodson had two Payday candy bars on the seat of his Chevy. When he offered me one, I took it because I hadn't eaten breakfast.

"If you did something, you know, a reaction to what Butler did, to the way he was treating you . . ."

"I didn't do anything to Dennis."

At the police station, it took longer to complete the paperwork than to conduct the actual procedures. I was told the fingerprint comparison would be concluded before the end of the day, but that the DNA comparison would take at least a week.

By the time I was done, my mood had plummeted and the rain that fell didn't do a thing to lift my spirits. I could have returned to the rehab center, but I just wanted to be alone somewhere warm and comfy.

At home, the red message light blinked on my phone, but when I tried to listen, the message was only air. Caller ID said out of state. Mac? No, probably Aunt Olivia. We were long overdue for a chat. I checked my cell phone for messages and sure enough, she'd called twice. I made some herbal tea while I thought about calling Aunt Olivia.

I hadn't talked to her since the day before my trip to Delaney. With her brother Pete having cancer, she had enough on her plate. The easiest solution had been not to call her at all. But she'd probably heard about Dennis. I'd have to bring her up to speed.

Continuing to delay the inevitable, I fell across my bed, TV remote in hand. The midday news was on and I caught the Montgomery County Police's official report in which the female officer confirmed the identity of the man found dead in Butler Automotive as Dennis

Butler, the owner of the shop and former NBA basketball star. His death was being investigated as a homicide. Details about the cause of death were unavailable pending an autopsy report, which was due back later today or tomorrow.

A couple of Dennis's former teammates bemoaned his death and then, lo and behold, Emma's sorority sister, Vivian Reese, appeared on camera, suitably distraught but elegantly coiffed. "I cannot believe this. Another life snuffed out senselessly. I've known Dennis's fiancé for years. I just pray she'll be strong enough to go on without him."

Triumphant footage from Dennis's basketball days ran for ten seconds, followed by a still picture of him with his year of birth and his year of death separated by a hyphen.

I rubbed my stomach. My babies were that hyphen in a sense, or a part of it. They were two of the good things he'd done between being born and dying.

I turned the TV off. The media hadn't been at the rehab center this morning, so maybe a modicum of decency remained in reporting. I hoped they would continue to give Emma her privacy.

I took a deep breath and called Aunt Olivia.

"Laurel, I just heard about Dennis. Why didn't you call me?"

"I know. I should have. Things have been crazy. I have so much to tell you—Dennis isn't even the worst of it, but I knew you were dealing with Uncle Pete. How is he?"

"It's a matter of time. Some good days, some not-so-good days. I'm just trying to make sure he's not in any pain. Did you say there's something worse than Dennis being murdered? Oh my God. You're scaring me. Why'd you change your phone number, and why do you have a Baltimore area code?"

"I'm selling my house."

"What? You love that house. What on earth has happened?"

"I'm fine. I'm perfectly okay and I would much rather wait and tell you in person, but that's not possible. This won't be easy for me to talk about and probably harder for you to hear, Aunt Olivia. Are you ready?"

"Go ahead."

I settled on my couch and started at the beginning, telling her about Dennis and me, getting pregnant, his insistence that I abort, and our decision to keep the truth from Emma. Near silence prevailed on her end, sprinkled occasionally with a flabbergasted *what?*

I continued with Bob getting shot, me getting shot at and meeting Mac. "Mac's a nice man. He's been a good friend."

"And this Mac fellow knows about you being pregnant?"

"Yes, he knows everything."

"Go on, Laurel. I want to know the details."

I told Aunt Olivia about the fire and Emma's subsequent injuries.

"Oh my sweet Jesus! That girl was decorating your place for a nursery, not knowing your babies were her fiancé's, and she ends up on fire and jumping out of a window? Is that what you're telling me?"

"Yes," I said, barely able to squeak out a sound.

"Umph. Umph. Umph. Now poor Emma has to bury her murdered fiancé and you still haven't been honest with her?"

"Not yet. Aunt Olivia, there's never a good time to tell her."

"Umph, if that ain't some mess. Awful doesn't come close to describing it. I'll come as soon as I can."

"Thank you." I waited for the rest of the lecture.

"Honey, you've been through a lot. Hold on. You know that song that talks about having to make it through the night to get to the day. That applies in spades here."

I sniffed back tears. It was kind of Aunt Olivia not to make me feel worse than I already did with questions about my morality, or lack thereof. I didn't need any more comments about doing the right thing. "I have the babies; they keep me strong, and I have Emma and Mac, so I'm going to be okay."

"What about your faith? Nothing or nobody can sustain you like ̄ıs can. He's the rock. Faith in Him creates a way out when there is

ʼ"

 ̄ave faith, Aunt Olivia."

"Don't ever lose that, Laurel. I love you. I'll let you know when I can come."

―――

The next day, I told Emma about replacing her house keys, explaining Dennis's car was missing, hence his house keys were too.

"Not missing," she said, shaking her head.

"What?"

"Dennis's car."

"The police found it? Did Woodson say something about it yesterday?"

"Yes, in a parking lot."

"Where?"

"In a parking lot."

"No, Emma. I mean where is the parking lot?"

"Two blocks from here."

The killer had driven to Baltimore? No wonder Detective Woodson's interest in me had increased and I had been right about them finding the car. I wouldn't talk to him again without a lawyer present. Finding the car so close to here wouldn't help my claim of innocence.

I hugged Emma and told her again how sorry I was about Dennis. "I'm here, Emma, whenever you want to talk."

"Thank you. I'm okay."

I cheered her on in physical therapy. Today she made it all the way to the end of the parallel bars. Next, in occupational therapy, she practiced handwriting. My phone rang and I excused myself.

"Laurel, this is Gabriel Butler, Dennis's brother."

"Oh, hello." This caught me off guard for a second. "I'm sorry about Dennis."

"Thank you. It's a shock. I'll be in town later this evening to make funeral arrangements. Laurel, I don't know how to say this."

"Say what?"

"I'm not sure how long the process will take and frankly money is a little tight—too tight for me not to stay at Dennis's place."

"Dennis's place? You don't mean the garage, do you?"

"No, he emailed me last month saying he was living with his girlfriend, Emma, but I know she's in the hospital, so I didn't call her. How's she doing?"

I glanced through the therapy room door at Emma. "She's doing well. Improving every day. How did you get my number, Gabriel?"

"Dennis told me about the fire. Actually, he called to ask if I could loan him some money, but I couldn't help him. Your name came up in that conversation. I tracked you down."

"I see. How can I help?"

"Can you ask Emma if I can stay at her place for a few days and explain why? If she says okay, I'll need a key to get in. I wondered if you could meet me there."

Although Gabriel and Emma were practically family, his request seemed a little odd to me. I quickly chided myself because I dealt with people's finances for a living and should know better. All it took was being out of work three months for most people to be on the verge of bankruptcy. "Okay. I'll ask. Call me back later this afternoon."

Emma hesitated, blinking, when I relayed Gabriel's request, but then she smiled and said, "Of course."

I shook Gabriel's hand when we met for the first time on Emma's porch. His snow-white dreadlocks were stark against a complexion like mine, sunburnt brown. Heavier and older, Gabriel had the pointed nose of his deceased brother, but no other resemblance.

Emma didn't believe in clutter or dust, so it was evident she hadn't home in a while. The mail basket on the marble half-table just he door overflowed onto the floor. Pizza boxes were piled on her glass coffee table. I picked up the boxes and headed for the trash can. In the kitchen, black bananas, home base for fruit flies, reeked with decay.

I showed Gabriel upstairs past the master bedroom to the guest room.

"Thank you, Laurel." He set his suitcase on the bed. "I should be here three days, four days max, depending on how quickly the funeral happens. I'm going to go see Emma first thing tomorrow and iron out the details."

"Okay. I'll plan to be there too and help where I can. I think she'll be able to attend the funeral."

"Good. Okay. Well, I think I'll take a stab at getting this house in some kind of order," Gabriel said, "in case folks stop by to pay their respects."

"Good idea. I probably should have thought of that."

I went back downstairs, stuffed the mail into the basket and took it to the kitchen table.

Most bills could be skipped a month, but it was time to look into these. I wondered if Emma's signature had improved in the last couple of days. If not, did I need to pursue a power of attorney order? I sorted through the mail, finding mostly bills interspersed with a few cards for Emma. Pepco, Verizon, Comcast, Master Card, Visa, Geico, Macy's, her mortgage and the water bill needed to be paid. And oh my gosh, what about Dennis's repair shop? It hadn't occurred to me to worry about that.

I couldn't imagine Emma wanting to keep it. What was involved in selling everything off, and would Gabriel take care of it?

I found a bag and deposited the mail in it. I'd take it with me. I went to Emma's office off the living room. Locating a checkbook and some stamps, I put them into the bag as well. A zipper pull sat in the slot where the stamps had been. I picked it up and examined it. It was the heavy-duty kind, probably off a suitcase or a man's jacket. Dennis's leather jacket maybe? I put the zipper pull back where I'd found it.

Gabe ran the vacuum upstairs, while I tackled the kitchen and kept waiting to feel sad. I hadn't shed one tear for Dennis, hadn't mourned his death at all really. Instead of feeling sad for him, for the first time I fretted about taking care of Emma. In the depths of my soul, I felt she would be one hundred percent again, but what if she wasn't? Would I be able to care for her while pregnant and after the babies were born? If it hadn't been for me, she wouldn't need care. One day at a time, Laurel, I reminded myself. One day at a time.

I started the dishwasher, and then sought out the powder room. I opened then quickly shut the door. I wasn't up to cleaning up after Dennis's pee. I dialed the maid service I'd used for my house.

———

Mac called me that night.

"Helin showed up," he said. "Insisted on taking a polygraph test to clear his name."

"You guys have a polygraph machine in Delaney?"

"No, we took a field trip to Philadelphia."

"And?"

"He passed. For what it's worth, he passed."

"Not surprising," I said. "Where does that leave Truman's story?"

"His story is unshakable. Something's wrong somewhere, but I don't know what."

"Mac?"

"What?"

"I like it better when you're here." I wondered, and not for the first time, what would have happened if Paula and Nathan hadn't shown up when they did.

His voice softened and seemed to curl around me. "I'm on duty for the next two weekends. If Emma's better, maybe you could take a break and come up to see me."

"She gets better with each passing day, but I'm not sure when Dennis's funeral will be."

"Okay. Well, I'll talk to you tomorrow, Laurel. You're feeling okay? The babies?"

"We're fine. Thanks for asking. Goodnight, Mac." I stood looking at the receiver a second, appalled that I had almost said I love you. It was hormones again. It had to be. Or else he was just a really wonderful person, the kind sane women fell in love with.

⁓

Gabe visited Emma's room late the next afternoon. While I introduced them, he threw his peacoat over the back of the maroon chair and sat beside her. I pulled up another chair and soon had to hold my hand so I wouldn't be tempted to pull lint balls off his black sweater. He certainly was different from Dennis. Dennis would have thrown that sweater away a long time ago. Emma's eyes lingered on the tiny protruding offenders before her gaze edged up to his face.

Gabriel got straight to the point. "I have limited funds. Hate to do it, but I need to ask you ladies for help with paying for Dennis's funeral."

I pushed my hair behind my ear, considering. "How much are we talking about exactly?"

"Seven thousand, minimum. That's for funeral and cemetery expenses." He handed me a folder from Douglas Funeral Home.

Inside the folder, I found a brochure and a worksheet with the numbers. I could come up with seven thousand, but did I want to? Maybe I should do it for the babies; a remembrance of their father. I knew it wasn't something typically done in the black community but I asked, "Have you considered cremation?"

"Gabe, I'll pay for it."

I looked over my shoulder to see who was talking before I jerked my head in Emma's direction. Emma? A whole sentence! "Emma?" I was up hugging her. "Are you back?"

"Back?" she asked.

"My God! Yesterday you were—your sentences were—and today . . ." Overwhelmed, I could only stand there with my jaw gaping and tears welling in my eyes.

"I guess I'm back," Emma said.

"Unbelievable. It's unbelievable!" I grazed my hands over her shoulders and arms, needing to touch her as I struggled to understand. "What? How? Everything just fell into place? How do you feel? This is what Tereka told me could happen!"

"It's probably the shock of Dennis's death sinking in," Gabe suggested.

I had forgotten he was in the room. I didn't know exactly what he meant, but I was grateful for whatever had given Emma her language skills back.

"Gabe, ask the funeral home to call me tomorrow. I'll take care of it over the phone."

"Thank you, Emma. I'm glad you're willing to step up to the plate like this. And thanks for the use of your place. You have a lovely home."

"You're welcome. I'll need my purse so I can conduct business. Gabe, I'd be happy if this could happen quickly. Will you do what you can to rush things along?"

He held up his palms. "Of course."

Amazed, I watched as Emma transformed right in front of my eyes. It was like her head injury had never happened.

"Emma, you might be home before the funeral," I said.

"Maybe you're right," she said. "I have a feeling that now that I'm talking again, other things will click into place."

We grinned at each other.

"You'll still need physical therapy and occupational therapy," I said, "but you could do those on an outpatient basis."

"I could." Her eyes twinkled with real animation, something I hadn't seen in a long time.

After Gabe said his goodbyes, Emma was ready to start packing. "Cool your jets," I said. "We need to let the doctors have a look. We don't want to risk undoing anything. Besides, there are practical considerations. Can we take this wheelchair or do we need to buy one? How are we going to get you in the bathroom and shower at your house? I'm excited too, but we can't just do this in a matter of hours."

"We can hire someone to help," Emma said.

"Sure, but who?"

"Tereka Moore. She could do it part-time."

"Really? Okay." I rubbed my forehead and tried to think while I paced. "We need to wait and have someone walk us through this." I couldn't wait to call Mac.

There was a happy pause in our conversation, then I said, "Emma, can I ask you something?"

"Go ahead," she said.

I waited for her to look up from her shirt. She'd been buttoning and unbuttoning, practicing one of the fine motor skills she needed to hone. When she looked up I said, "Dennis's murder. I don't know what I expected, but you are very matter-of-fact about it."

She nodded. "I know. I should feel something more, shouldn't I? It's like a distant cousin died. I'll ask the psychologist about it tomorrow." She looked at her left hand. "I had an engagement ring, didn't I? Where is it?"

"Dennis took it. I think he may have returned it to get money."

Eyebrows pinched she said, "He did what?"

I gave a helpless shrug. "Emma, it was cubic zirconium. I saw the pawn shop receipt."

"No way! No fucking way!" She chuckled, then giggled, then laughed.

I joined her, and we couldn't stop laughing.

The loss of Dennis's life juxtaposed with the loss of the fake ring should not have been funny, but it was. We laughed until our sides hurt. We laughed until tears rolled and an aide came to see what the matter was. Then we laughed more, saying goodbye to the hardest part of what Emma had gone through. We laughed in celebration because as bad as things had been, they would get better.

As our raucous conviviality abated Emma said, "Laurel, I remember everything clearly up until the fire. The doctors gave me a version. Can you tell me about it?"

Bad segue. Nothing funny about that. "Ahem. You know it happened at my house, right?"

She nodded.

"Umm, do you remember bringing the space heater up to the extra room?"

"Space heater? I think the doctors mentioned one."

"There was one in my garage, and it ended up where you started to decorate a nursery for me."

"Oh yes, the space heater. It was always cold in that room and you refused to get baseboard heating installed."

"Yeah, I wish I had now because that space heater caused the fire. We don't know exactly how it happened, but your clothes caught fire and you jumped from the window."

"Out the window? The fire must have been too much."

"Apparently. You jumped into about eight inches of snow. Someone driving by stopped and called for help. I'm so sorry, Emma."

She stared at her right hand instead of me, holding it up, turning it to different angles.

"The scars will fade," I said.

"Eventually. I fell asleep on a heating pad last year and I still have the scar on my back. Look at my legs."

"Well, you can wear pants until you feel comfortable."

She looked at me and said, "And one glove like Michael Jackson? If only it were that simple. You sound like that stupid psychologist they make me talk to. 'Yes, Ms. Yates, this is a blow to your self-image, but you are so much more than your physical appearance.' Please, don't even try to spoon-feed me that garbage. Right or wrong, I have traded on my looks my whole life. Now I have to live with stares and snickers and the long-faced 'oh so sorries' while people talk behind my back."

"Emma, true friends won't act that way."

"True friends? Now there's a concept."

She was angry at the world and she had every right to be. I didn't take her comment personally.

CHAPTER 26

"Mac, Emma is so much better today," I said when I phoned him.

"Is she walking on her own?"

"No, not yet, but she's talking like her old self. I mean, completely back to normal, Mac. She's Emma again and God, I didn't realize how much I missed having a conversation with her."

"That's wonderful. Start at the beginning."

I told him about Gabriel and the funeral expenses.

"And the best news of all is her doctor thinks she'll go home the day after tomorrow! They need time to set up treatment for her closer to Takoma Park."

"That's fantastic. So, now, does that mean you will move again to be close to her?"

"I guess it does."

"Are you moving in with Emma?"

"I don't know. Emma and I will have to talk about it. It depends on how much help she needs. There's truth in the saying that fences make good neighbors or however that goes. We might drive each other nuts actually living together."

"You have other options. You still have your house."

"I had a message right before I called you. Someone placed a contract on the house last night, and they're in a hurry to settle. If their bid is approved, I won't have that option any more."

"Your nomadic lifestyle is getting old. We have to do something about that."

I loved that he'd said *we*. "Yeah."

"What would you do about it, if you had your druthers?" Mac asked.

LIES TOO LONG

My druthers? I would move to a tropical island with him and drink coconut milk all day between trips to mineral spring spas. But if I said that and he didn't say what I wanted to hear, my feelings would be hurt. "I'm going to have to get a grip. Get back to work because I'm paid on commission, you know, and maybe rent a house until, well . . . until."

"Until what?"

"Until nesting urges overtake me, I guess." I patted my stomach, wishing Mac's hand was under mine, like in Dr. Patel's office. "Tomorrow will mark the first day of my second trimester and I've been doing my reading, Mac. Mothers prepare their nests for their young and women get the urge to make sure everything is clean and ready for their baby."

"I know. And now that Emma is better, are you going to tell her about Butler and about the space heater?"

Mac wasn't one to let sleeping dogs lie, so once again I winced as this issue came between us. "I'll know what's best to say to Emma and when to say it."

Mac sighed and said nothing.

I picked up the slack. "Things aren't always so black and white for you, are they, Mac? How come I can see all this gray area and you can't? There's not always a definitive right or wrong answer. We do the best we can in life."

"With the correct mindset, right answers and right actions are possible." We endured another long pause. "If you are willing to live with this lie, won't it be easy to live with others?"

He was questioning my character again. I didn't answer because I figured the anger I needed to let loose would be counterproductive and was bigger than could be adequately handled on the phone.

"I'll tell you what. We'll pray about it, Laurel."

That did it. "Thank you, Mac." I hung up the phone, not bothering to hide my irritation. He reminded me of a priest holding out absolution, and I resented it.

Mac and I couldn't have a relationship where he needed to control my decision-making. That's what he was trying to do, even though he might not admit it. Someone telling me what to do had never set right with me. This was never going to work between him and me, and I was nuts for thinking for even a second that it would.

Needing to channel my anger, I dug out Emma's bills. I would make out the checks and take them for her to sign. After the occupational therapist helped her practice her signature, Emma could give it a go. If that failed, she could call in her payments using her credit card. Navigating those darn voice menus that businesses seemed so proud of would be a challenge, but she had plenty of time on her hands.

Ten minutes later, the only mail left unopened was her bank statement. I hesitated for a minute, then ripped through the envelope. Double-checking to make sure no checks would bounce was my excuse for being nosy.

Whoops. Her checking balance was down to forty-seven dollars and seventy-two cents, but there was over eleven thousand in her savings account. That was a substantial sum to have on hand, even for a car salesman. Where had that come from? Then I remembered: When Emma's sister passed, she'd left Emma cash.

On the bank statement, the maximum ATM withdrawals jumped out at me. Three hundred dollars appeared six times. The dates of the withdrawals were after Emma's hospitalization.

I kept re-reading, trying to get this information to make sense. Emma could not have used the ATM, so that meant Dennis had a card and her pin number and he had cleaned out her checking account. I reasoned the ATM couldn't access her savings account or Dennis would have tapped that too. But she must have overdraft protection and that's why Dennis had tried to get her to sign a check. Why had he been so desperate for money?

I pulled the magnetized calendar from the refrigerator to scrutinize the ATM withdrawal dates. They'd been done over two days, starting the day after the fire. That didn't tell me a whole lot except the ATM limits kept Dennis going back for more. The gnawing feeling in my stomach remained. Whatever Dennis had been up to couldn't have been good.

The phone rang. It was Mac.

LIES TOO LONG

"Listen," he said. "I didn't like how our conversation ended earlier tonight."

I sighed. I couldn't stay mad at a man who clearly cared about my feelings and had such good intentions. "You have strong convictions, Mac."

"Yes, I do. And I'm proud of them. But you're certainly entitled to think and do what you feel best. It's not my place to point a finger."

"And if I decide to handle the situation with Emma differently than you would?" I asked.

"No worries. We'll cross that bridge when we get there. In the meantime, since weekends are out, how about you drive up tomorrow and spend the day with me?"

"Tomorrow? Hmm." I paced the three feet my kitchen would allow. The only thing I needed to do tomorrow was make sure Emma got her purse. I could ask Gabe to do that.

"You could see my place and maybe spend the night."

If he were any other man, an overnight invitation would have sexual connotations.

"I can't spend the night because I want to be at the rehab center early to take Emma home."

"But you'll come for the day?" he asked.

I hesitated. "Delaney and Mayberry have a lot in common. What will the good townsfolk say when they see me coming and going?"

"I would like you to take a look at Truman, listen to him. Maybe you know him under a different name."

I stopped pacing and placed my hand on my hip. "Mac, is that the real reason you want me to come? It's not about seeing me? It's about Bob's murder?"

"I'd want to see you even if I didn't have Randall's murder to solve."

That didn't answer my question. I waited.

"I have to do my job, but if it helps to hear me say it again, I know you're not a murderer. Would I have been at your place last weekend if I thought that?"

"I don't know. Would you?"

"Laurel."

"Okay, I'm sorry. Of course solving Bob's murder is the priority. It's just that Woodson fingerprinted me and took a DNA sample yesterday. I'm probably a little sensitive."

"Really? I'll bet they found Butler's car and he wants to be sure they can't connect you to it with trace evidence. They won't be able to, will they?"

"No, I've never been in Dennis's car and yes, they did find it."

"They found his car? Do you know where?"

"Here in Baltimore."

"And you've never been in it?"

"Never."

"Then don't worry. So, did you say you would come to Delaney tomorrow?"

"Yeah, I'll come."

"Great. Call me before you leave."

"I will."

"Is there something else bothering you? Woodson's just working the case. Don't let him get you down."

"It's not only that. I went through Emma's bills before you called." I told him about her bank statement.

"We already agreed. Whatever Butler was involved in and needed cash for was related to his death," Mac said.

"If you ask Woodson, would he tell you what they've turned up so far?"

"I doubt it. He's got to be thinking I'm not totally neutral where you're concerned."

"Oh." Not neutral. I was sure that if I gave myself a chance, I'd read more into that than he meant.

"Why don't you bring the bills and everything when you come? We'll take a look."

CHAPTER 27

Delaney, Pennsylvania, had only eight traffic lights. I'd never gone past the second one in my trips here before, but today I shuddered as I went by the Ramanda Inn where Bob had died.

I drove through downtown, made a left at the fifth light and stayed on that road for a half-mile until I came to a dairy farm called Boyle's Best. Mac had said I should wave to the cows in the pasture, continue to where the electrified fence ended, and I'd see his house at the top of the hill.

It was a bumpy ride to the top of the dirt road. Getting out, I slammed my car door. Cow manure, thy name is stink, and that distinctive odor had followed me up the hill. Reddish-brown sandstone covered the bottom half of the house. The top was painted pale yellow. There wasn't much of a porch, and two windows were on either side of the red door. I immediately looked for the chimney because this house reminded me of the kind little kids draw with stick figure families standing to the side. Yep, there it was, a chimney. Brown shutters added nice detail, but if I were living here, I'd paint them to match the door. If I were living here? Laurel, girl! Fantasy got you in trouble last time. Keep it real.

I banged with a brass doorknocker. A surprised Mac swung open the door, buttoning his pants. Tightly muscled biceps and curly hair above the edge of his T-shirt drew my gaze.

"You didn't call me before you left," he said. "How was the drive?"

Stepping inside, I smiled. "The drive went quickly. A lady likes to pop into a guy's house unannounced; you know, to gain a variety of perspectives. I hope I haven't been too rude just showing up this way."

"I hope I'm not too busted." He winked and kissed my cheek, smelling like cigarettes and coffee. "Come on in."

"Mac, your place is cute!" Peach walls, brown sofa and two yellow and brown plaid armchairs contrasted nicely with the tan sheers with a woven design in them at the windows.

"Contemporary, yet homey. How long have you lived here?" I asked, shucking off my coat and hanging it on one of the black hooks near the door.

"Five years. Got the job, got this house. It's about seventy years old."

"Looks great." The rooms were an L-shaped open design. "You're a carpenter too?"

"No, I wish. I paint, can read directions and hammer a nail. I rely on the Internet and UPS for everything else."

"Me too." We stood facing the kitchen. It was small, like mine in Baltimore, but homier despite the exposed brick wall, which might tend to make it have a colder feel. To the contrary, it had a welcoming effect. "You've done a great job. How many bedrooms?"

"Sit down," he said, "while I get you some coffee."

I sat before the unlit fireplace and Mac sat next to me, offering me a mug.

"That's the only drawback. There are only two bedrooms, and it's tight when the boys are here."

I smiled, cradling my coffee and taking little sips. I was weaning myself off caffeine. It wasn't good for the twins. "Yeah, five guys. I can see how it would be tight."

"Not that the five of us get together much these days, but that just makes the couple of times a year we do manage it more special."

"Sure." I nodded. "You want to move or build on?" I asked.

"I rent."

"Oh, but you like it here? The town?"

"Yeah, it's been good to me. I've even grown accustomed to the cow smell. After New York, this has been like heaven. I was able to find humanity again."

"I know exactly what you mean. There's so much inane violence and cruelty in the world."

LIES TOO LONG

"I meant I found the humanity in me again, Laurel, or maybe I should say the Divinity in me. I had become hard inside. You just don't know." He looked at his watch. "We have time for breakfast. How about some of my banana pancakes?"

The manure smell seemed to linger in the air and I didn't want to risk adding too much food to a potentially upset stomach. "How about just toast?"

"Sounds good."

"And Mac?"

"Yes?"

"I'd like to know. Anytime you want to tell me about anything, I'd like to know."

On his way to the kitchen, he squeezed my shoulders.

At the Delaney police station, Mac's small office smelled of coffee and cigarettes, but thankfully no dairy farms were next door. It contained two metal desks with maple veneers, a couple of extra chairs, a trashcan, and a bookcase. An African violet grew on the lone windowsill, beneath a hanging dream catcher. The dream catcher spoke of hope. If they were supposed to catch bad things, a police station was the perfect spot for one.

"Laurel, come here. Take a look at this."

I couldn't imagine what he was showing me until I saw the thirteen-inch TV/VCR with a tape in it. I pulled up a chair for the show.

A big man with a full beard and mustache sat at a table, handcuffed hands resting in front of him, not so much by choice but because his hands were bolted to the table. I hoped the table was bolted too, because this guy could make light work of a Sumo wrestler. He had a pleasant, intelligent brown face, what I could see of it around all the facial hair.

I heard Detective Spoon's voice off-screen. "Here you are, driving a black Mazda through our fair town without friend or purpose in sight. We've got the gun that killed Randall. And guess what we found under the carpet in the trunk of your car? The matching 9 mm ammo. We've even got a witness who saw a black Mazda 626 driving away from the murder scene on the night in question. A blind man could connect the dots. A jury is going to convict you nine ways from Sunday for murder one. If you're smart, you'll do yourself a favor by talking."

The big guy sweated so profusely, I wondered if they had turned up the heat in that room for effect.

"Truman? I asked Mac.

"Yeah. You recognize him?"

I shook my head, unable to take my eyes away. "Nope. Twenty years old?" I asked incredulously.

Mac nodded. "This was shortly after he was booked."

Spoon continued, "Dumbing up is an option. You keep your reputation for not ratting out. Not that anyone on the street is gonna remember your name next month, but you'll have your reputation to hold onto while your fellow inmates tie you down at one of Pennsylvania's fine federal prisons."

Truman broke his silence. "I want a lawyer." His voice lacked emotion, certainly showed no fear. More like he was ordering off a menu.

"Sure, sure," Spoon said. "Ike Bankhead is on his way now. I told you, he's seventy-three and can't move as fast as he used to. Who knows? Maybe he had to stop for hearing aid batteries, or else maybe he went to the library to see what he could find out about representing a murderer. Up until now, I think the most he's had to handle was Louise Lansky's DWI." Spoon offered Truman a cigarette. "Smoke?"

Truman shook his head, lowered it, wiping his brow with his palm, handcuffs notwithstanding. He looked at the sweat gathered there until Detective Spoon shoved some napkins into his hands.

"On the other hand," Spoon said, "a man your size might learn to control that overeating habit you got there. Working out every day, you could be buff in six months, if your heart held out, that is."

Spoon moved in close as if he had a secret to share. "You won't see a woman again in this life, so I guess it doesn't matter how buff you get. You can be damn sure Leroy, Jose and Big Dick Gunther like something to hold on to." He got in Truman's face. "They gonna love it when you buck like a wild stallion they need to tame."

"Raise up off me, man." Truman was starting to tense up.

Spoon's laughter trilled, making the atmosphere uneasy. "Oh yeah, sure. You better practice saying that."

A door opened and a bald man with beady eyes shuffled into the room as if he had a pebble in his shoe. His suit jacket was buttoned unevenly and he swung his brown briefcase as if it had nothing in it. "Fred." The elderly man nodded an acknowledgement to Spoon.

Spoon nodded back.

Truman shook his head and closed his eyes as if this could not be happening to him. "Pops, who you supposed to be?"

"Who am I? Who are you?"

"Who is he?" I asked Mac.

"That's Ida Louise's daddy."

"He's not Ike Bankhead, is he?"

"Nope."

"Is he even an attorney?"

"Actually he is, he just doesn't work for the court. A tactic we use sometimes to turn evidence. It worked. Keep watching."

"How is that ethical?" I asked.

"We never said he was the court-appointed attorney."

"You twisted the truth."

Mac looked at me, clearly surprised by my objection. "You could look at it that way, or maybe we untwisted it."

A bit hypocritical, I thought. Seemed Mac recognized a gray area after all.

I focused on the screen again. Ida Louise's daddy inexplicably excused himself.

Spoon eased into a chair across from Truman. "Who got you involved in this?"

"Where'd my lawyer go?"

"I'm not sure. You want me to go get him?"

Truman shook his head, rolling his eyes in disgust. "I never got a name."

Both men looked up as someone else entered the room. Mac came into camera range on the small screen, sleeves rolled up, ready for work.

"Let's hear it," Mac said.

"This gonna get me something, right? I get a deal?"

"Depends. If you give us something we can use, chances are excellent the DA will work with you. You got nothing to lose and everything to gain," Spoon said.

"Like I said, I never got a name. Dude told me where the car would be and said everything I needed would be in the trunk."

"So what, this dude just picked your name out of the phone book?" Mac asked.

"I was hanging out with my boys front of the liquor store on Fulton. This old dude gets out of this black Nissan and waves me over to him."

"He called you by name?" Spoon asked.

"Naw, uh-uh, think he said, 'You in the red,' or something like that."

Spoon took notes. "What did he look like?"

"Had to be fifty if he was a day, but still holding it down—you know—fit."

Spoon said, "You seen him before?"

"I think so. Maybe around the hood."

"White or black. Tall or short."

"Black, tall. Had on shades, a blue jacket and a hat."

"What kind of hat?"

"An old man's hat. The kind Dr. King used to wear."

"Complexion?"

"Kinda dark."

"We'll show you some pictures. What about who you were hanging out with? What are their names?" Mac asked.

"Reg, Kovan and Junior."

"Full names?" Spoon asked.

"I think it's Reggie Sams and Kovan Stewart. Junior I don't know."

Spoon asked. "What exactly did this old dude say to you?"

"Say 'I got a personal problem that needs a permanent solution.' I say, 'What you talking about, Pops?'"

"He say, 'I know you've done a little time. Heard from people who know who say you can handle yourself. Four thousand now, six thousand later. Everything you need is ready to roll. You'll roll. This other person don't do nothing ever again. You understand?'"

Mac urged Truman to keep talking.

"Well, you know. I ain't trying to say no to money like that. Told me to go to White Marsh Mall. Say I should pick up a Mazda in Section C, next to the red ragtop Benz. The key was under the mat, the money was in the trunk and so was the gun and the cell phone."

"Then what?"

"I turn on the phone and wait for a call. Phone finally rings. I say who's this? He say just call me Helen."

"Helen? A woman?" Spoon asked, leaning forward with renewed interest. "You were talking to a woman?"

"I don't think so, man, that's just what he say I should call him. Said the target was a tall, dark-skinned woman driving a black Lexus. Say she stay at the Ramada in Delaney. She wasn't hard to track to the hotel, but I ain't never killed nobody just cold like that. I ain't no punk, but when that white dude came right back out to the car like that, I flipped. I bugged completely out. Next thing I know, I was back in the car, trying not to speed and looking for a place to get rid of the gun."

"Let me fill in the missing moments," Mac said. "You fired the gun and murdered that white dude, who happened to have a name, Robert Randall, who happened to have a perfectly good life you snatched away from him and a daughter and a mother who loved him. Then you took a shot at the lady in the car, but you missed."

Truman shook his head full of regret, as if he'd missed the final basket that could have won the game.

A tremble coursed through my body. "I was who he wanted to kill? Why would Helin or anyone who worked for him want me dead? Bob would have decided if his company stayed invested with Helin's firm or not. I only made suggestions."

Mac covered my hand with his. "Could have been a way to scare Randall into compliance."

On the screen, Mac conferred with Spoon and then addressed Truman. "You know someone with the last name Helin?"

"Nope."

Spoon asked, "When the job was over, how were you going to get paid?"

"After I checked in saying it was done, he was gonna let me know."

The interview ended with Truman pleading for a younger attorney. Mac pushed stop and the small screen faded to dark.

He excused himself and came back with cones of water from the water cooler. Handing me one, his concerned eyes inspected me.

"I'm okay," I assured him. "Shocked, of course, to hear that, but I'm all right." I emptied my cup and pitched it into the can, hoping my bravado was convincing. "No incoming numbers in the call log on his phone?"

"He deleted it and *69 was blocked so we can't call back the last number. This phone company is still working on finding it. A lot of effort is involved because calls are relayed through various satellites and pre-paid phones don't generate account statements."

"Truman didn't recognize any of the pictures as the guy who set him up?"

Mac shook his head.

"So, basically, Truman will do the time but we'll never know who put him up to it."

Mac shrugged. "It's about perseverance. Maybe something will break, sometimes it does. It's frustrating, I know."

So that was that. I drew in a breath and looked around still needing a better answer. I tried to tell myself that if this was the closest we came to getting at the truth, at least Bob's murderer would be brought to justice and his family would have some measure of peace. That should be enough for now.

"Do you need some fresh air?" Mac asked.

"No, I'm okay for now. So, what else do you do all day?"

"Well, detectives in small towns are not limited to homicide, you know. Let's see . . ." He looked at some paperwork on his desk. "A bold perpetrator stole a bag full of game CDs from the local video store in broad daylight. The night receipts for Pizza Hut came up missing. Mrs. Blumberg swears somebody is breaking into her basement at night to do laundry. But, on the other extreme, we have a man who says an adult day care provider abused his father. Not to mention this murder."

"Tough job, Mac."

"I enjoy the challenge."

"Well, speaking of account statements—you were a minute ago—is this a good time to go over Emma's stuff?"

"Sure, let's see what you've got."

I handed him my bundle from my purse. He looked at the various bills, then opened the bank statement.

"Hmm." Mac stroked his chin. "It's a smart thing she has the ATM hooked only to her checking and not to both accounts. We know he needed cash, but we don't know why."

"No, except he mentioned needing to fund their lifestyle in the hospital one day."

"Wonder if Emma knows, and if she would confide in you now that she's talking again and Butler is dead?"

"I can't imagine Emma knowingly being involved in anything illegal."

Mac lined up the Verizon phone bill and the Sprint cell phone bill next to each other. He looked them over for a minute in silence, his expression becoming increasingly disturbed.

"What do you see, Mac?" I sounded as if I were asking a fortune teller to predict my future.

"Wait a sec. I want to be sure." He quickly selected a red folder, opened it and let his finger trail to the spot he wanted, then looked up at me with astonishment in his eyes.

CHAPTER 28

"What is it?" I whispered.

"I'll be damned. Truman's prepaid cell number is on both the Verizon and the Sprint bill."

"What?" A fog of denial prevented the truth from penetrating.

"Look." He took a yellow highlighter and marked what he wanted to show me.

I looked, then shook my head. "I don't understand? What does this mean?"

"It means Butler arranged the hit on you."

I snatched the bills to compare dates. "This can't be right. Is this right?"

Mac paged his partner and while he waited he said to me, "Dennis talked to Truman the afternoon Randall was shot. At 12:18 p.m. to be exact, using the Verizon phone. He called Truman's prepaid cell number from his house. Butler called Truman again at 4:13 p.m. using his Sprint cell phone. I guess he was checking on progress, probably getting anxious."

I plastered my palm to my forehead. "My God! My first instinct was right. It was Dennis all along."

Mac said, "I'm thinking the man who approached Truman, 'the old dude,' brokered the deal. Dennis contacted him first. His number is probably on one of these bills too, but I'll lay odds we'll find out it belongs to another prepaid anonymous number after we run them. Too bad Truman couldn't identify this guy when he looked through the books."

Mac excused himself by putting an index finger up. He shared his discovery with Spoon over the phone.

I had a headache, my heart pounded, but the puzzle pieces were falling into place. It had been Dennis, not Nathan or Paula. Had the person Truman talked to really said Helin or had Truman invented that on his own?

Mac hung up. "Spoon is still wondering how the person talking to Truman came up with the name Helin."

"That's exactly what I was thinking," I said. "Is Spoon on his way now?"

"No, he's tied up. My question is, why did Dennis keep tapping the ATM? I'm figuring this broker dude must have given Truman the four thousand down payment out of his pocket, thinking Butler was good for it. But why would Butler hire someone if he knew he didn't have the money?"

"He knew Emma had money."

"But he didn't know Emma would be in a fire," Mac said.

"Dennis probably owed more than four thousand because he had to pay the broker a finder's fee, don't you think?"

"That's quite possible. The total price for a hit could be anything these days." Mac looked impressed. "If you ever change careers, Laurel, you should seriously look into law enforcement. You'd be good at it. When Spoon gets back, we'll have a little talk with Truman again. We'll get to the bottom of this."

"So, it really was Dennis's shady dealings that got him killed. This broker wanted his money and Dennis, even with all of his basketball connections, couldn't raise the cash."

"That would be my guess."

I took Mac up on his earlier offer of fresh air. We drove to Delaney Park and walked around. I breathed deeply for several breaths, exchanging the bad for the good, the doubt for the truth. The headache I had been nursing faded.

The winter light bounced off tree limbs like frogs in a pond covered with lily pads. Babies rode in carriages, ducks waddled military-style from a lake to another location. I smiled, thinking of Aunt Olivia.

In spite of all that had happened, my babies and I were thriving, Emma's recovery was going well, and a man I cared a great deal about

189

walked next to me. Truman would do serious prison time for murdering Bob, and Dennis, the man who had prompted his hire, was dead.

I slipped my arm through Mac's as we strolled. "Mac, I wanted to tell you the night Bob died that Dennis was behind it, but part of me just didn't want to believe he hated me that much."

"That's understandable."

"I only wanted to give the babies a chance. Is murder the normal reaction to that?"

"No, of course it isn't, but self-preservation can make someone do crazy things. You threaten them or the image they want to create and they go on the offensive."

"This is what I've decided. I'm going to give Emma a week to get back home and settled and then I'll tell her the whole thing from beginning to end."

Again, he nodded, keeping any commentary he may have had to himself.

"Ohhh," I groaned.

"What?"

"Dennis's funeral is in a couple of days. It was a stretch trying to pull off going for Emma's sake when I thought Dennis just really didn't want to be a father. What am I going to do now?"

"If you went home and told Emma the truth, she wouldn't expect you to attend the funeral."

"Tell her now?"

He shrugged. "She's entitled to mourn the man he really was, if she wants to. You keep thinking you need to protect Emma. Maybe you're underestimating her ability to handle the truth. I had another thought . . ." He stopped walking and turned to me, his gaze searching mine to know if he should continue or not.

"Go ahead."

"Maybe you're hiding from the consequences. You know, thinking it's about protecting Emma when you're really protecting yourself."

"I didn't imagine the fire and her injuries, Mac. I don't think that's fair of you to say that."

"All things being equal, if the situation were reversed, wouldn't you want to know the truth?"

I had never thought of it that way. I started walking again, pondering. Faced with the ordeal of rehabilitation and losing my friend, would I want to know the complete truth? "Yes." I nodded. "I would."

"And you could handle it, just like Emma will. You're strong, Laurel. Emma is strong."

I mulled over his words in silence again.

"May I say one more thing, Laurel?"

I chuckled dryly and looked him in the eye. "You're on a roll. Why stop now?"

"When you made the choice to sleep with Emma's man, you sacrificed the trust and your right to expect her friendship from that point on. Whatever you are left with, is what you are left with."

The starkness of his words forced me to divert my eyes from his and squint at a ray of light for a second. Finally, I found my voice. "I can't say you're wrong, Mac. With everything else happening, I thought salvaging our friendship, if possible, would be a good thing. But you're right. People are allowed to make informed decisions about who they're friends with."

"I can be with you when you tell her, whenever that is," Mac said softly.

"That's sweet of you, but no. It's between Emma and me."

Mac put his arm around my shoulder. "This isn't me telling you what to do, Laurel. It's me being honest with you about my feelings. Is this going to be okay? This kind of honest exchange between us?"

"Of course. I'll always appreciate your point of view. It just seems so easy for you. Maybe that's what I resent a little."

"What do you mean?"

"You've got a solution for everything. I envy you."

"My beliefs, you mean. Well, what's the purpose of having beliefs if you don't live them?"

I didn't have an answer for that. He was right.

"I'm not perfect, Laurel. Not now and certainly not in the past."

LIES TOO LONG

We settled on a bench and I waited for him to go on. Mac pulled out his pack of Viceroy Lights, shook one free and got it halfway to his mouth before he looked at me. He reversed his actions.

"Six years ago I turned a man's head into a basketball and grinned harder each time I bounced it off the floor."

In the seconds it took to process that, I remembered something Aunt Olivia was fond of saying: Life will take you through some changes; it's how you cope with the changes that point to your character. "Why? What happened?"

"He shot my partner during a drug buy."

"Oh Mac. I'm so sorry. What went wrong?"

"We were undercover. This guy they called Pockets recognized her. Came to find out his brother used to date her in college. Pockets knew about her criminal justice major. He killed her."

Why is the world so small like that some days, and then other days you can stand on a corner naked and shout, "See me! Know me!" and people never look up? I shook my head in sympathy.

"I thought the only fallout would be him changing his mind about the transaction. He said, 'No, man. We'll do this another time,' and turned away. But then he turned back around and shot her in the neck."

I gasped at the horror of it.

"I couldn't believe it had happened, Laurel. I held her, watched the life slip from her eyes. I'm looking at her die and Pockets says to me, 'You owe me, man. That bitch was a narc.'

"I'm telling it like it took minutes, but it took all of six seconds. I lunged at him, two more cracks of his skull on the concrete and he would have been dead. Back-up came and saved his life."

"God, Mac." I uttered what I hoped were soothing words and stroked his arm through his jacket.

"She was twenty-five years old and I was in love with her, even though she had a husband and a son."

He looked at me for my reaction. I hoped only compassion showed.

192

"I think she would have left him. I regret we never got around to talking about it. Her son was only three." He shrugged. "I had four kids of my own I was trying to father, and she and I were happy the way things were. But still . . ."

Mac looked at me. His eyes shimmered, and his voice wavered. "I hesitated one second too long. I should have had my gun drawn when he turned back around. I see it over and over in my head. I still have nightmares about it. One stupid thug with a clown name erased her from the planet just like that."

"Hindsight, Mac. You did what you thought was best in the moment."

"They put me on leave for anger management and post-traumatic stress issues. But not having a job made it worse. I would stay in my apartment for days at a time."

"How did you get through it? Your faith?"

"Indirectly. The trick was to find one thing I cared enough about to make getting out of bed worth it. I had four of them, my boys, and I remembered that. I got back to work after six weeks. But even before Kelly died, things were starting to get away from me. You have any idea how many times a day it would have benefited me to look the other way? To take a bribe in New York City? Police work is not what you do to get rich.

"She died on June 10, 2001. And then there was September 11. At Ground Zero my job was to put up crime scene tape, and collect body parts."

"Oh Mac!" I caressed his face with the back of my hand, catching a tear as it fell.

"I still grieved for Kelly, and then on top of that I had 9/11 nightmares to beat the band. I didn't sleep until I passed out from exhaustion. Whatever they prescribed to help me sleep, I was becoming addicted to. I still needed counseling, and then I needed a six-pack after the counseling."

The magnitude of what he'd gone through dictated a few moments of respectful silence. How long should I wait before asking the inevitable questions? "Mac, are you telling me you have a drug and a drinking problem?"

"No, I saw where things were headed and pulled up in time."

"And were you on the take?"

"I thought about it, but I couldn't do that to my boys."

I nodded, relieved.

"Gary Thaxton and I were in the reserves together, deployed to Kuwait in Desert Storm together, and we had kept in touch through the years. He told me he was getting remarried and moving to Pennsylvania. He suggested I check it out. Said a change might do me a world of good."

"You took his advice."

"Not right away. The problem wasn't what was happening around me. It was that emptiness inside of me that needed to be fixed. When I came down to check out Gary and Melina's B&B, I liked what I saw. I talked cop to cop with the chief here in Delaney, applied for the job and he hired me. I've been building a new life every day since then."

"Wow. And you ended up with me in your life."

He smiled with affection warm enough to seal our friendship for the rest of our lives. "How about that?"

CHAPTER 29

On the drive back to Baltimore, my thoughts buzzed like bees. Mac's traumatic past. Him kissing my forehead, telling me to call him as soon as I got home. I had wanted to grab him by his tie, press his lips to mine until I forgot my name, and my recently declared mission, but I had resisted.

Why did Dennis tell Truman to call him Helin?

Thinking about Helin made me think about calling Nathan and Paula to get things straight between us.

Thinking about Paula got me thinking about work. I wanted a change, but where could I make a comparable income? Besides, I needed the health benefits.

Thinking of the health benefits pregnancy required brought me back to Emma. Even though I had fought not to lose her, I had no right to keep her friendship under false pretenses. I had to let her make her own decision. Maybe she would forgive me after she got over the shock. She had to agree she was better off without Dennis. Heck, maybe she would even thank me for bringing the real Dennis to the surface.

I sat taller in my seat. Maybe she and I could weather this after all. That would be almost too much to ask, but I sent up a prayer. "God, please see what you can do." Instead of dreading our talk, I looked forward to it.

I pushed Emma's number on speed dial. No time like the present.

"Hey, you're back," she said. "How was Delaney?"

"I'm still en route. Be home in about an hour. Delaney was interesting. I have a lot to tell you, Emma. I thought I'd come straight there to see you."

"Nope."

"No?"

"I get to go home today instead of tomorrow!"

"That's wonderful news!"

"I'm so ready to get out of here, but I want to stop by your flat first, if that's all right?"

"My place? Sure. Do you mean you want me to come get you?"

"Oh no. Gabe is going to drop me off and then take me home after I leave your place."

"Great. So you've made arrangements to have help once you get home? You've spoken with Tereka?"

"Yes, we've worked out a four-day-a-week schedule for the first couple of weeks. I'm still looking for someone for the other times, but I really think I'll be walking independently in no time, Laurel. I may not need someone on a daily basis."

"Yes, you will be. You can do it and it won't take long."

A moment passed, then she said, "Was it a productive trip to Delaney?"

"Yes. I'll fill you in when I see you." An hour to showdown. I was ready.

Standing near the front window of the flat, I saw Gabe and then Emma getting out of a black late-model sedan. I heard Emma's soft murmur and Gabe's deeper voice, but couldn't make out the details of their conversation. I opened the door to greet them.

"Hey. She wants to practice using her walker," Gabe said, turning toward Emma at the foot of the steps.

Gabe stood behind Emma, ready to catch her if she fell, and I stood in front. Thank goodness there were only three steps, a small porch landing, and then the threshold step into my place. Emma was doing great. I beamed at her progress.

She angled the walker sideways across the bottom two steps as she repeated "Walker, strong leg, weak leg" a couple of times. Her reminders to herself.

Gabe helped her remove her coat before she positioned her back to the kitchen chair I had brought out into the living room for her. She lowered herself into it, cheeks flushed, breathing hard, but smiling. "The good news is I'm going to have killer biceps and abs. Madonna, eat your heart out." We laughed.

Gabe said, "Page me when you're ready."

"Wait, Gabe, don't forget the hot chocolate," Emma said. "We stopped on the way. This is a celebration."

Gabe brought in the cups of hot chocolate, then said goodbye.

"To freedom," I said, taking a swallow. The boys, I had decided my babies were boys, could tolerate a little bit more caffeine—this was a special occasion.

As Gabe left, I gave Emma the raised-eyebrow tell-me-all look.

"You mean Gabe?" she asked.

"Yeah, Gabe. What's going on?"

"I figure we can offer each other mutual support."

"Is he planning to stay after the funeral?"

"We haven't talked about it. Red couches! How daring. Let's see the rest."

That ended the Gabe discussion. After Emma took a few breaths to fortify herself, she stood up using the walker and got the full tour. We ended up back in the living room.

"I'm impressed, Laurel. You did a good job. Red is bold, but I like it. And you brought your Jacob Lawrence prints with you. They make a bold statement, too. I always liked the one with all the people walking around in two's. I'd think this other one with the tombstone and babies in close proximity would give you the willies. Especially now, being pregnant and all."

I shrugged, sitting on the couch. "Thank you. Boldness is called for at some point. The life and death symbols in Lawrence's work keep me grounded. Isn't that what I always say when you ask me why I like it?" I smiled.

"Yes, that's what you say." Emma lowered herself into the kitchen chair again. "Let's make a toast. To boldness, and to people we loved who now are gone."

We clicked our cups of chocolate and drank in silence for a minute.

"When is the funeral?" I asked.

"Saturday."

"I won't be able to make it, Emma."

Coughing as if something had gone down the wrong way, she set her cup down and reached for a tissue. "Why?"

I moved closer and lifted the box of tissues to her. "A couple of reasons."

Her eyes drilled through me. "What are these couple of reasons you can't come to Dennis's funeral?" It was as if she were daring me to tell her the truth.

I set my cup on the coffee table. "Emma, there's no easy way to say this. I'm carrying the reasons. Dennis is the father, and that's just the start of it."

She grunted sharply, as if I'd jabbed her with a large stick. Then I heard nothing except the hum of the refrigerator. Her fixed gaze slid from my eyes down to my stomach. She turned away slightly, probably unable to stand the sight of me. "I see. There's more?"

"The day of the fire, Dennis hired someone to shoot me because I refused to have an abortion."

She raised her hands to cover most of her face and her fingertips massaged her forehead. "This confession is just too perfect."

"Please, please try not to hate me, Emma. I'm so sorry. I could never find the right time to tell you."

Not looking at me, she continued. "You were my best friend. How could you do that to me?" Her voice kept its soft, modulated tone.

"I had this attraction to Dennis from way back, you know that, and when he showed interest I couldn't say no. I was infatuated with him. One thing led to another. I know I don't have any right to ask, but I hope you can forgive me."

"Forgive you?" She turned to me with pure hatred flaring in her eyes. "Forgive you for lying to me? For sleeping with the man you knew I wanted to marry? Forgive you for treating our friendship with absolutely no regard? Forgive you and your stupid space heater for doing this and this and this to me?" She jerked back her right sleeve and pants legs.

Technically, when I first slept with Dennis, I'd had no idea Emma wanted to marry him, but that wasn't much of a defense. "I know, it's too much to ask," I mumbled.

"I want the details. Write it out."

"What do you mean?"

"I want to know when you betrayed me. I'll look at it whenever I want to remember the time I trusted two people who used me like toilet paper."

Stunned, I sat there, probably with my mouth hanging open.

"Do it, damn it. You owe me at least that much after making a fool of me."

I moved to the edge of the couch slowly. A strange feeling came over me when I tried to stand. Probably just the tension of the moment.

I tried again and made it to the kitchen table where my laptop sat attached to a printer. I quickly pecked out 4/14, 9/4, 9/5 and 9/6. The days Dennis and I were together. I'm sorry, Emma.

"Here." I handed her what the printer ejected, smiling. Maybe it was the relief of having this off my chest, but I felt giddy.

"Sign it," she said.

"Why?"

"Humor me."

Shrugging, I found a pen and signed it. My eyelids wanted to close as I handed the paper to her. She took it with a white hand.

"Emma, why are you wearing a glove on your hand?"

She looked at me, but didn't answer. If Emma wanted to wear a latex glove, that didn't bother me. In fact, I thought it was funny and giggled.

LIES TOO LONG

"You're really starting to feel it now. Good. Thanks for this note. It will add the touch of authenticity I was missing. Without it, I had planned to tell the police you had confessed to your nasty little deeds, we argued bitterly and you must have decided to take your life because of your guilt and shame." She scanned the note a second time. "Wait, you left off October 31, but that's okay."

The room rocked like the pirate ride at Six Flags. My vision blurred. I held on to the wall for support. The words coming from her mouth seemed to bounce off the floor and drift into space.

"What did you do, Emma?"

"Do?"

Emma placed the note I'd typed on the coffee table in front of her. Then rising to her feet, ramrod straight, she kicked the walker aside. I laughed out loud, covering my mouth too late to stop guffawing. She reminded me of someone magically healed on a midnight evangelism TV show.

"I'll tell you what I did. I measured windows for curtains, and room size for a damn bunny border. I tried out different paint colors. By the time you came back from Pennsylvania, I'd planned to have enough done to let you know I was with you through this pregnancy. I don't think I could have been a bigger fool if I'd tried.

"And then I needed a bathroom break. From then on, my world as I had known it went out the window."

I interrupted her mildly interesting story with a statement of fact. "I'm going to be sick." Everything was oddly out of focus and strangely amusing.

"Uh-huh, that's the whole idea. I put Tylenol with codeine in your Tylenol bottle, but that didn't do the job. What I put in the hot chocolate will. You'll see."

I blinked at her and wiped my eyes. What was she talking about?

"Anyway, the towel hanging out of your hamper had black grease stains on it. Hmm. Where have I seen that before, I asked myself. Oh yeah, I got Dennis his own special set of towels for that very reason. Why would Dennis be in your bathroom upstairs?"

The bathroom. That's where I wanted to go, but my head might as well have been on backwards. The more I walked, the farther from the bathroom I seemed to get.

Emma trailed behind me. "Then I remembered the zipper pull I found in your kitchen and an earring I had found of yours. Remember? Shortly after your birthday, which, according to your suicide note, is the first time you two betrayed me."

Images, light and sounds floated by, but nothing made sense. Did she say suicide?

"So now I had the earring, the zipper pull and a greasy towel. I'm not paranoid, but I'm not stupid either. I did some looking around. Underneath the bed I found unmistakable proof. You want to guess what it was, Laurel?"

No, I wanted to lie down. I'd feel better if I could just lie down.

"I can see you're dying to know. I found a Band-Aid with a blood-stained cotton ball attached to it. Dennis and I had a matching set from taking our marriage license blood test in D.C.

"I called the bastard and told him to fix it. I told him he would not treat me with this disrespect after all I had done for him. I'd invested enough in his shop to padlock the door if I wanted to. 'You don't want to fuck with me, Dennis,' I said. 'Fix it or have your shit out of my house by the time I get home.'"

I made it to the bed, gratefully collapsing face down.

"You should have heard him beg. 'Baby, oh baby, it didn't mean anything. I've tried to reason with her. She's trying to ruin both our lives. You're the woman I really love' . . . blah, blah, blah. Not his finest moment, but he had his uses. You know all about that.

"Then I smelled that electrical burning smell, heard the popping, saw that damn heater glowing red and then instead of unplugging it, I decided to let it burn your house down. You deserved it.

"But my jacket was in there and my car keys were in my jacket pocket. That's the last thing I remember about that day of hell. It's been at least fifteen minutes, Laurel. Are you asleep yet?"

LIES TOO LONG

Not yet. One part of my brain told me sleeping was not a good idea, but the other part tried to pull the bed covers over me. Just a little nap, I telepathized to my teddy bears with their shiny bright, lifeless eyes.

"You and Dennis did this to me. But you obviously didn't know who you were dealing with if you thought I was just going to lie down and take it. You never suspected for a minute that I was faking it in the hospital, did you? Of course you didn't. You were too busy being guilty to see anything but what I wanted you to see. Laurel, you should know by now I let people think they've outsmarted me right until the time I show them how stupid they truly are. And don't try and play possum with me!" Emma's voice blasted through the ever-enclosing darkness.

"I cut your phone line, just in case you're plotting how to use it, and I'm going to drop your cell phone off the curb near your car. Can you think of anything else I'm overlooking?" She cackled.

This wasn't right. Fear jumpstarted my sleepy brain into action. Think, Laurel! God, can you help me?

I took a deep, slow breath. Blissful sleep, so close. No! Wake up, Laurel. Think! I needed help. I needed a phone. No. No. She just said that wasn't possible. I needed . . . the panic button that came with the burglar alarm! Where was it? Where was I? My bed. My pillow. Thank you, God. I told my hand to feel for it.

Emma said, "You can't make it to Dennis's funeral. Damn skippy you can't. You'll be getting dolled up for your own. Laurel!"

Her voice screamed right in my ear. I could feel her breath on my face, but I didn't feel like waking up. I wanted to sleep.

She shook my shoulder so hard my head jiggled. "Look at me!"

My eyes squinted open to something making glittering, ribbon-like arcs. So beautiful.

"This is the knife I used to cut the air hose," she said.

My gaze followed the sparkling blade. Its shine flitted through the air like the sun. I smiled. I liked it when the sun did that, especially in the wintertime. Then fear penetrated the drug haze. Instinct told me I wasn't going to see the sun again if I didn't do something. My fingers, silent like butterfly wings, opened and closed beneath the pillow. There it was! Something small with buttons. I pushed and prayed I hadn't turned on the CD player.

"I should do you like you did me. Stab you in the back and then stab you in the heart. I'm going to slash your wrists instead. As soon as you're still, I'll put this knife in your hand to get your fingerprints on it, and then I'll slice your veins wide open. You have to admit my plan is brilliant. Hurry up and sleep, Laurel, so you can wake up dead."

CHAPTER 30

The medicinal smell layered on top of the pain made me open my eyes.

A white bandage started below my left wrist and moved halfway up my arm. I stared at the bandage thinking something else had been white recently that shouldn't have been, but I couldn't remember what. "What happened?"

"What do you remember?"

Startled because I hadn't realized I wasn't alone, I turned to Mac's voice.

He kissed my cheek and stroked my hair. "Didn't mean to scare you, honey. You're all right. What do you remember?"

Dazed, I took in my surroundings. White bedcover, yellow walls and a blue and white shiny tiled floor. "Is this a hospital?"

"Yes, and everything's going to be fine."

"How long have I been here?"

"About four hours."

"What happened?"

"You were drugged, and someone cut your wrist to make it look like a suicide."

I repositioned my head on the pillow to see him better. His face was gaunt and his eyes were lit with a fierce intensity that I'm sure intimidated. "Say again?"

"What do you remember, Laurel?"

"Mac, help me raise my head higher." After I was upright and had drunk some water, I answered his question. "I remember leaving Delaney. Talking to Emma. Her coming over and then feeling sleepy, kind of high actually. I think I told her about Dennis and me."

"Could Emma have done this to you?"

"No, I—it's all fuzzy. What time is it?"

"It's almost eight. You tested positive for Rohypnol. Emma must have done it. Otherwise, why isn't she here? While you were knocked out, she cut your wrist, thinking it would look like a suicide. How did she get you to type that note?"

"Whoa. What? Rohypnol? Emma gave me the date rape drug?" I closed my eyes and could hear Emma's voice and see her holding something shiny. Had it been a knife? "Rophynol?" I repeated. "Why do you think that?"

He leaned close and brushed back my hair "It's a lot to take in, I know. Emma wanted to incapacitate you. You tested positive for the drug and even though the police first called that list of dates a suicide note, I know you better than that. There's no way you would kill yourself."

"Kill myself? No, of course not! Dates? I remember typing that. Emma asked me to tell her the dates of something. But I didn't try to kill myself. Where is Emma?"

"Exactly. Where is Emma? I don't know, but I'm going to find her."

I squeezed my eyes shut and rubbed my forehead. "Am I dreaming? Are you in my dream, Mac?"

The door opened and Dr. Patel rushed in. A sob broke free unexpectedly—this was actually happening. And if he had come all the way to Baltimore, it had to be bad news. I looked at Mac and grabbed the rail with one hand and protectively covered my stomach with the other. Mac wrapped his hand over mine on the cool metal bed frame. Had he waited until Patel got here so they could tell me together? Patel acknowledged Mac before taking my hand. A mewing sound of distress came from somewhere and I realized it had come from me.

"You came all this way?" I squeaked out.

"I had a call saying one of my pregnant patients tried to kill herself. Of course I came all this way."

"No, no. I promise you I didn't!"

"I see." He took my arm, staring at my bandage, his lips puckering and unpuckering. "These babies were fine the last couple of times."

LIES TOO LONG

I squeezed my eyes shut. My heart stopped while I waited for his next sentence.

"And they are fine this time, but how many times can you put them at risk?"

I spurted relief, able to breathe again. "Everything's okay?"

Much of the darkness in Mac's expression lifted as he joined me in my elation. "Thank God."

"They were a little groggy." Dr. Patel continued, "which would be expected based on your toxicology report, but they are fine. A cut a centimeter to the left and you would have bled to death in minutes. You promised me that you are going to take better care of yourself, Ms. Novak."

"I will. I swear it. I'm going to be the model patient from here on out. I don't have to stay in the hospital then?"

"Yes, you do. Overnight. And in the morning, we'll see how you are feeling. When you leave, may I suggest you go to a less turbulent space, like we spoke of earlier." He looked at Mac for added affirmation. "No more hospital visits until it's time for you to deliver. I mean that, Ms. Novak."

"Whatever we have to do to have healthy babies, she'll do, Dr. Patel," Mac said with conviction.

Rest seemed like a good idea, not that I could get Emma out of my mind, but then Detective Woodson paid me a visit next.

Mac whispered to me as Woodson approached. "I've got a hunch that the knife Emma used to cut you will prove to be the same knife that cut the air hose at Butler's shop. I called Woodson about that."

"Ms. Novak, sorry for your trouble. I understand you'll be fine," Woodson said.

"Thank you."

"I also understand from McKnight here someone slipped you a roofie and then cut you. You had drinks with someone?"

"I remember having hot chocolate Emma brought with her."

"Emma Yates?"

"Yes, she came to see me. I remember wanting to tell her about Dennis being the babies' father. I remember typing something on my laptop and feeling sleepy, but I don't remember anything else."

"Rophynol has that effect." Detective Woodson flipped open a small notebook. "So, she's done with the rehab center, huh? How did Emma Yates get to your place?"

"Dennis's brother brought her."

"Butler's brother?" He looked perplexed.

"Yes, Gabriel Butler."

"That's interesting. Officer Nadine Lipton drove to Harper's Ferry, West Virginia, and spoke with Gabriel Butler in person. He was recuperating from a ski injury and had metal pins sticking out of his ankle."

"What?" Mac and I spoke in unison.

"Lipton is thorough. A positive ID was made. There's no way Gabriel Butler took Ms. Yates anywhere."

I was stunned. Someone was posing as Dennis's brother? I'd been alone with him in Emma's house? I groped for words. "Who—who is he?"

Mac gave Woodson one of those cop exchange looks I'd seen him give to Detective Spoon. "Give us a minute, Laurel," Mac said as they moved toward the door.

"No, wait. Tell me."

Mac put up his finger. "Hold on."

I figured it out on my own. Gabriel's imposter must have been the broker looking to recoup his costs for arranging the hit in Delaney. Who else could he be? How had Truman described him? Tall, dark-skinned, blue coat and a black car. Literally shuddering as a chill came over me, I was thoroughly humiliated at my naiveté with this Gabriel, or whatever his name was. And with Emma. My God. She'd tried to kill me?

LIES TOO LONG

That next day at noon, I was back in my flat on Addison Court because Mac thought being there would help me remember more details.

"I'm surprised Rachel didn't change the locks," I said when Mac opened the door to my place.

"I spoke with Rachel last night when the police were here. I told her you would be moving. We have to get your furniture put into storage." He had two large empty boxes with him and he put them on the kitchen table.

"You got the police to come? I thought they were treating it as an attempted suicide? How come there's no crime scene tape?"

"Woodson has contacts. He got a local team to come out and process the place. Didn't find much. No need to hold the scene. They already had the knife, but no prints on it. They took pictures, took the sheets. The cups that had the hot chocolate in them weren't here."

"And they are still looking for the man pretending to be Dennis's brother, right?"

"Right." Mac's hand paused on the bedroom doorknob. "Ready?"

I nodded. He pushed the door open.

I gasped at the blood-stained mattress. What I saw gave the expression bloody hell an all-new meaning. Prickles rose along my whole body. "Emma was in this room with me, and I remember needing to sleep."

"You lost a lot of blood, but you were blessed." He took the panic alarm button off the dresser and handed it to me. "This is what saved your life."

I left the bedroom holding it as if it were a talisman, knowing another house had evicted me. Studying my Jacob Lawrence prints, I wrapped myself in my own arms. Oh, what I would give for a spell that would suck me into that world. But I'd have to settle for moving to the opposite coast. "Mac, I'm going to California."

Mac came out of the bedroom fuming. "What? And let Emma get away with this? You didn't cut your own wrist! You didn't give yourself Rohypnol." He slammed the bedroom door behind him.

208

I turned toward him. "I'll have a scar the rest of my life, but I'm going to walk away a winner because I'll have the twins."

"No!" I had never heard him yell before. "Emma cannot be allowed to get away with this."

I could only look at him, too weak to argue.

He rubbed his hand over his face and came to me. "I'm sorry."

"It's okay. I know you want to help. How did you know to come yesterday anyway?"

"You didn't call me to say you made it back safely. I had expected to hear from you by three. When six o'clock rolled around and I couldn't get you on your cell, at your house and even the rehab center, I came here and Rachel told me what had happened." He hugged me. "Here's your phone, by the way."

I took it. Turned it on. It was still working.

"Laurel, I can't stand the thought of anybody hurting you. Really, I cannot bear it. Don't you know I'm in love with you? I want to be with you. I need to be with you all the time. I want you to marry me."

My eyes brimmed over and the cadence of my heart matched a marching tune Sousa wrote. I reached for Mac's cheek. Those were words I had longed to hear, but now were they enough?

"Oh Mac, I've fallen in love with you too, but in a few months I'm going to be forty-one, as big as a house and then I'll be a crazy person with two brand-new babies to take care of. Did I mention I'm homeless and people keep trying to kill me?"

"I'm here for you. You'll move to Delaney. It's going to be all right."

"I don't know, Mac." I sighed and sat down.

Mac sat next to me. "What don't you know?"

I immediately stood again. "How am I going to protect my babies, Mac? I keep trying, but I keep . . . things keep happening. I didn't know Emma was faking it. I should have known that. I can't believe how stupid I was. How gullible! And to make it worse, I was alone with this man who arranges murders for a living. He could have done anything he wanted to do to me.

"I can't . . . I'm so tired of being weak and wrong and vulnerable. I can't be vulnerable anymore. Do you understand? I can't risk one more failure. I can't risk having one more thing in my life turn out to be something other than what I thought it was."

I hid my face with my hands and cried. Mac stood and wrapped his arms around me, riding out my meltdown with me, saying nothing.

As my final shudders left me weak, I wiped my eyes and searched Mac's.

"Laurel, sweetheart. It's going to be okay. Let me take care of you. You know I would never hurt you or let anyone hurt you or the babies. Trust me. Let me love you the way you deserve to be loved."

A heavy sigh left my body, but then his lips were on mine, soft yet demanding. Maybe this was the man I should be with. Maybe this was real love and if it was, I'd be a fool to walk away.

"Mac, is getting married feasible or are we nuts for considering it? We've known each other less than a month. Can I find work in Delaney? We'd have to find a place big enough for you, Drew, me, the twins and your other boys."

His eyes twinkled. "Details. What else?"

I sighed again, feeling myself waver. "I've never relied on anyone in my adult life. I've fantasized about having the perfect life mate, but that never turns out right. I've fantasized about you, Mac, but it might be too late in the game for me. I have to be realistic. It's easier not to get involved than to have to clean up the mess afterwards. Look at the mess I'm in now. And it's not just me anymore. The twins will learn by my example."

He took my hand in his. "Don't be scared, Laurel. You can count on me."

"I know you wouldn't intentionally let me down, but things happen. Or I might disappoint you. You've been married twice, so you know how that happens. Romance is impossible. And look how hard the non-romantic relationships are. I didn't let Emma down on purpose. My mother didn't wake up one day and decide she'd rather drink than take care of me. Dennis . . ." I shook my head after saying his name, not needing to say more.

"Yes, relationships are incredibly hard," Mac agreed. "People often don't live up to our expectations and we disappoint ourselves, falling short. Sometimes we end up hurt, sometimes we hurt others unintentionally."

"Whose side are you on?" I asked.

He smiled. "You love me. I love you. With God's help, we'll make it work. Stop struggling. Surrender and trust, Laurel. It's the right thing for both of us. We can't give up on each other because we're afraid of getting hurt. We belong together."

Another kiss infused with unadulterated passion lasted for several thudding heartbeats. When we finally broke apart, he looked at me with his honey-brown eyes, pressed his forehead against mine and captured my face between his hands. "After we've tried our best for fifty years and it doesn't work out, you can always move to California."

I laughed. "Thank you, Mac. You're incredibly sweet. I need to think about it."

"That's fair and I'm a patient, if persistent, man. Now Laurel, tell me what else you remember about yesterday, please."

"I think Emma told me she killed Dennis. But if she did, he got what he deserved." I ran my hand over my taped wrist. "Just like I got what I deserved."

He winced, shaking his head. "Please don't talk that way. You're feeling depressed, and that's probably an aftereffect of the drug. Let's think this through. Butler was killed the day before Emma transferred to the rehab center. That meant she left the hospital, drove or was driven an hour to Takoma Park, killed Dennis and then came back to Baltimore. She probably needed help slipping in and out of the hospital. Probably needed help with transportation. Any ideas?"

It didn't take me long to answer. "One of her nurses. Tereka Moore or Cheryl Darden."

"Not this guy posing as Dennis's brother?"

"No, I don't think so. Why would he need to pretend to be Dennis's brother if he and Emma were already in cahoots at that point? I think it was Tereka. If I'm remembering correctly, she'd changed shifts and was working late that night before Emma moved to the rehab center. She and Emma are chummy. Plus, we talked about her wanting to move to Columbia so her daughters would be in a better school district. She could have done it for the money."

Mac pulled out his phone, but looked at me before placing his call. "You'll have to come with me, because I don't want to leave you alone. I'm going to contact Woodson and then talk to Tereka."

"I'm honestly not sure I'm up to it, Mac. I'll be all right here as long as you won't be gone long. It's creepy, but for a short time, I'll be fine."

"I won't take more than a couple of hours at most. Are you sure you'll be okay?"

"Sure, I won't let anyone in, and I have my cell phone."

"Okay. I'll arrange for a patrol car to sit outside if possible or at least cruise the neighborhood. I'll check the back door and you lock the front door after me. Oh, and don't worry about packing. We'll do that when I get back. You shouldn't overdo it."

As Mac opened the door to leave, Nathan came up the steps.

"I was between meetings, passing through the neighborhood and thought we could talk." His stare settled on my belly. "Are you pregnant?"

"Yes, I am." I beamed, standing straighter. "Mac, this is Nathan Stroud. Nathan, Wendell McKnight."

Nathan nodded. "Is this a bad time?"

"No," I said. "Mac was just leaving." I ignored Mac's frown, happy to have someone to talk to. "I'll be fine, Mac. Nathan and I have a few things to go over."

"Just make sure I can reach you because if I can't, expect the guys in blue," Mac said as he left.

"What's going on?" Nathan asked, settling on the couch.

"I've got so much to tell you. You want something to drink?"

I brought him his Diet Coke, started at the beginning and told Nathan about Dennis, Truman and Emma. He held me in his arms for a long time and even kissed my bandaged arm. "That is some wild drama."

"Yeah, can't argue with that. I'm sorry, Nathan. And I'll apologize to Paula too. Truman insists the caller said Helin, and that's what led us to barking up the wrong tree."

"Helin. You know what that sounds like, don't you?" Nathan asked.

"What?"

"L.N."

"What? I don't get it?"

"L as in Laurel, N as in Novak. Now that I know Butler made the call, he probably used your initials."

"Oh! You're right!" The ah-ha moment blossomed into a welcomed bit of clarity. "L.N. would sound like Helin on the phone. Makes sense, and ties up that loose end."

"I've been trying to tell you all along I'm more than just a pretty face," Nathan said.

I chuckled. "You wouldn't happen to know any fifty-year-old guys who deal in murder for hire, would you?"

"Locally? I know a lot of people who know a lot of people. I'll ask around."

"Nathan, I was kidding. I'm not even going to mention how scary that answer is."

He shrugged, glancing at his watch. "What can I tell you? Lots of bad dudes out there. I'm not surprised a cat like that would have access to roofies. Listen, I've got a meeting at two, but I can cancel it and wait here with you until Mac comes back."

"No, I'm all right. Don't cancel your meeting. I've already thrown enough monkey wrenches into the works. Go, become a billionaire with my blessing."

"If you insist." He smiled and began putting on his coat. "Mac seems like a good man. You already let me slip through your fingers. A word to the wise is sufficient."

"Thanks, Nathan." I kissed his cheek.

Mac called ten minutes later. "We can't find Tereka. I spoke with Cheryl Darden. She denies knowing anything. We'll check her out more thoroughly, but I think she's telling the truth. I'm going to stake out Tereka's place for an hour or so and see if she shows up. She could know enough to crack this case wide open. I'll be back soon. Did Nathan leave?"

"Yes."

"Make sure the alarm is on, charge your cell phone and I'll be there as soon as I can."

"It's done, Mac. Be careful. Oh Mac, wait. Let me tell you what Nathan figured out." I told him about L.N. and Helin.

"What?" His voice ended half an octave higher. "Man, wait until I tell Spoon. Can't believe we overlooked the obvious."

"I know. They're my initials and I missed it too."

CHAPTER 31

After I hung up, I took an extra blanket from the linen closet and got comfortable on the couch, making sure everything I needed was in easy reach. The panic alarm, my phone and my book about having twins were on the coffee table. I began reading that raisins and strawberries were natural sources of iron, but when my thoughts wandered, I could almost hear the Harlem street traffic in the Jacob Lawrence picture. In reality, the noise was closer.

The refrigerator hum and the occasional rattle of the wind against a pane kept me company. From upstairs, I heard the murmur of conversation—two female voices, and then a thump, some running, children's laughter and a yell to stop running. Rachel's visitors had kids. I felt another ah-ha moment descending. Tereka had kids, and Tereka was Rachel's cousin.

What had Mac and I just been saying about overlooking the obvious? I pressed Mac on my speed dial.

"Put the phone down, Laurel."

I went three feet straight up in the air from a sitting position. Putting the phone down was moot. It had flown halfway across the floor toward the prints, spinning in a dizzying circle.

Emma pointed a gun at me while she walked over to the phone, picked it up and ended the call.

I eased myself off the couch and stood, maybe six feet in front of her. Rachel had the code to disable the alarm. Emma apparently had it too, as well as a key to the back door. "It's you. You scared me. How . . . how did you get in?" Keeping her talking was the only chance I had.

"No, it's you," Emma said. "The bitch that won't die. You didn't die in Pennsylvania, the codeine didn't do it and I was sure you'd bleed

LIES TOO LONG

to death, but no. The whore lives. You're probably carrying the devil's spawn, that's why."

"Maybe you should leave well enough alone, Emma. Right now, no one can prove you did anything. You don't want to kill me, because you'll rot in jail if you do. What would have been the point? Take your sister's money and some time off. I think you'll look at things differently later."

"Oh dear. Are we having one of our sisterly chats? Well, since we're chatting, tell me this. Where is my Caribbean cutie with the light brown eyes? Where are my kids? Why do you get to have it all while I end up with nothing except burn scars? Frankly, I'd rather be dead than to see you have all of that at my expense."

"Emma, please. All of this over a guy? Dennis was a mistake for me and for you, too. Your marriage wouldn't have worked."

"Nobody asked you, and that's not the point. You betrayed me. Once was unthinkable, but then you did it over and over again. Nobody is going to treat me like that and get away with it. I won't stand for it. Do you hear me! There will be retribution. There has to be."

Emma had always had her own standard for justice, but this was beyond extreme. She needed to save face, but I couldn't think of what to say to make this possible. I was shaking, crying and not above begging. "I'm sorry, Emma. You know I care about you. Wasn't I at the hospital nearly every day? Weren't we the best of friends before this happened? Killing me isn't going to change anything, and you'll never get away with it."

"That's not true. I've been feeling so put-upon lately. Being rid of you will allow me to breathe again. But you're probably right about one thing. Caribbean cutie wouldn't let me walk. So, let's see how you live with my death on your hands."

Emma put the barrel of the gun in her mouth.

"Emma! Emma, no!"

Two questions fought through the confusion in my mind. Was she serious, and had my call to Mac gone through? Either way, I needed to stall.

"Wait, Emma. Why is this the best solution? It's not. Talk to me."

A single tear dropped from Emma's left eye. Those kinds of tears fell when pain on the inside overflowed. Her pain sucked the air out of the room. I thought I was going to faint.

"Baltimore Police! Open the door!"

The ripping sound of wood splitting from the doorjamb didn't bother Emma; she held her pose. The door tumbled forward, off its hinges. She held me mesmerized. She's going to blow the back of her head off, I thought. Someone would search for Emma's gray matter the way Jackie Kennedy had searched for her husband's, yet I couldn't turn away.

One person pointing a weapon at Emma spoke. "Ma'am, you don't want to do that. Put the gun down and step away." With three guns and one rifle aimed at her, Emma's eyes remained locked on mine. I'm not sure she even saw my helmeted and vested defenders form a semi-circle in front of her.

From the corner of my eye, I sensed Mac edging through the officers near the fallen door, but I couldn't turn to him. Emma's gaze wouldn't release me.

"Emma, please," I whispered. "Please don't kill yourself." Please don't make me watch. Please forgive me, I silently beseeched. Emma took a step backwards into the wall.

Someone dropped a twenty-pound dictionary on a marble floor, or at least that's how it sounded to me. I closed my eyes at the last second and Mac moved to block my view. He held me while I screamed in total anguish, screamed with pain almost beyond human endurance, screamed like I'd lost my best friend.

"Oh no, no, no," I moaned.

"Shh, it's okay, Laurel," Mac said. He slowly disengaged himself while I grasped at his jacket, willing him to never let me go. He tilted his head to the side and back, indicating I should look behind him.

I shook my head, staring at him in disbelief, appalled at the suggestion. Everything had a surreal, nightmare effect. Slowly my gaze shifted behind him. I didn't want to look but felt compelled. My God!

LIES TOO LONG

Emma was alive. An officer clicked handcuffs behind her back. "You should at least name one of those kids after me," she said, "because I'm going to be all over them like scales on a fish."

I blinked, too full of emotion to say anything. Thrilled she wasn't dead. Horrified at the thought of dealing with a vengeful Emma the rest of my life. Hopeful the penal system was effective and she'd live a long time in a state institution, unable to perpetrate her threat against my children. And sad. I felt heartrending sadness.

The police removed Emma, clearing the way for me to see the Jacob Lawrence's *Tombstone* print on the floor. It weighed at least twenty pounds and had taken a vertical drop, but was leaning upright against the wall. I would replace the cracked glass much the same way I would eventually lose my sorrow and put a different perspective on my new life as Mrs. McKnight.

EPILOGUE

Aunt Olivia tried to orchestrate the twins' birth the way she had orchestrated fundraisers and Mac's and my wedding reception. "Laurel, thirty-eight weeks is considered full term for twins. I'll be there for your birthday. That's a week ahead of schedule. That way, we'll be ready."

"Okay, Aunt Olivia," I had said, but the twins didn't cooperate, they came early.

Mac did great, not missing a beat. He had been present at the births of his four sons, and had faithfully attended birthing classes with me, so he was the breathing master. Of course, by the fifteenth contraction, I wanted to snatch his Jamaican accent right out of him.

Fortunately, the twins were eager to be born. At 2:04 on a Sunday morning, after several more humdinger contractions, our first daughter, Annalise Olivia McKnight, made her appearance. The veil still covered her face, but when that was removed her cries released a collective shriek of delight from everyone in the room.

Mac and I cooed like drunken pigeons over her, me attempting to breast feed, waiting for her sibling's birth and, since Annalise wasn't the boy I'd sensed they both would be, I thought maybe she would have a twin brother.

Ten minutes passed without a contraction. Just as I was starting to worry, despite the nurses' claims that this delay was normal, another contraction and urge to push hit me. Soon after, Arianna Madeline McKnight popped out, calmly observing the world.

While grinning and kissing each other, Mac and I tearfully examined every inch of our beautiful, healthy girls. Although I was gratefully afloat in all this bliss, thoughts of what we had gone through to get to this moment still wrangled their way to the surface. Our lives were on such an optimistic track now, but what of the others who would reside in my memory for the rest of my life?

Tereka had provided Emma with codeine-laced tablets and had assisted her in leaving and returning to the hospital the night Emma killed Dennis. She'd also told Emma my alarm code and had given her a key to my place. Tereka's confession had cost her her job and nursing license, but her cooperation saved her from criminal prosecution. The consequences of her actions would make life that much harder for her two young daughters, and that made me sad.

Kendrick Truman eventually identified the impersonator of Dennis's brother as the person who had hired him to kill me. They are both awaiting trial. Seems this broker was close enough to Dennis to trust he would make good on the payment.

Emma. When I think of Emma I remember Aunt Olivia's advice: *Be careful who you let into your life, Laurel. Use your head.* Well, I had used my heart, set off-kilter by my emotional baggage, and let the wrong people into my life. Despite my poor choices and irreversible mistakes, I've been blessed with immeasurable joy. Grateful for the tremendous progress I've made, I can honestly say I value the person I am today the way I never did before. Maybe there was another road I could have taken to get here, but I'll never know.

The End

ABOUT THE AUTHOR

Pamela Ridley's writing credits include her novel, *Between Tears*. Readers enjoy seeing her well-drawn characters overcome life's often harrowing circumstances by relying on love and faith. Ms. Ridley lives in Maryland and is the proud parent of two genius sons. Watch for her next novel and visit her web site: *www.p-ridley.com*.

LIES TOO LONG

2007 Publication Schedule

January

Corporate Seduction
A.C. Arthur
ISBN-13: 978-1-58571-238-0
ISBN-10: 1-58571-238-8
$9.95

A Taste of Temptation
Reneé Alexis
ISBN-13: 978-1-58571-207-6
ISBN-10: 1-58571-207-8
$9.95

February

The Perfect Frame
Beverly Clark
ISBN-13: 978-1-58571-240-3
ISBN-10: 1-58571-240-X
$9.95

Ebony Angel
Deatri King-Bey
ISBN-13: 978-1-58571-239-7
ISBN-10: 1-58571-239-6
$9.95

March

Sweet Sensations
Gwendolyn Bolton
ISBN-13: 978-1-58571-206-9
ISBN-10: 1-58571-206-X
$9.95

Crush
Crystal Hubbard
ISBN-13: 978-1-58571-243-4
ISBN-10: 1-58571-243-4
$9.95

April

Secret Thunder
Annetta P. Lee
ISBN-13: 978-1-58571-204-5
ISBN-10: 1-58571-204-3
$9.95

Blood Seduction
J.M. Jeffries
ISBN-13: 978-1-58571-237-3
ISBN-10: 1-58571-237-X
$9.95

May

Lies Too Long
Pamela Ridley
ISBN-13: 978-1-58571-246-5
ISBN-10: 1-58571-246-9
$13.95

Two Sides to Every Story
Dyanne Davis
ISBN-13: 978-1-58571-248-9
ISBN-10: 1-58571-248-5
$9.95

June

One of These Days
Michele Sudler
ISBN-13: 978-1-58571-249-6
ISBN-10: 1-58571-249-3
$9.95

Who's That Lady
Andrea Jackson
ISBN-13: 978-1-58571-190-1
ISBN-10: 1-58571-190-X
$9.95

2007 Publication Schedule (continued)

July

Heart of the Phoenix
A.C. Arthur
ISBN-13: 978-1-58571-242-7
ISBN-10: 1-58571-242-6
$9.95

Do Over
Jaci Kenney
ISBN-13: 978-1-58571-241-0
ISBN-10: 1-58571-241-8
$9.95

It's Not Over Yet
J.J. Michael
ISBN-13: 978-1-58571-245-8
ISBN-10: 1-58571-245-0
$9.95

August

The Fires Within
Beverly Clark
ISBN-13: 978-1-58571-244-1
ISBN-10: 1-58571-244-2
$9.95

Stolen Kisses
Dominiqua Douglas
ISBN-13: 978-1-58571-247-2
ISBN-10: 1-58571-247-7
$9.95

September

Small Whispers
Annetta P. Lee
ISBN-13: 978-158571-251-9
ISBN-10: 1-58571-251-5
$6.99

Always You
Crystal Hubbard
ISBN-13: 978-158571-252-6
ISBN-10: 1-58571-252-3
$6.99

October

Not His Type
Chamein Canton
ISBN-13: 978-158571-253-3
ISBN-10: 1-58571-253-1
$6.99

Many Shades of Gray
Dyanne Davis
ISBN-13: 978-158571-254-0
ISBN-10: 1-58571-254-X
$6.99

November

When I'm With You
LaConnie Taylor-Jones
ISBN-13: 978-158571-250-2
ISBN-10: 1-58571-250-7
$6.99

The Mission
Pamela Leigh Starr
ISBN-13: 978-158571-255-7
ISBN-10: 1-58571-255-8
$6.99

December

One in A Million
Barbara Keaton
ISBN-13: 978-158571-257-1
ISBN-10: 1-58571-257-4
$6.99

The Foursome
Celya Bowers
ISBN-13: 978-158571-256-4
ISBN-10: 1-58571-256-6
$6.99

LIES TOO LONG

Other Genesis Press, Inc. Titles

A Dangerous Deception	J.M. Jeffries	$8.95
A Dangerous Love	J.M. Jeffries	$8.95
A Dangerous Obsession	J.M. Jeffries	$8.95
A Dangerous Woman	J.M. Jeffries	$9.95
A Dead Man Speaks	Lisa Jones Johnson	$12.95
A Drummer's Beat to Mend	Kei Swanson	$9.95
A Happy Life	Charlotte Harris	$9.95
A Heart's Awakening	Veronica Parker	$9.95
A Lark on the Wing	Phyliss Hamilton	$9.95
A Love of Her Own	Cheris F. Hodges	$9.95
A Love to Cherish	Beverly Clark	$8.95
A Lover's Legacy	Veronica Parker	$9.95
A Pefect Place to Pray	I.L. Goodwin	$12.95
A Risk of Rain	Dar Tomlinson	$8.95
A Twist of Fate	Beverly Clark	$8.95
A Will to Love	Angie Daniels	$9.95
Acquisitions	Kimberley White	$8.95
Across	Carol Payne	$12.95
After the Vows (Summer Anthology)	Leslie Esdaile T.T. Henderson Jacqueline Thomas	$10.95
Again My Love	Kayla Perrin	$10.95
Against the Wind	Gwynne Forster	$8.95
All I Ask	Barbara Keaton	$8.95
Ambrosia	T.T. Henderson	$8.95
An Unfinished Love Affair	Barbara Keaton	$8.95
And Then Came You	Dorothy Elizabeth Love	$8.95
Angel's Paradise	Janice Angelique	$9.95
At Last	Lisa G. Riley	$8.95
Best of Friends	Natalie Dunbar	$8.95
Between Tears	Pamela Ridley	$12.95
Beyond the Rapture	Beverly Clark	$9.95
Blaze	Barbara Keaton	$9.95

Other Genesis Press, Inc. Titles (continued)

Blood Lust	J. M. Jeffries	$9.95
Bodyguard	Andrea Jackson	$9.95
Boss of Me	Diana Nyad	$8.95
Bound by Love	Beverly Clark	$8.95
Breeze	Robin Hampton Allen	$10.95
Broken	Dar Tomlinson	$24.95
The Business of Love	Cheris Hodges	$9.95
By Design	Barbara Keaton	$8.95
Cajun Heat	Charlene Berry	$8.95
Careless Whispers	Rochelle Alers	$8.95
Cats & Other Tales	Marilyn Wagner	$8.95
Caught in a Trap	Andre Michelle	$8.95
Caught Up In the Rapture	Lisa G. Riley	$9.95
Cautious Heart	Cheris F Hodges	$8.95
Caught Up	Deatri King Bey	$12.95
Chances	Pamela Leigh Starr	$8.95
Cherish the Flame	Beverly Clark	$8.95
Class Reunion	Irma Jenkins/John Brown	$12.95
Code Name: Diva	J.M. Jeffries	$9.95
Conquering Dr. Wexler's Heart	Kimberley White	$9.95
Cricket's Serenade	Carolita Blythe	$12.95
Crossing Paths, Tempting Memories	Dorothy Elizabeth Love	$9.95
Cupid	Barbara Keaton	$9.95
Cypress Whisperings	Phyllis Hamilton	$8.95
Dark Embrace	Crystal Wilson Harris	$8.95
Dark Storm Rising	Chinelu Moore	$10.95
Daughter of the Wind	Joan Xian	$8.95
Deadly Sacrifice	Jack Kean	$22.95
Designer Passion	Dar Tomlinson	$8.95
Dreamtective	Liz Swados	$5.95
Ebony Butterfly II	Delilah Dawson	$14.95
Ebony Eyes	Kei Swanson	$9.95

LIES TOO LONG

Other Genesis Press, Inc. Titles (continued)

Echoes of Yesterday	Beverly Clark	$9.95
Eden's Garden	Elizabeth Rose	$8.95
Enchanted Desire	Wanda Y. Thomas	$9.95
Everlastin' Love	Gay G. Gunn	$8.95
Everlasting Moments	Dorothy Elizabeth Love	$8.95
Everything and More	Sinclair Lebeau	$8.95
Everything but Love	Natalie Dunbar	$8.95
Eve's Prescription	Edwina Martin Arnold	$8.95
Falling	Natalie Dunbar	$9.95
Fate	Pamela Leigh Starr	$8.95
Finding Isabella	A.J. Garrotto	$8.95
Forbidden Quest	Dar Tomlinson	$10.95
Forever Love	Wanda Thomas	$8.95
From the Ashes	Kathleen Suzanne Jeanne Sumerix	$8.95
Gentle Yearning	Rochelle Alers	$10.95
Glory of Love	Sinclair LeBeau	$10.95
Go Gentle into that Good Night	Malcom Boyd	$12.95
Goldengroove	Mary Beth Craft	$16.95
Groove, Bang, and Jive	Steve Cannon	$8.99
Hand in Glove	Andrea Jackson	$9.95
Hard to Love	Kimberley White	$9.95
Hart & Soul	Angie Daniels	$8.95
Havana Sunrise	Kymberly Hunt	$9.95
Heartbeat	Stephanie Bedwell-Grime	$8.95
Hearts Remember	M. Loui Quezada	$8.95
Hidden Memories	Robin Allen	$10.95
Higher Ground	Leah Latimer	$19.95
Hitler, the War, and the Pope	Ronald Rychlak	$26.95
How to Write a Romance	Kathryn Falk	$18.95
I Married a Reclining Chair	Lisa M. Fuhs	$8.95
I'm Gonna Make You Love Me	Gwyneth Bolton	$9.95
Indigo After Dark Vol. I	Nia Dixon/Angelique	$10.95

Other Genesis Press, Inc. Titles (continued)

Indigo After Dark Vol. II	Dolores Bundy/Cole Riley	$10.95
Indigo After Dark Vol. III	Montana Blue/Coco Morena	$10.95
Indigo After Dark Vol. IV	Cassandra Colt/ Diana Richeaux	$14.95
Indigo After Dark Vol. V	Delilah Dawson	$14.95
Icie	Pamela Leigh Starr	$8.95
I'll Be Your Shelter	Giselle Carmichael	$8.95
I'll Paint a Sun	A.J. Garrotto	$9.95
Illusions	Pamela Leigh Starr	$8.95
Indiscretions	Donna Hill	$8.95
Intentional Mistakes	Michele Sudler	$9.95
Interlude	Donna Hill	$8.95
Intimate Intentions	Angie Daniels	$8.95
Ironic	Pamela Leigh Starr	$9.95
Jolie's Surrender	Edwina Martin-Arnold	$8.95
Kiss or Keep	Debra Phillips	$8.95
Lace	Giselle Carmichael	$9.95
Last Train to Memphis	Elsa Cook	$12.95
Lasting Valor	Ken Olsen	$24.95
Let's Get It On	Dyanne Davis	$9.95
Let Us Prey	Hunter Lundy	$25.95
Life Is Never As It Seems	J.J. Michael	$12.95
Lighter Shade of Brown	Vicki Andrews	$8.95
Love Always	Mildred E. Riley	$10.95
Love Doesn't Come Easy	Charlyne Dickerson	$8.95
Love in High Gear	Charlotte Roy	$9.95
Love Lasts Forever	Dominiqua Douglas	$9.95
Love Me Carefully	A.C. Arthur	$9.95
Love Unveiled	Gloria Greene	$10.95
Love's Deception	Charlene Berry	$10.95
Love's Destiny	M. Loui Quezada	$8.95
Mae's Promise	Melody Walcott	$8.95
Magnolia Sunset	Giselle Carmichael	$8.95

LIES TOO LONG

Other Genesis Press, Inc. Titles (continued)

Matters of Life and Death	Lesego Malepe, Ph.D.	$15.95
Meant to Be	Jeanne Sumerix	$8.95
Midnight Clear (Anthology)	Leslie Esdaile Gwynne Forster Carmen Green Monica Jackson	$10.95
Midnight Magic	Gwynne Forster	$8.95
Midnight Peril	Vicki Andrews	$10.95
Misconceptions	Pamela Leigh Starr	$9.95
Misty Blue	Dyanne Davis	$9.95
Montgomery's Children	Richard Perry	$14.95
My Buffalo Soldier	Barbara B. K. Reeves	$8.95
Naked Soul	Gwynne Forster	$8.95
Next to Last Chance	Louisa Dixon	$24.95
Nights Over Egypt	Barbara Keaton	$9.95
No Apologies	Seressia Glass	$8.95
No Commitment Required	Seressia Glass	$8.95
No Ordinary Love	Angela Weaver	$9.95
No Regrets	Mildred E. Riley	$8.95
Notes When Summer Ends	Beverly Lauderdale	$12.95
Nowhere to Run	Gay G. Gunn	$10.95
O Bed! O Breakfast!	Rob Kuehnle	$14.95
Object of His Desire	A. C. Arthur	$8.95
Office Policy	A. C. Arthur	$9.95
Once in a Blue Moon	Dorianne Cole	$9.95
One Day at a Time	Bella McFarland	$8.95
Only You	Crystal Hubbard	$9.95
Outside Chance	Louisa Dixon	$24.95
Passion	T.T. Henderson	$10.95
Passion's Blood	Cherif Fortin	$22.95
Passion's Journey	Wanda Thomas	$8.95
Past Promises	Jahmel West	$8.95
Path of Fire	T.T. Henderson	$8.95

Other Genesis Press, Inc. Titles (continued)

Path of Thorns	Annetta P. Lee	$9.95
Peace Be Still	Colette Haywood	$12.95
Picture Perfect	Reon Carter	$8.95
Playing for Keeps	Stephanie Salinas	$8.95
Pride & Joi	Gay G. Gunn	$8.95
Promises to Keep	Alicia Wiggins	$8.95
Quiet Storm	Donna Hill	$10.95
Reckless Surrender	Rochelle Alers	$6.95
Red Polka Dot in a World of Plaid	Varian Johnson	$12.95
Rehoboth Road	Anita Ballard-Jones	$12.95
Reluctant Captive	Joyce Jackson	$8.95
Rendezvous with Fate	Jeanne Sumerix	$8.95
Revelations	Cheris F. Hodges	$8.95
Rise of the Phoenix	Kenneth Whetstone	$12.95
Rivers of the Soul	Leslie Esdaile	$8.95
Rock Star	Rosyln Hardy Holcomb	$9.95
Rocky Mountain Romance	Kathleen Suzanne	$8.95
Rooms of the Heart	Donna Hill	$8.95
Rough on Rats and Tough on Cats	Chris Parker	$12.95
Scent of Rain	Annetta P. Lee	$9.95
Second Chances at Love	Cheris Hodges	$9.95
Secret Library Vol. 1	Nina Sheridan	$18.95
Secret Library Vol. 2	Cassandra Colt	$8.95
Shades of Brown	Denise Becker	$8.95
Shades of Desire	Monica White	$8.95
Shadows in the Moonlight	Jeanne Sumerix	$8.95
Sin	Crystal Rhodes	$8.95
Sin and Surrender	J.M. Jeffries	$9.95
Sinful Intentions	Crystal Rhodes	$12.95
So Amazing	Sinclair LeBeau	$8.95
Somebody's Someone	Sinclair LeBeau	$8.95

LIES TOO LONG

Other Genesis Press, Inc. Titles (continued)

Someone to Love	Alicia Wiggins	$8.95
Song in the Park	Martin Brant	$15.95
Soul Eyes	Wayne L. Wilson	$12.95
Soul to Soul	Donna Hill	$8.95
Southern Comfort	J.M. Jeffries	$8.95
Still the Storm	Sharon Robinson	$8.95
Still Waters Run Deep	Leslie Esdaile	$8.95
Stories to Excite You	Anna Forrest/Divine	$14.95
Subtle Secrets	Wanda Y. Thomas	$8.95
Suddenly You	Crystal Hubbard	$9.95
Sweet Repercussions	Kimberley White	$9.95
Sweet Tomorrows	Kimberly White	$8.95
Taken by You	Dorothy Elizabeth Love	$9.95
Tattooed Tears	T. T. Henderson	$8.95
The Color Line	Lizzette Grayson Carter	$9.95
The Color of Trouble	Dyanne Davis	$8.95
The Disappearance of Allison Jones	Kayla Perrin	$5.95
The Honey Dipper's Legacy	Pannell-Allen	$14.95
The Joker's Love Tune	Sidney Rickman	$15.95
The Little Pretender	Barbara Cartland	$10.95
The Love We Had	Natalie Dunbar	$8.95
The Man Who Could Fly	Bob & Milana Beamon	$18.95
The Missing Link	Charlyne Dickerson	$8.95
The Price of Love	Sinclair LeBeau	$8.95
The Smoking Life	Ilene Barth	$29.95
The Words of the Pitcher	Kei Swanson	$8.95
Three Wishes	Seressia Glass	$8.95
Through the Fire	Seressia Glass	$9.95
Ties That Bind	Kathleen Suzanne	$8.95
Tiger Woods	Libby Hughes	$5.95
Time is of the Essence	Angie Daniels	$9.95
Timeless Devotion	Bella McFarland	$9.95
Tomorrow's Promise	Leslie Esdaile	$8.95

Other Genesis Press, Inc. Titles (continued)

Truly Inseparable	Wanda Y. Thomas	$8.95
Unbreak My Heart	Dar Tomlinson	$8.95
Uncommon Prayer	Kenneth Swanson	$9.95
Unconditional	A.C. Arthur	$9.95
Unconditional Love	Alicia Wiggins	$8.95
Under the Cherry Moon	Christal Jordan-Mims	$12.95
Unearthing Passions	Elaine Sims	$9.95
Until Death Do Us Part	Susan Paul	$8.95
Vows of Passion	Bella McFarland	$9.95
Wedding Gown	Dyanne Davis	$8.95
What's Under Benjamin's Bed	Sandra Schaffer	$8.95
When Dreams Float	Dorothy Elizabeth Love	$8.95
Whispers in the Night	Dorothy Elizabeth Love	$8.95
Whispers in the Sand	LaFlorya Gauthier	$10.95
Wild Ravens	Altonya Washington	$9.95
Yesterday Is Gone	Beverly Clark	$10.95
Yesterday's Dreams, Tomorrow's Promises	Reon Laudat	$8.95
Your Precious Love	Sinclair LeBeau	$8.95

ESCAPE WITH INDIGO !!!!

Join Indigo Book Club©
It's simple, easy and secure.

Sign up and receive the new releases every month + Free shipping and 20% off the cover price.

Go online to www.genesis-press.com and click on Bookclub or
call 1-888-INDIGO-1

Order Form

Mail to: Genesis Press, Inc.
P.O. Box 101
Columbus, MS 39703

Name _____
Address _____
City/State _____ Zip _____
Telephone _____

Ship to (if different from above)
Name _____
Address _____
City/State _____ Zip _____
Telephone _____

Credit Card Information
Credit Card # _____ ☐ Visa ☐ Mastercard
Expiration Date (mm/yy) _____ ☐ AmEx ☐ Discover

Qty.	Author	Title	Price	Total

Use this order form, or call 1-888-INDIGO-1

Total for books _____
Shipping and handling:
  $5 first two books,
  $1 each additional book _____
Total S & H _____
Total amount enclosed _____

Mississippi residents add 7% sales tax

Visit www.genesis-press.com for latest releases and excerpts.